"Nik Kor... mesmeriz... adventure... as-hell no... couldn't put it down."

Paul Tremblay, author of A Head Full of Ghosts *and* Disappearance at Devil's Rock

"*The Rebellion's Last Traitor* is an explosive tale of betrayal and revenge in which allegiances prove as dangerous and unreliable as the memories the citizens of Eitan City buy and sell. Korpon crosses genre lines with ease, and imbues this post-apocalyptic tale with the rhythm and immediacy of crime fiction."

Chris Holm, Anthony Award-winning author of Red Right Hand *and* The Killing Kind

"'Reach off the page and grab you' characters, and brutally intricate world building."

SFF World

"Korpon's take on speculative fiction is unique."

Crimespree Magazine

"A sharp and clever novel that manages to discuss difficult themes without ever being sneaky about it."

Dead End Follies

BY THE SAME AUTHOR

NIK KORPON

QUEEN OF THE STRUGGLE

ANGRY
ROBOT

ANGRY ROBOT
An imprint of Watkins Media Ltd

20 Fletcher Gate,
Nottingham,
NG1 2FZ
UK

angryrobotbooks.com
twitter.com/angryrobotbooks
Sing a song of liberty

An Angry Robot paperback original 2018

Cover by Steve Stone
Set in Meridien and Q Type Square by Argh! Nottingham

Distributed in the United States by Penguin Random House, Inc., New York.

ISBN 978 0 85766 659 8
Ebook ISBN 978 0 85766 660 4

Printed in the United States of America

9 8 7 6 5 4 3 2 1

To all of our ghosts.

1.
HENRAEK

They took their time dying.

After the water distribution center collapsed, before the flames of the Gallery were even smoldering, the Tathadann declared Eitan under riot law, allowing their troops to use any force necessary – including lethal – to subdue the rebels. It should have been a death knell for us. It should have crushed the nascent uprising. It should have set the streets of Eitan City awash in blood. And it did.

But not with our blood.

Citizens of all ages, colors, races, abilities, we armed ourselves with pistols, knives, rocks, rebar, pieces of wood. Everyone drew on anything within their means and ability to strike a blow against the Tathadann and reclaim the city as our own. The Tathadann's soldiers were massively outnumbered, yet we were just as massively outgunned. Still, although technology and armaments gave them a tactical advantage, there was nothing they could use to compensate for our heart.

All of this, six months' worth of battles and operations and bullets and bodies runs through my head as I crouch behind the chest-high crumbling rock wall that rings Lady Morrigan's estate, the last vestige of the Tathadann's rule, inside of which cower the remaining Tathadann soldiers, driven into hiding by a Ragjarøn squad. "Estate" is a generous term for the place – I've seen bigger farmhouses back in Westhell County – but it's a term propagated by the party for stature's sake. Although the rest of the Tathadann has been destroyed and we could walk away from this place, let these soldiers run off to whatever hollow they choose, we need the sense of finality, in the same way that you cut away all of the gangrenous flesh, lest the smallest portion of disease begins to multiply again and rot away the rest of the body.

I press on the comm device in my ear. We took them from a group of soldiers we captured two weeks ago. As much as I loathe the party, I have to say their toys make fighting a hell of a lot easier.

"Are you in position yet?" I say to Emeríann.

"Yet?" She laughs. "Me and Lachlan already ordered food. We needed something to do while you all were taking your sweet-ass time."

Yeah. She's taken to the whole revolution thing pretty well.

"Once you're done eating, care to finish this?"

"We've got your cover."

I smile to myself and motion for the four people in my squad – one from Eitan, three from Vårgmannskjør,

Ragjarøn's base – to advance. We hoist ourselves up over the wall, digging the toes of our boots into the gaps between stones, and roll down the other side. Bullets from Tathadann soldiers ricochet off the nearby surfaces, plumes of dust sprouting around us, but they're quickly pushed back into the house by suppressing fire from Emeríann's squad, hidden behind the burnt husk of a military transport vehicle that sits on a slight hill to the east of the estate. We duck behind the statues dotting the yard, spreading out over the area to ensure we can cover Emeríann's squad as they advance to take over the house. Macuil had these installed not long before he died, each monument a variation on himself or Fannae, depicting selected accomplishments throughout the Tathadann's history, ensuring they'd live on long after he was gone. However, the one above me is currently missing half its head, a bird's nest now occupying the space where the left side of Macuil's face should be.

I glance up and down the line, make sure everyone is safe.

"Now would be a great time for a power outage," says Vanda, the boy crouched two statues away. "Though I never thought I'd be wishing for one."

"I was thinking the same."

Vanda's skin is still shiny from the burns he sustained in the alleyway six months ago. I feel a little bad, for how slow his healing has been and for the amount of scarring that remains, but he and his friends *were* trying to murder me before that lagon father immolated himself. Once the uprising began, and Vanda realized his father and I fought together during the Struggle, he changed his tune pretty damn quick. He's not a bad kid, aside from giving his friends more credit than they deserved. If only we could marry the passion of the young with the experience of the old.

When everyone is ready, I radio Emeríann.

"We're in place."

"Time to pull up your socks," she says.

We all peer around the statues, our rifles ready, waiting for the report of gunfire, the bright points of light from the soldiers trying to pick off Emeríann's squad while they're in the open, but the Tathadann soldiers must be waiting for perfect shots, conserving their ammo in preparation for a prolonged fight. I'm surprised they haven't surrendered yet, thrown themselves on the mercy of the rebels, but perhaps they don't realize they're the last of the Tathadann. I heard a story once, about soldiers who had been stationed on a remote island during a war. They lost radio communication with the mainland and stayed isolated for forty years. The whole time, they operated under the assumption they were living in wartime, unaware that their country had surrendered within months after their last transmission. It made me wonder if those forty years were pleasure or purgatory.

Vanda lets out a long breath and looks over at me. I can't get a clear read on his expression, but he doesn't look good.

"You're going to be OK," I reassure him. "Take cover behind me if you're unsure."

"I'm OK."

"You look scared."

"I am a little worried," he says. I cock my head. His words are wavering but his voice is steady, strong. He nods toward the house and says, "I'm worried because I don't know what I'm going to do when this is over. This is what I'm best at."

"What, killing?"

"No," he says. "Fighting."

I can't help but smile at him. "Don't worry. Even when this is all over, the real fight will just be starting."

Vanda considers this for a minute, but as he opens his mouth to reply, I see a shadow in the window nearest Emeríann's squad.

"We've got movement," I say into the comm device. "Second floor, third window from the edge. Advancing toward you."

"You got him?" Lachlan says through my earpiece, his voice a low whisper. I can hear the other rebels grunting in the background as they advance on the house. The shadow moves back from the window, staying out of the line of fire. I fix my rifle sight on the spot where it had been.

"As soon as he appears, he'll disappear."

"Keep them off us. We're almost to the house."

And he no more than says the words when the shadow appears at the edge of the window. I set my crosshairs on him, then exhale as I pull the trigger.

Shattering glass. An agonized scream. Bursts of gunfire. A bullet smacks the statue, chipped cement hitting my face.

Emeríann's squad stays tight to the house, a few

feet below the bottom of the windows, unable to point up and return fire.

"We need to advance. Stay low," I say to my people, then pop off a few shots before we move to get a better position. We leave the statues, running at a crouch, and slide behind one of the two ornate fountains in the yard. A small puddle remains in the bottom, the last bit of water after six months of evaporation. I wager a glance around the corner and see no barrels sticking out of the windows.

Then a bright explosion near the base of the house makes me take cover. White stars float before my eyes. I blink as quick as I can, trying to clear my vision.

"Everyone OK?" I ask the other squad.

"That was too close," Emeríann says, her voice strung tight. "We need to end this."

"We've got you," I say. "Wait for our cover."

"Hurry."

"Get ready to move," I tell my people. I point at the three on the end. "You give us cover. Vanda and I will draw fire, taking pressure off the others. You understand what I'm saying?"

"It's insulting that you keep asking us," one of the men says in heavily accented English.

"I'm sorry, but now's not the time for something to be lost in translation." I turn to Vanda, clap my hand on his back. "Now's your time. Keep moving and don't go straight."

"Got it."

We set the rifle butts against our shoulders and break from the fountain. Bullets pepper the ground around us but we zig and zag and make abrupt turns on our way to the other fountain. As I strafe across, I take three potshots in the general direction of where the fire is coming from but hit nothing. Behind me, I hear the rattle of my people's guns, punching scores of holes in the exterior walls. One of them screams when he's hit and the rattling dampens slightly. Vanda pauses a moment, sets his feet to aim. I start to yell at him to keep moving, but before I can, a soldier appears in a second-story window.

I imagine Riab all over again. His blood splashing on my lips, his death hanging on my shoulders.

Then the soldier's head explodes in a red bloom, his body toppling forward and crashing through the window.

Vanda doesn't react, just turns two ticks to the left and fires again, killing another soldier I hadn't noticed.

I want to hurry over to him, to tell him he's a great shot or offer my condolences because someone so young shouldn't be so at peace with killing. But before I can, a concussive blast vibrates the thick air around us. A tongue of flame reflects off Vanda's eyes. Screaming erupts inside the house, coupled with calls for a medic, which just makes me laugh. We're way past that kind of military order. There's another explosion after Emeríann's squad launches a second pulse-grenade. I do my best to hold it in but I flinch slightly, not because of fear but because I so badly wanted to be in the group that ended the Tathadann.

After some discussion – and, to be fair, some hard-handed persuasion – we came to the decision that Emeríann's group was the best to go in. Several of the fighters in her squad had extensive hand-to-hand experience, and my people were better shots and could provide cover. Plus, she planned the bombing of the water distribution plant that sparked this uprising – along with Forgall, Nahoeg hold him close. Still, as I stand outside with my rifle trained on the windows, listening to the cacophony of shouting and the occasional gunshot, I have to consciously tell myself that I made the right choice.

Vanda and I duck down behind the fountain and keep our rifles on the house, though it doesn't look like they'll fight any longer. A few minutes later, members of her squad emerge from Morrigan's house, guns pointed at the Tathadann soldiers – no, *our prisoners* – with their hands atop their heads. One of the men calls out to us: "Clear."

I survey my squad. Everyone in position, rifles at the ready, just in case. I look over to Vanda. "You ready for this?"

He nods.

"Watch the squad while I check on the house."

His chest inflates, back straightens. "Sir, absolutely, sir."

"Don't call me sir."

"Right." He readjusts himself. "I can handle it."

"Good." I clap his shoulder, then hurry across the yard, passing two small tombstones set to the side. Macuil's name is etched on one of them, though given the family's penchant for excess, I'm surprised to see such a reserved resting place. On the other is a name I don't recognize, but the birth and death dates are only six years apart, which makes me feel both sad and disgusted at myself for feeling sad. I've never heard that the Morrigans had any children.

I climb the dull, scratched marble steps up to the looming mahogany front doors, split open and held by a length of rope wrapped around the brass handles. Inside the lavish living room, two rebels mill about, talking conspiratorially and pointing at some of the more ostentatious decorations. The gold candle sconces. The ornate ravens carved into a cabinet at least ten feet long, holding rows of crystal decanters, filled with gallons of water. The animal skins hanging on the walls like grotesque tapestries, striped and spotted and furry and scaly, some with the head still attached, featuring long, twisted horns or jagged, sharp teeth. I've never even seen some of these creatures before. Three prisoners sit on a thick rug with their hands and ankles restrained. One has blood leaking from his ear, dripping down and mixing with the burgundy and gold pattern of the rug.

The rebels glance over and straighten their backs when they see me standing behind them. "Ceanasaí Laersen," they say in unison.

"Comrades."

"Ceanasaí Daele was looking for you," the shorter rebel says.

"Where is she?"

"Two rooms over."

I nod and thank them, then head toward her, pausing in the grand archway between rooms. "The water can go. But everything else stays."

I can feel them shifting uncomfortably behind me.

"We're not wasteful, but neither are we thieves. Got it?"

"Understood," they say.

"But after you've removed the water, if, say, the cabinet becomes unstable, tips over, and crashes into those abominations hanging on the wall, then so be it."

"How would the cabinet knock all of those down?" the smaller one says.

"Guess that's the question now, isn't it?"

I pass through the dining room. The table and chairs are a style similar to the dry sink Emeríann and I carried into Johnstone's – the one that landed us on the news – though I doubt that these rock on uneven legs with every touch. What's most striking about this house isn't the golden accents or ridiculous displays of wealth, but how sparse and empty it is. It's bordering on depressing. Despite existing at the highest strata in Eitan for sixty years, Fannae Morrigan was still an old widow who lived alone in a big house.

I find Emeríann in the sitting room, holding a ceramic teapot in her hands, something like sadness playing across her face.

"You OK?" I rest my hand on the back of her arm.

"My mom saved my tea set for me, from when I was little." She turns the kettle over, running her finger along the soft curve of the handle. "She said she wanted to play tea time with her granddaughter one day."

I nod because I don't know what else to do. This is not quite the conversation I expected to have at this moment, but the last six months have shown me that, if nothing else, nothing will ever turn out like you expect it.

"Are you saying you want to have a baby?" I say, my voice unintentionally searching.

She barks out a laugh. "Holy shit, are you serious? Can you imagine what it would be like to have a kid now? It's crazy enough with Donael and Cobb. A baby would be a terrible idea."

I almost say *OK, good* but manage to bite my tongue.

"It just made me think about Mom, is all. It'll be fifteen years next month…" she says, her voice trailing off.

"You can bring that home for the boys if you want. I'm not sure they're really into tea, but–"

"There is no way in hell I am bringing anything from Fannae Morrigan into our house unless it's her head mounted on a pike."

"That, the boys might be into."

Emeríann holds the teapot up as if she's presenting it, then hurls it at the ground, shattering it into a hundred jagged pieces.

"Let's do this," she says, setting her backpack on the ground.

As we pull out a dozen charges, delay timers, and blasting caps, a wave of nostalgia washes over me. It's only fitting the actions that will complete this uprising are the same as those that incited it. This time, though, there are no pulse-charges, no atomizers, just old-fashioned, highly potent bombs – courtesy of a raid on the armory led by Brighid, Daghda Morrigan's daughter – that will reduce this house to no more than a pile of rocks and wicked ghosts.

The lights flicker as we attach the bombs to the critical points, the power grid groaning under the strain. Emeríann and I pause, making sure the lights will stay on. During the uprising, the Tathadann destroyed three power plants that fed rebel neighborhoods. It was a logical move – given that the plants not only supplied electricity but also powered the jerry-rigged water distribution system – except they failed to take into consideration that we could just siphon energy from other streets. That required the remaining plants to produce twice the electricity, resulting in the rolling blackouts we've been seeing for the last few months. While the lights stay on, we sweep the house quickly to ensure there are no remaining rebels.

Outside, we call for everyone to take cover, then move beyond the blast radius. Emeríann pulls the detonator from her bag, the big red button smiling like an old friend.

"You ready?" she says.

"Never more."

The neighborhood lays largely quiet, echoes of gunshots and shouting from a few streets over, the murmuring of rebels around the yard, the thrum of anticipation seven years in the making.

She takes my hand in hers, kisses me on the lips, then guides our hands to press the button.

A loud click, then a burst of light from inside and a thunderous clap. The windows shatter outward, shards of glass hurled into the yard, piercing the body of a dead Tathadann man lying in the grass. Great sections of brick and mortar fly in all directions, blinding light blasting through the gaping holes. One of the fountains crumbles as a tire-sized chunk of wall smashes into it. With little first-floor wall remaining, the top half of the house comes crashing down, throwing a huge cloud of dust and debris up into the heavens. Within a moment, the heat of the explosion sets the wooden roof aflame, tongues of fire lighting the area.

And as the ringing in my ears begins to subside, I hear voices. Some shouting and cheering. A few praying. Then I realize it's not just our squads, but that a crowd has gathered, hundreds of people watching, and they're all singing.

Down near the river where our brothers bled…

I look over at Emeríann, rivulets of sweat cutting through the dust on her face, slivers of wood and other debris sprinkled through her hair, and she's the most beautiful woman I've ever seen.

I lean over to her, my lips brushing her earlobe. "I love you."

With the Tathadann now totally destroyed, we all head to Johnstone's, the unofficial gathering point for the uprising.

"Are you sure?" Emeríann says to me as we stand across the street from the door.

"Yeah, go on."

Emeríann kisses me hard on the lips before joining the stream of people, ready for celebratory drinks and regaling one another with various and sundry war stories. I stand beneath the flickering streetlight and watch her disappear inside, some part of me sinking, wishing I could be there, not just to commemorate the occasion with my love and my partner and my fellow Ceanasaí – the two architects of the uprising – but because I can finally show my face in public without hearing the taunts of *traitor* and *bhfeallaire*. As much as I would love to though, I can't, because I have more important tasks at hand.

Because, Donael informed me this morning, tonight is movie night.

2.
EMERÍANN

The bartender pours shots like his hands are broken. I snatch the bottle from him and run it down the row. Bourbon – *real* bourbon, finally – fills the lined-up glasses. I hand them out to whoever's standing around me.

Lachlan calls for everyone to shut the hell up. When the room finally quiets down, he climbs up on the bar.

"A year ago, I came to Eitan because the people were tired of living with the boot-heel of Fannae Morrigan and the Tathadann on their necks. I knew only one man here, me cousin and brother-in-arms Forgall Tobeigh, the one who convinced me to leave me home in the mountains. I told him he was crazy. And I was right." Everyone bursts into laughter and cheers. Lachlan waits a moment before continuing. "But he was also right. The people of Eitan wanted to live better. They deserved to live better. And so, with the help of our lovely host Emeríann Daele, who is so kindly allowing us to drink all her booze tonight, we started planning. It would never be easy, we knew, but it was important – vital – that we succeeded.

"Six months ago, our Emeríann and her partner Henraek Laersen started this uprising. And tonight, with the help of Daghda and Brighid Morrigan, as well as Ødven Äsyr and his Ragjarøn troops, we finished it."

Everyone breaks out in cheering, whoops and screams filling the bar. Through the crowd, I catch Brighid's glance. She raises her glass to me and gives a salute.

Then the lights go out, and the shouting gets louder. But it's not fear: it's frustration. Even after they're gone, those Tathadann bastards still find a way to screw us.

A minute later – a blessedly short outage, this time – they flicker back on. Everyone calls for Brighid to make a speech. At first she brushes it off, but relents when she realizes they won't stop cheering until she does. She stands next to Lachlan.

"I'll make this quick so you can get back to what really matters – getting drunk."

This elicits a lot of shouting.

"My father and his brother Macuil founded the Tathadann years ago in order to rescue Eitan from the carnage of the Resource Wars and rebuild the city. They knew that in order for the city to prosper again, everyone must prosper. So you can imagine my father's surprise when his brother and wife betrayed him, removing him from his own organization and exiling him into the mountains, destined to watch from afar while the city he loved was ruled with an iron fist, where only the wealthiest were allowed water or freedom."

Everyone boos and hisses, some calling for Lady Morrigan's head, even though Henraek already put a bullet through it.

"My father and I travelled across continents, helping others achieve liberation, and we put everything we had learned to work in helping to liberate our homeland, Eitan. Now that we all have thrown off the shackles of the Tathadann, my goal is to help the city prosper the way my father envisioned many years ago. That is my promise to you."

She waves to everyone and they all hoot and holler, raising glasses and singing. I can practically hear Henraek's teeth grinding from across the city. He never liked Brighid and thought we should fight for our own independence. He hated to admit that he couldn't liberate us by himself, that we wouldn't have been able to defeat the Tathadann without Brighid and Ragjarøn.

Lachlan calls out, quieting the crowd. "I raise me glass to the lot of you. I congratulate you on completing something that will live on long past our lifetimes. I commend you for making your children's children's children's lives better. And I thank you for all of your hard work, your sacrifice, and most importantly, your heart." Lachlan raises his glass. "To those who are still living, and to the many who we've lost, may Nahoeg hold us all close."

Everyone calls out *Hael Hael Nahoeg* and throws back their drinks.

"Now somebody turn on the music," Lachlan calls out. The bartender flips a switch and kicks off a blast of raucous guitars and whinnying fiddles nearly as loud as the shouts from the crowd. Then he goes back to getting people drunk. A few people give me hugs and try to hand me more drinks, but I already have a glass in each hand. Others jump up and down in time with the music. I weave my way through the throngs of people, spilling half of one drink I really didn't want over some man whose clothes are still splattered with blood, and make my way to the door.

Outside, people stumble up and down the street. Some of them blow on homemade horns, while others shout and slur rebel songs and chants. Most of them have a bottle of something in their hands. The streetlight flickers in the darkness as the power ebbs, and it should make everything seem more romantic. But it doesn't. Aside from the noise, everything feels the same. The heavy, wet air. The stink coming from the dark corner across the street that I still haven't been able to identify. The piles of rocks and burnt boards. Everything has changed yet everything is the same.

The noise from inside the bar swells, then dies.

Lachlan's voice rings out behind me. "I'd wondered where you'd gotten off to, then."

"Needed a little air." I sip at one of the glasses.

"Everything all right, love?"

"Yeah, fine. Why?"

He looks at me like, *Do I really need to answer that?*

"I just thought things would be different."

"Out here, or in there?" He points somewhere in

the distance, meaning home.

"Out here." I take a big swallow from my glass, emptying most of it.

"A bit anticlimactic, innit?" Another group of revelers walks by. Lachlan takes a drink, waiting until they pass. "You plan for something a whole year, putting your whole self into it, yeah? And it's going and it's going and then it's done."

"Yeah, exactly. I thought I'd feel something more. Something different."

"You're not relieved?"

"Sure I am."

"But also a bit sad that our Forgall isn't here."

I nod in response, finish the rest of my drink, then pitch the glass into the shadows.

"Never did figure out where that wretched smell is coming from," Lachlan says, almost to himself. He clears his throat. "How's the home life, then?"

A smile spreads over me, just thinking about it. "Good. Really good. It's really hard, but the boys are really good. Most times, honestly, I don't think I've ever been happier." I start on my other drink, but he's waiting for me to continue. "It does take some getting used to." I laugh to myself. "And it's kind of nice to be away for the night."

"I'd imagine. Especially as the wee ones aren't even yours."

"Trust me, they're not so small. I cook for them most of the week."

"They're growing because you're a great cook."

"It's not Tathadann food, but I guess they're adjusting."

Lachlan waves to someone on the sidewalk across the street, a man with a stump for a left arm and a rifle propped up against his right.

"I think it's tough for Henraek, you know. I mean, he loves having Donael again, obviously. And I love them both being around. But Henraek, seeing Cobb every day, knowing he was Walleus's, knowing what Walleus did, hiding Donael and all..."

I shake away the mental image of Henraek's silhouette in the middle of the night, standing over the boys, watching them sleep on the couch as he wraps his arms around himself or bites his hands to stop sobbing. For a good two months after they came to live with us, I don't think Henraek slept more than a couple hours a night. He'd either stand in the living room, like he was afraid someone was going to sneak in and kidnap Donael, or he'd wake up screaming and spend the rest of the night sweating and staring at the ceiling. I figured for as many people as he's killed over the years, Walleus would've been just one more body. But I've never killed anyone I loved, so what do I know?

"Well, love," Lachlan says, "you're welcome to celebrate in whatever manner you see fit. It's your night, then. But me? I'm going to go inside, listen to some good music, and toast the demise of those rancid *spirad olcs* with a couple dozen of me closest friends. I have a feeling that tomorrow, all this will feel much different."

He leans over and kisses me on each cheek, squeezes my shoulder once, then returns inside. I sip at my drink. Before the door can close fully, it swings back open.

Brighid holds her arms up in the air. "What are you doing?"

I hold up my glass, like that's some sort of answer.

"Drinking alone on this night of all nights?"

I gesture toward the people passing on the sidewalk. "I'm not alone."

"Seriously, Ceanasaí?" she says with something like a smirk at the formal title.

"I'm coming. I just needed some air."

She lays her arm across my shoulders. "I know we haven't always agreed while on the battlefield, but you are a hell of a commander, and you should be proud of all that we've accomplished. This is just the beginning of something much bigger. I promise you that."

I feel a flush run across my skin, and I'm not sure if it's the alcohol or the rare compliment.

"It's been a privilege to fight alongside you." She gives a wry smile. "But you need to get your ass inside, because this is your night."

After a minute, I think to myself, *they're right*. This is my night. I'd rather have Henraek here with me, but he's fine at the apartment with the boys. And I'll see them in a couple hours when I get home, because that's what we've made: a home. Tomorrow, when Daghda and Brighid stand on the steps before Clodhna and announce that Eitan is once again self-ruled, everything will feel a hell of a lot different. So tonight, we'll celebrate. And besides, I started this. Me and Forgall. Others helped us along the way, but it was our idea.

I lift my glass up to the sky. "Hael hael Nahoeg. Hael hael you, Forgall." Brighid joins in and we cheer again.

Then we head inside and join the party.

3.
HENRAEK

It's not until my hand touches the doorknob that I realize I'm shaking. It's not fear, for there's no longer anything to fear. Maybe it's residual adrenaline, or the realization that this chapter in my life has finally come to an end. I tell myself that's not a bad thing, not by any means. I say it twice.

I give myself a once-over as I do every time I come home – Emeríann and I both promised the boys that we'd never bring the streets inside our apartment – and decide I'm clean enough. No blood.

I open the door and find the boys sitting on the couch, Donael sketching something on a piece of paper and Cobb clicking at him, telling him what to draw. Silas is perched on the back of the couch, as if supervising. The three of them look up as soon as they hear me. Donael sits up straighter. Cobb clicks. Silas coos.

"You were supposed to be home an hour ago," Donael says to me.

I slide my field pack off my shoulder and set it on the ground. "Things took a little longer than I'd expected. Are you OK?"

"Yeah," he says, returning to his pad. "But I was starting to get nervous."

"I'm sorry. I didn't have a chance to call."

When they first came here, they would both tackle me every time I came home, so terrified were they of being left alone again. After their seeing what happened to Walleus, I can't blame them. But in the last two months, they've been much more reserved – uninterested might be a harsher way to put it – upon my arrival. Emeríann says they're just becoming comfortable here and that it's a good thing, but I can't help wondering if Donael figures there are only a certain amount of times I can go out before I don't come back, and if he's preparing himself for that day.

I kick off my boots then go to the kitchen, grab the water pitcher, and pour myself half a glass of cloudy liquid. I could really go for more, but we won't be able to refill it for another day and I want to leave some for Emeríann and the boys. I plop down beside Donael, glance at his drawing.

"Is that a race car?"

"Targeted bomb. Like a spaceship, but, you know, it blows up."

Wonderful. This is definitely what I need.

"Cobb used to make them with a modeling tablet but…"

He doesn't need to finish his sentence. *He can't anymore after your rebel friends blew up the Gallery and destroyed one of Cobb's favorite toys.*

I change topics. "Have you two eaten yet?"

"I heated up some leftovers for us," Donael says. Cobb clicks and points at something on the paper. "I know. That's what you told me to draw." This seems to satisfy Cobb well enough.

"You still want to do movie night or are you otherwise occupied for the evening?"

I try not to let an edge creep into my voice, though it's hard. Not so much because Donael is distracted, but because it is Cobb who is distracting him. I understand that he has had about the worst luck imaginable – on top of suffering from a crippling blood disease, his mother died when she tried to abort him, and he saw his father's dead body lying in a pool of blood on the carpet of their rowhouse – but that doesn't stop me from not liking him very much. One of the first thoughts I had after hugging Donael for the first time in years was a vision of us becoming the halcyon nuclear family, him and Emeríann and me. Then Cobb came out from the panic room and has been tarnishing that vision ever since. I've never been able to say this aloud, not even to Emeríann, because I realize it makes me a horrible person. But that doesn't mean I can't feel it. For six years all I wanted was to be with my son, and now that I finally have him, I'm still not completely with him.

"Well, I guess I'll go do something else for a little while and you just let me know when you're ready."

I start to push myself up off the couch when Donael grabs my arm.

"Dad, just chill. I'm trying to finish this for Cobb."

And the way he says *Dad* coupled with the lazy

admonition, with its implicit intimacy and familiarity, makes a warmth bloom inside my chest.

"OK. I'm going to grab some food while you're finishing. Should I bring something for you two or are you just going to eat my dinner?"

Donael says, "Probably the second." Cobb clicks in accord.

"Fair enough."

In the kitchen, I sniff the container of grey meat in some sort of curry sauce that Emeríann concocted, deem it good enough for an empty stomach, and dump it on a relatively clean plate along with some browning carrots. I put a few chunks of salt on the side for Silas. Since we've been so busy rooting out and beating down the Tathadann forces, we haven't had much time to focus on logistical issues, like public transportation or rebuilding the education system. Or getting the water plants properly up and running again. What seemed like such a brilliant tactical plan six months ago has since become a gigantic pain in the ass.

The water will be one of the first things addressed after the ceremony tomorrow, with constant power a quick second. Once Eitan is officially ours again, we will issue a call for a citizen-based congress to work with us to rebuild the city, each person having as equal a vote as the next, a true egalitarian government comprised of the people, working for the benefit of the people through direct action. No one will get paid, so it will truly be a labor of love and weed out those looking for a cushy, worthless job. Which was mostly what the Tathadann was.

The trickiest part will be navigating the various interests. While everyone was in favor of destroying the Tathadann, there have been divergent positions on how far this citizen congress goes. The majority is in line with my and Emeríann's vision. Some conservatives think we've gone too far, but a small cadre of insurgents – some from Eitan proper, some bussed in to help the fight – has been agitating for a complete dissolution of rule. My problem with them isn't that I don't think the people of Eitan can govern themselves – that's what this congress is supposed to be, after all – but more an issue of semantics. We don't see this congress as a ruling party, but instead a reflection of the people's will. The people tell the congress what to do and they do it. If the people don't like it, the members are removed and replaced with new representatives. It seems intuitive to me, but the cadre has been vocal in its displeasure. For now, they're just going to have to deal with it.

Donael hands the pad to Cobb when I come back, then grabs the coffee table and adjusts it to rest his feet as he slides down into the couch. Surprisingly, in the time he's been here, he's never once complained about the couch, or *a somewhat-ergonomic petri dish* as Emeríann has called it on occasion. Cobb examines the drawing a moment before setting it on the floor, while Silas struts over to the arm beside me and pecks at the salt.

"Which one tonight?" I say to them. Donael hands Cobb a thick black cloth, identical to the one in his hands, and they drape them over their eyes.

"Can we do a funny one?"

"I do those all day long."

"I mean an actually funny one." Donael lifts up the edge of the cloth and eyes me, a small smirk dancing across his lips.

"Now who's the comedian?"

Unlike the setup at Walleus's place, our television only gets two channels – neither of which is interesting to near-teenagers – and we don't have any kind of projection machines. And the last thing I'd want to do is show them memories, even if I hadn't smashed my viewer after seeing the memory of Donael's supposed-murder. I finally learned how to adapt various devices into portable memory players, but I keep them hidden beneath the floor under the couch next to the memory vials from Walleus. My son sleeping above them every night prevents me losing more of my life watching Walleus's past, cataloging the moments with my son that he stole from me. I know in my heart what's true, but that doesn't stop his words about being Donael's real father – or the shocked expression on his face as my needle pierced his temple – from ringing against my skull every time I close my eyes.

So, instead of watching movies, we tell movies to each other. Theirs are usually disjointed, with scores of non-sequiturs and ridiculous tangents that are funny only to them. Mine aren't much more organized, mostly whitewashed accounts from the Struggle or the shenanigans Walleus and I used to get into, the names changed and profanity erased.

"All right," I say as I settle into the couch. "A long time ago in a country far away…"

• • •

A rattle and scrape in the living room. My eyes bolt open, my hand instinctively going to the axe handle beneath our bed. Then there's a hushed curse, then an apology for cursing. I let go of the axe handle.

Emeríann's home. And fairly drunk from the sound of it.

Good for her. She deserves it. She's put a ton of work into this, risking things larger than I think she realized. The last thing I wanted to do was put a damper on her celebration by having to come home and watch the boys. We've had enough to adjust to as it is already.

I spring up from the bed, hurry to the living room. She's leaning against the wall, trying to muscle off a boot she hasn't yet untied, still cursing quietly under her breath.

"Let me help you," I whisper, leaning in and providing my back for support while I unlace her.

"Fascist-ass boots, the pricks," she slurs. "Whoever made these?"

I don't have any kind of answer for that, so I tell her to lean on my shoulder while I take her boots off. Her hands grip my back.

"You feel muscly. You been working out?"

I set her boots beside the door and take her hand. "Let's get some water for you."

"We can be quiet. Won't wake them up."

As I lead her across the bedroom, I swear a cloud of vapors follows us. After she passes out, I'm going to need to find some of that medicine she gets from a Brigu woman. Tomorrow is about the last day she'll want to be hungover for.

In the bedroom, she climbs onto the bed in a manner that teeters between seduction and sleepwalking.

"I can't get my pants off," she slurs, then hiccups. "Can you help?" The combination of her complete drunkenness and attempts at sex kitten are as adorable as they are hilarious.

"Sure, sweetheart, I can help."

"Mmm," she says, "my strong man."

I come over to the bed, grab the bottom of her pants, and tug. "Em, you have to unbutton them first."

No answer. I tug again.

"Em."

A slight snore.

Yeah. Figured as much.

I take her pants off to avoid further contaminating our bed, then roll her on her side, and pull the covers up to her chin.

After setting out the packet of medicine and a glass of water for her, I check on the boys once more, lingering on Donael's face.

In my head, I run through the hours of Walleus's memory that I watched. Aside from a few awkward looks he and Aífe exchanged over the years, there's never been anything to substantiate his claim that Donael is his son. Still I stand here nearly every night, looking at him, that jawline, the cheekbones. I was never one for identifying physical characteristics, could never say *your baby's got your eyes and his mother's ears*, but I know in the primal part of me that operates on instinct instead of logic that I am Donael's father. I can just feel it.

Yet that hasn't stopped me from questioning it every night.

The crowd gathered before Clodhna in the morning is so immense that I cannot even see the back of it as I look out from my elevated vantage point on the side of the stage. I initially balked at the idea of raising ourselves above the citizens, thinking it too reminiscent of the Tathadann's pomp and circumstance. But Emeríann and Brighid convinced me otherwise. They said the people needed to see this was not a rag-tag rebellion that would dissolve into chaos within the year, but a proper citizen-centric government, one that could rebuild and allow us – every one of us – to prosper. With the amphitheater on the southern edge of the city damaged during the uprising, it was easier to build this platform. And the carpenters did a nice job, painting the salvaged plywood blue with a white trim to give the illusion of carpeting, angling the trusses to make it look more official.

Emeríann sits in the chair beside me, her skin slightly peaked beneath her radiant smile but otherwise ready to go. It's not until I'm seeing us side-by-side that I realize these are the same clothes we wore to Forgall's funeral, just before we took down the water distribution plant. Macabre, but appropriate. We look down to the crowd, and in the front row are the boys. Donael runs his finger inside the collar of his shirt, the expression on his face saying we tied a noose around his neck. Cobb just plays some type of game with his fingers.

In the center of the stage, sitting on a larger chair to support his shrunken form, is Daghda Morrigan. He wears the boar mask I first saw him in so many months ago, the tusks on it since chipped but polished to a high gleam. What most impresses me about him isn't what covers his face, but what covers his body – normal clothes, the same as anyone in Eitan would wear. He is an exalted rebel, a myth of a myth, the savior of Eitan, yet he's just one of us. His daughter stands to one side of him, in clothes similar to Emeríann's. It's a gesture big enough to tamp down my cynicism about the Morrigan lineage and temper my hurt in not being recognized as I feel I should've been.

Even more than with the Morrigans, I never really approved of Ragjarøn's involvement in our rebellion. I thought the people of Eitan should take back the city on their own. Now Ødven, his severe clothing – a nicer version of the grey fatigues his troops wear – sits on Daghda's other side. Beads of sweat dot his forehead, his body still unaccustomed to the heat and humidity down here. From what I've always heard about Vårgmannskjør being a land of savages, I'm half-surprised he's not wearing a jacket made of human skin. Then again, he does have a ceremonial sword at his side, reminding me that we wouldn't have been able to take down the Tathadann without Ragjarøn's support – and their weapons.

This is the moment I've been looking forward to for almost all of my life. But there's still something pulling at the back of my skull. Part of it is saying *You did it. You defeated the Tathadann.* But the other part is saying *Are you actually ready for this?*

When the time seems right, Emeríann stands up and walks to the middle of the stage. I try hard not to stare, but it's damn tough because, even with a sizeable hangover, she still looks stunning.

She takes the microphone, then pulls hair away from her face and tucks it behind her ears, a few of her fingers sporting significant gashes. Somehow, I think that makes her even more attractive, which briefly causes me to question what's wrong with me. She clears her throat twice, pushing down the nerves, then speaks.

"Thank you all for being here today. This is a very special day, a historic day, for Eitan City, for all people who have been oppressed, and I'm very glad you all are here to witness it." She looks over at me, maybe for support, maybe for me to guide her. I'm not sure why, because she needs nothing from me. She was born for this. I motion with my hands, telling her she's great, then wink once. When she looks back to the crowd, something settles inside her. "There are a lot of people who aren't here today, people we lost along the way. Friends, sons, daughters, mothers, fathers. But I think they're still watching, even if they aren't here, looking down with pride on all we've accomplished."

A breeze passes through the crowd and my arms turn to gooseflesh. I blink twice and feel tears involuntarily welling. I rub them away, smile at Emeríann, then glance down at the boys. They've stopped their fidgeting, both of their eyes on Emeríann, transfixed, and my chest swells.

Our life is not perfect. We have had to deal with many issues. We will have to navigate many more. We have lived under a constant threat of death for the last six months, and likely will for many more to come. Our food and water are never guaranteed, and all the sacrifice and blood expended during this uprising – and, for that matter, the Struggle that laid the blueprint – can easily be erased if the next few months of rebuilding go awry and the space between factions grows too large. Despite all that, I don't know that I've ever been happier in my life.

"And I want to make sure you heard that," Emeríann says. "*We*. There is no longer an *us* and a *them*. We are all one people, we are all Eitan, and we are all reclaiming the city as ours."

The crowd erupts into a sustained cheer, some shouting and some fireworks and, in a few pockets that quickly spread across the crowd, our song.

Down near the river where our brothers bled...

But it's different this time.

We knelt on the banks and our fathers said, "This is our land, all that we can touch, and we've watered our crops with Tathadann blood."

Emeríann senses the shift in the crowd and gestures for Daghda to come forward, to say the words we've been waiting to hear for countless years. He pushes himself up slowly, but as he walks, there's a sense of purpose. His general countenance is like a giant boulder: impenetrable, indecipherable, indestructible. Hard to budge at first but impossible to stop once he gets moving. Brighid and Ødven stiffly stand and join in the applause.

Daghda lumbers up to Emeríann, seemingly riding in on the current of cheers and hollers and supplications. The prodigal son – once cast out by his own wife and brother – has returned a prophet. Of war. Of violence. Of freedom.

Emeríann gives him an awkward hug – because how do you hug someone who is as much a god as he is a ghost story – and hands him the microphone before retreating to the opposite side of the stage. Behind Daghda, Brighid and Ødven step forward, creeping toward the front of the stage, trying to absorb some of the adulation. I can't blame them, wanting some credit for their efforts. As much as Daghda is an inspiration and an omen to cast upon people, he is also an old man. He gave the rebels a reason to fight – which was priceless – but in all the times I saw him on the battlefield, I rarely saw him leave his transport vehicle.

Daghda holds the microphone for a long pause, waiting for the crowd to quiet down.

"Much has changed in Eitan since I left my home in the mountains to come here, to fight the resource companies. But one thing has never changed…" He pauses, expecting applause, which he gets, "… and that is the heart of its people."

The crowd screams itself hoarse and Brighid and Ødven are now only a few feet behind Daghda, as close to the limelight as they can be without knocking the old man over.

Eventually, the people fall quiet.

"And so, many years later, it is my utmost pleasure to say that Eitan City is no longer beholden to the tyrannical rule of the Tathadann."

As the crowd erupts in shouts and song, the swell of energy is palpable, especially from up here, the nexus of the revolution. I want to close my eyes, to soak it all in, to imprint this on my memory because I will never have sensations such as this for as long as I live, but I can't. Something deep in my reptile brain prevents me. I scan the crowd, looking for rogue Tathadann members, ones we haven't yet executed. But I see none.

"And now I present," Daghda says, but the cheering is too loud and he can barely be heard.

The line of Ragjarøn troops behind us shifts, and my skin prickles. There is a threat. I know it. I feel it. I scan the crowd surrounding the boys, then the space behind Emeríann, but still see nothing. Then, six rows back, two men shuffle to the side. My arms tighten. These men are about to rush the stage, weapons concealed beneath their clothing. But then they stop, shout something to a woman beside them, and start clapping and cheering. I've been at war for too many years. Looking for threats for too long, seeing them where there are none.

Eventually the crowd quiets enough for Daghda to audibly clear his throat. "And now I present, the people who will usher in a new era of equality and self-sufficiency into Eitan–"

But as he says the last words, Brighid gives a quick nod to Ødven, who turns to me and flicks his wrist. "What?" I say, completely confused. Then I realize he was not gesturing to me but instead to the troops behind me. A rifle stock confirms this as it smashes into the back of my head. I tumble forward, catching myself before my face hits the ground only for a soldier to yoke up my elbows and cinch them together with a metal restraint, then yank them high above my head. I glance up and see Emeríann in a similar position, a soldier's thick forearm wrapped around her neck, her legs flailing. My head snaps to the crowd, but blessedly, no one has touched the boys.

The collective shock is audible.

The shouting only gets louder when a massive soldier restrains Daghda, pushing his head downward.

Daghda lashes out with his foot, trying to break free, but he is no match. I try to throw myself backward, knock the soldier off-guard, but two more have appeared from nowhere and my arms are cinched so far back that any movement unleashes a shower of hot knives in my shoulders.

Ødven strides forward, unsheathing his sword, which I now see is not in the least bit ceremonial. It appears so sharp it could slice the air before it. He extends his arm, giving Brighid the hilt. She takes it as if she has been preparing for this moment her entire life, and in a flash, I see what's happening.

I turn toward the crowd, scream as loud as I can at Donael and Cobb, "Close your eyes!"

Then I hear the blade split the air before slicing through Daghda's neck. His head hits the stage with a dull thump and rolls to the edge, twirling around before falling over the edge like an olive dropped from the dinner table.

The crowd displays a mixture of horror and

disbelief. Some are screaming, some yelling. I hear people inhale sharply and even titter.

Emeríann's face is beyond pale, as if her body is trying to implode but just can't summon the willpower to do it.

Brighid stabs the sword into the stage, right in the middle of the blood squirting from her father's torso, then picks up the microphone and hands it to Ødven.

"I, Ødven Äsyr, leader of Ragjarøn, hereby declare this land be called Självastand from this point on. You are now a satellite of Vårgmannskjør, under the command of your new Befälhavare." He gestures to Brighid. "All who do not comply will be dealt with thusly."

He drops the microphone into Daghda's blood and walks off stage.

The last thing I see before they pull a black hood over my head is Donael and Cobb in the front row, tears streaming down their faces, mouths open in a horrified scream, and then there's nothing at all.

They drag me off stage and across the ground. A soldier throws me forward, and I lose my feet under me, my face slamming against a hard, metallic surface. The smell of my own breath inside the hood mingles with something like dirt and old sweat. With my hands restrained behind my back, it's hard to push myself up. I press my forehead into the ground to get my torso up, then work my knees beneath my chest. Then the soldier's foot in my ribs flips me over on my side.

I hear his breathing, which means his face is close

to mine, and I'm about to swing my head forward, slam my forehead against his ear or face and stun him, when he yanks the hood away and light stabs my eyes. Then it goes dark again as he slams a door.

After a moment, things come into focus, light seeping in through the small oval windows. I glance around. Grooved metal floor spotted with dirt and rust. Formed metal benches attached to the walls, restraining belts every few feet. Three vertical storage units with metal grates covering them, used for housing weapons. This is some variation of a transport vehicle.

Outside I can hear the chaos of the crowd, shouting and crying and screaming, a few gunshots, the crack of batons crushing bones. I must not be far from the stage, which means I'm not far from the boys. I have to get out of here and find them, regardless of what it costs me. Something slams against the side of the vehicle, followed by an agonizing howl.

Our uprising did this. We overthrew one dictator only to be colonized by another. Removed one tyrant and replaced her with someone even worse. I knew a Morrigan could not be trusted.

I should have known this would happen. My life has been a warzone for the last fifteen years. As a father I'm supposed to protect Donael from all of this, and now I've dragged him into the middle with the landmines all around us. And the thought arises before I can squash it, *Would Walleus have done this?*

There's a squealing near the doors, the sound of the bolt lock sliding. I shift my head down to keep the light from blinding me so that I can see when I spring out and away from this truck.

The doors fly open, the soldier standing at the rear with a rifle trained on me. This is it, Henraek. This is what you've been preparing yourself for. Can you fight him off with your hands tied behind your back, or will you sit placidly and accept your fate? Is there any point in going on without Donael? Again?

Rifle still trained on me, the soldier steps aside, making room for one of his compatriots, a soldier with skin so pale it's nearly blue. Then the pale one shoves someone forward, and as he tumbles forward and curses, "Damn sonofabitchamadan," my heart liquefies.

"Donael," I say, trying to position myself to break his fall. I'm not quick enough and he slams against the floor, his hands restrained as well.

"Asshole," he spits at them. Clicking follows, and Cobb is tossed in with us before they slam the door, sliding the bolt lock over to secure it.

I do my best to help Donael to his feet, slipping my legs beneath his chest and straightening them, trying to lever him upright.

"Are you OK?" I say when he's up on his knees.

"My wrists hurt. My face hurts."

"Turn around. Let me see if I can release your hands."

The restraints look like ones I've seen before – simple steel ovals with a binder in the center – but there's no keyhole. Instead, a red light pulses, indicating the lock function is activated.

"They're remotely operated. You're going to have to get used to them." I turn around. "Are mine the same?"

"Yeah," he says.

Cobb clicks at us from the floor. We turn our back to him, then crouch down and grab his arms, do our best to pull him upright. His skin scratches against my palms.

Once everyone is upright, Donael and I look out the back windows. Ragjarøn soldiers herd citizens into smaller, more manageable groups. Those who protest and swing pieces of wood are promptly subdued, some lethally. The stage is a good three hundred meters away, and from this orientation, I can't tell where we are. As I scan the crowd, scouring faces, I can't see Emeríann either.

"Dad," Donael says, "what's going on?"

"I don't know."

Cobb clicks.

"I thought they were supposed to help us. Isn't that why they came?"

A soldier bashes his baton against the back of a protestor's head, splitting it open. He wipes the blood off his uniform and flings it on the ground, then resumes watch over his group as if nothing has happened. The man lies limp, the blood from his skull seeping into the ground.

"I thought so." I swallow hard. "It appears I was wrong."

4.
EMERÍANN

The soldier amadan wraps his arm around my neck so tight I can barely breathe. I slam my heel on his foot as hard as I can. He doesn't let go, but it shocks him enough to loosen his grip. That seems like a positive development until I look up and see Brighid take a sword from Ødven and then bring it down across her father's neck. His head clomps against the stage floor and rolls, making eye contact with me on every revolution – accusing me – until it tumbles off the edge into the crowd.

My legs disappear. My body burns. We had it. We were so close. We were minutes from having the city be ours again.

And now it's gone. It's my fault. I planned the bombing. I started the uprising that called Daghda. Brighid wouldn't have come without Daghda. Ødven wouldn't have come without Daghda. Daghda wouldn't have come without the bombing. The city is going to burn again and it's all my fault.

Ødven picks up the microphone and I can barely hear what he says through the blood rushing in my ears, the anger pulsing through my arms. I go to smash my heel again but the soldier has gotten wise, so I throw my head backward, catching him on the cheek instead of the nose like I'd planned. The soldier squeezes tighter, breath rushing from my chest. He puts his mouth next to my ear and I smell old tobacco and raw meat.

"I don't care what she says, I will gut you where you stand if you don't stay still."

I start to fight back until I feel a sharp point in my side.

Ødven announces that Brighid will oversee the city and that we are now property of Vårgmannskjør. Colonized again, and not even by a native. At least the Morrigans were ostensibly trying to make Ardu Oéann a stable country again. He's just going to exploit us.

Across the stage, Henrack is hemmed up about the same as I am. Our eyes meet for a second; then his dart to the crowd. I turn mine too and see the boys in the front row.

I start to call out to Henraek that it will be OK, that we'll figure out something and the boys will be safe, but they slide a black hood over his head and drag him off. I lunge forward to help him and feel a white line of heat in my side.

"I said stay still, you satkäring," the soldier grunts. He leans back, yanking me off my feet, the sliced skin parting even farther, then whips me to the left and propels us forward through the people gathered at the side of the stage. Ragjarøn troops swarm in all directions with rifles slung across their shoulders, some holding back the crowd, others climbing up the scaffolding for a better shot while the remainder spreads out to cover the flanks. Watching them pull wartime maneuvers just minutes after we were supposed to take the city back is goddamned terrifying. In the middle of all the chaos, Daghda's body lies on the stage, pumping out blood.

My feet finally touch the ground as the soldier slams me down, pushing me forward by poking a rifle into my back. I run through every move I know, every technique Henraek and Forgall taught me for disarming an attacker, but something tells me that not only is this bastard quick enough to shoot me dead before I make a decent attack, he'd goddamned enjoy it. Probably put a couple extra in me just for the hell of it. We wind through a mess of people, everyone scuttling like they've already been told their orders, which leads me to believe that Brighid and Ødven had been planning this for a while. How the hell were they able to keep it hidden from us for so long?

We come around the back of Clodhna when the soldier signals to one of the men standing by a door. He swipes a card and opens the secure entrance. My stomach drops. This is not good.

I plant my feet and the rifle jabs into me.

"I don't think you understand how much trouble I'll get in if I shoot you," the soldier growls.

"I don't think you understand how few shits I give." I do my best to steel my voice. His hand lands on my shoulder but I expected it and softened my knees to stay in place. I hear him exhale really hard.

Then I feel both of his hands on my shoulders, pushing me forward. Which means his rifle is hanging freely from the strap.

I drop to a knee and kick out my right leg like a mule, connecting squarely with his kneecap. He grunts hard and doubles over so I swing my leg out and around like a hook punch, aiming my heel where his head should be. But he catches my foot, yanks it and twists. I flip over on my side, landing hard on my right hip, then stab my left leg out, hoping to land somewhere near his face. He tries to snatch it but misses, deflecting my leg. His rifle is hanging from its strap between his legs. I make a grab for it but the soldier has recovered. His fingers wrap around my wrist so hard I can feel the bones grinding against one another. He yanks my arm forward, bringing my face within inches of his.

"This is the last time I will say it." He pushes the words through his teeth. "We are to bring you to a secure location. Unharmed. Those are our orders, with a severe punishment should we not follow them." He squeezes even harder, and I didn't think that was actually possible. The pain is so bad my field of vision narrows. "But I will deal with the consequences if it affords me the joy of gutting you on the steps and leaving you to bleed out. So, I will tell you one last time to knock this shit off. Next time you'll be grabbing for your innards, not my gun. Do you understand?"

He doesn't really ask it so much as he says it. And

while it's my instinct to push him, make him angry and get him to make a mistake, his thing about being given orders makes me hesitate. If I'm to be taken safely, does that mean Henraek is too? Where is he? Surely they know about the boys, so where are they? More important, if I cooperate, can I pry that information out of one of the lower-ranking soldiers?

"I understand," I tell him.

"Good. Now get your ass up and go inside."

I push myself to my feet with as much composure as I can muster and step into the cryptorium. The inside is completely marble, marble that used to be white before we bombed the shit out of the city and sent these roaches scattering, tracking soot and blood all over the place. The building has the eerie feeling of a tomb, like the temperature is just right to keep a body from spoiling. Despite racks of Ragjarøn troops scurrying around, the place is nearly goddamn silent.

The soldier leads me down the hallway to a solid metal doorway, where he scans a badge then veers off to the right.

That badge, man, it scares the shit out of me. Because this is the hub of the Tathadann, which means that in order for there to be so many Ragjarøn troops inside Clodhna – and to have access to so many places – they must have stripped Tathadann personnel of their badges several weeks ago. And all without us knowing. How long has that cunt Brighid been planning this? And to think that this whole time I'd been telling Henraek, *No, relax, stop worrying, we're all fighting for the same thing, that's just residual paranoia from working under the Tathadann for too long.*

If I ever see him again, I'll never be able to tell him he was right. His head might explode. No, don't talk like that, stupid woman. Of course you'll see each other. We'll get out of this somehow. We always have.

The soldier leads me down a hallway that seems to go halfway to forever, but every room we pass makes me more concerned. At first, they are small, like personalized waiting rooms. Then there are rooms with toilets and beds inside. Now, there are bars on each of them. This isn't a waiting area: this is a detention center.

I stop walking for a second and am quickly greeted with a rifle barrel in my back.

"Did you forget what we talked about no more than five minutes ago?" the soldier says.

I mutter something about a pebble in my shoe then continue walking. How the hell am I supposed to get out of this? I don't think I can take him out. He's already proven he's as quick if not quicker than me. Not to mention he's trained for this for years, instead of picking up a couple things from his co-worker and boyfriend. And besides that, he gets off on shooting people. Talking him out of it won't work.

As some vague notion of a plan starts to form in my head, he grabs my shoulder, grunts, "This one," and stops me dead in my tracks.

He swipes his badge and the metal bars slide open. I can feel his frustration mounting with every second I don't step into the cell.

"What do you expect me to–"

His hands land on my shoulders again, shoving me forward. Before I can spin around, the bars slam shut, locking me in.

He starts to walk away, then pauses and sets his face between the bars. "You have no idea how lucky you are, sweetheart."

I feel something barreling up inside me, pushing through my legs and arms. But I tamp it down, keep myself under control. Instead, I cough a few times then spit it in his face.

"I've got a good idea."

The spit drips off his nose, his rage barely contained by whatever threat Ødven has issued on behalf of Brighid to anyone who harms me. I'm tempted to push it further, but instead err on the side of caution. Never know how shitty his home life is and how much more relief he'd get from killing me.

"Just remember what I said." He spins on his heels and stomps away.

I survey my new surroundings. A slab of wood juts out from the wall, an inch of torn padding on top of it. A metal bowl with a drainage hole in the center of it. A small window overlooking the street outside Clodhna.

God damn it.

I press my face against the window. Outside in the street, soldiers gun down protesters, shove people into pre-categorized groups, forcibly disperse the groups that might be able to rebel, batter anyone who dares stand tall.

This was supposed to be a new beginning, an opportunity for the people of Eitan to be responsible for our own future. To throw off the yoke of the Tathadann and revel in our freedom. And now look what we've done. Cold-blooded murder. Separation according to age, race, ability.

Things weren't great under the Tathadann. They were really shitty.

But, I think as my forehead touches the warm, smeared glass of my window, they sure as hell weren't this.

5.
HENRAEK

We've only been driving for twenty minutes when more slaps hit the side of the transport vehicle. As if from a receded memory, I recognize the sound, the pitch.

Heavy-gauge artillery and assorted projectiles, likely thick pieces of wood and metal.

The vehicle judders, wobbling from the smack of the shells and the driver's swerving attempts to be more elusive. While he does succeed in not getting us blown to bits, he also tosses us around the back like ragdolls. I slam against the metal bench, the back of my head hitting the floor. Bright white points speckle my vision for a moment. When they clear, I see Donael and Cobb on the floor near me, their feet in the air and backs against the walls. I shuffle down to them, pulling myself along the grooved floor with the soles of my boots. The driver swerves again but this time he helps me roll closer to the boys. I stretch out my legs and catch them, pull them in close to me.

"Try to hold on," I shout over the whine of the engine and thumps of artillery.

Donael says, "How?" and while it's a reasonable question, I choose not to answer.

The vehicle cuts and weaves down the road – a road? Where are we? – and I clench my legs tighter to keep them safe, my muscles burning with every passing minute.

Before long, our path begins to straighten, and the threat passes. We cruise on at what feels like a good clip and I feel I can release my legs. My thighs burn from the exertion. The boys scoot out from our cocoon, but this time stay on the floor, leaning up against the bench.

I work my way up to my feet and look out the window. Despite the long slabs of wood and metal littering the road, I can't see any people. I suppose out here they stay hidden as a matter of survival.

"What was that?" Donael says.

"I don't know. I've heard stories about bands of scavengers who live out here, scraping by on whatever little bits they can find. Some of them set up shelters in the old resource company outposts. Repurpose whatever's left."

What I can see is mountains in the distance, beyond the scrubland of what might be Westhell County. I haven't been outside Eitan in nearly twenty years. No one really comes out here as far as I know. Looking over the scorched fields, I can see why. Houses long abandoned poke out from the barren ground like rotten teeth in decomposing gums. Scattered over the vast nothing are the heavy-duty trucks resource companies used to scour the ground, though these ones were picked over for parts years ago, only the frames remaining like steel carrion skeletons. I see a single tree in the distance, seemingly towering above the scads of stumps, its black branches reaching for the sky, beseeching the heavens for rain. Its calls go as unheard as ours have for decades.

There's a click, and my wrists feel looser. A second later, our restraints land with a clunk on the floor.

"Did they break?" Donael moves away from them as if they might become self-aware and reattach themselves.

"Remotely controlled." I rub my wrists, working blood-flow back through my fingers. "I guess they're not concerned about us escaping anymore."

Looking outside, I have no idea where we'd go if we did escape.

Two hours later, the transport vehicle slows, then turns right. The boys fell asleep so hard that even two additional attacks from scavengers didn't wake them, and I spent most of the time focusing on the feeling of Donael resting against me. But this change in speed rouses Cobb, his gnarled body nestled on my other side. He unleashes a great yawn. After a few minutes, the road becomes bumpier, jostling Donael awake.

"Where are we?" he says, blinking as he looks around.

"Don't know." I'm about to get up and check out the back window, but the vehicle comes to an abrupt stop, tossing us forward. We land on the floor again, and before we can even stand up the back doors open, the three of us grunting and covering our eyes from the sudden exposure.

"Get up," one of the soldiers says.

"Where's Emeríann? Is she safe? Where did you take her?"

"Get up. Your ride's about to leave," he says, now climbing inside and pulling us to our feet. I push him back, tell him to keep his hands off us. Then there's the click of a baton. He rears back, ready to bash me across the face, when someone shouts out behind him.

"Stand down, soldier."

Rage passes across the soldier's face, but he duly lowers his baton.

"Apologies, Befälhavare Slåtann," the soldier says. "Just keeping the prisoners in line."

"They're not prisoners," Slåtann says. "They're guests. Now help them out."

The soldier is far from pleased by this but does it regardless.

"Henraek, I am Ibra Slåtann," our host says, and I'm a little disconcerted that this man knows my name. "I assure you, Emeríann is safe. I guarantee no one will harm her."

"You're not surprised that I don't believe a word you say, are you?"

"We haven't killed you, have we?" He gestures absently. "So why would we kill her?"

I can think of several reasons but I don't have much choice other than go along with what he says. When I step out of the vehicle, I feel an instant difference in the air. The land in the distance is scorched but greener where we are, and there's a rushing, rhythmic noise under a mechanical drone. I step around the vehicle and see a long makeshift dock comprised of wooden shipping pallets and assorted planks. The dock leads to a nondescript boat, painted red below the midpoint and bright white on the top. Satellites and antennae jut out at angles, and each corner of the boat features a rotary gun that looks to fire shells the size of my fist.

Beyond the boat is water. Water that rushes, water that flows. Water that stretches until the horizon and then far beyond that.

My knees weaken and I nearly collapse. All the stories my father told me, about streams and rivers and oceans, about green hills and blue skies, about bright red birds and silvery scaled fish, stories I'd thought he'd made up for my benefit, to give me something to believe in: those stories were true.

"Are we still in Ardu Oéann? What country is this?" I don't ask anyone in particular, more a question to the universe, a query as to whether we're still in the same reality or if I finally watched too many memories and have now fallen into one. "Where are we?"

"We haven't left the country. This is barely two hundred miles from Eitan," the man says. "You should really expand your horizons."

I walk toward the water, my hand instinctively reaching out for Donael and Cobb. Several men work on the boat, tightening lines and shouting to each other in a foreign tongue.

We pass the beginning of the dock and the ground abruptly turns from grass to sand. I kneel down near the edge, scoop a handful of sand and let it slip through my fingers. I take two steps, the water lapping against the toes of my boots, and run my fingers through it. It's cold on my skin, and it is wonderful, an explosion of sensation. After not having water for so long, I want to stick my face in it and drink, but even in Eitan we know you can't drink salt water. I stick my whole hand in, cupping it then pouring it back. Such a simple thing, yet so significant.

"I'm sorry to break this up, but we need to leave," Slåtann says behind me. "The tide is going out and we'll be stranded for hours if we miss it."

I swirl my hand in the water one last time, then stand, rub some across my face. It's like waking for the first time. If this is true, that there are oceans and green land, then that means anything can be true.

Slåtann leads us up to the dock, nodding toward the boat.

"We're getting on there?" I say.

"Härskare Äsyr needs your advisement in Vårgmannskjør, so you're going there one way or another." He adjusts the bandoleer wrapped around his chest. "And I'm guessing you're not much of a swimmer."

I take the boys' hands and lead us down the dock, the pilings shifting beneath us as we walk across the wood planks suspended over the water. When we get to the boat, I glance back before helping the boys over the threshold. The surface is white like the rest of the boat, but textured and gritty to avoid slipping.

Tools line the underside of the walls. Slåtann shows us to a door.

We enter a surprisingly large room. Four bunks hang from the wall, held up by chains at either end so they can be folded back into the wall for space. Beneath them are formed benches, much like those in the transport vehicle but more comfortable looking. On the far side is a U-shaped blue vinyl booth ringing around a white table. There's a narrow door in the corner that probably leads to a bathroom. And hanging by the door are three heavy coats with fur-rimmed hoods, one large and two mediums.

I let out a little laugh and nod at them. "Really?"

"You may think it funny now," Slåtann says, "but I would wager in a couple days you won't."

"Why won't I find it funny?"

I glance out the window and see we're already several hundred meters from shore. I didn't even feel us take off.

Slåtann tips his imaginary hat then says he's headed to the bridge to see the captain, leaving us alone as the shore slowly recedes into the distance. I stand with my palms pressed against the glass, as if I could project myself across the distance and contact Emeríann, let her know we're alive, ask her where she is. The boys come up beside me, and we watch our homeland grow smaller and smaller, until it's eventually overtaken by the water.

6.
EMERÍANN

I'm lying on the hard mattress with one arm draped across my eyes when I hear the door creak open. I tighten my grip on the knife I keep strapped against my calf, now hidden under my back. Someone steps inside my cell. I wait for them to approach me, get close enough that I can jump to my feet and slice their throat all in one motion. But they stay near the door.

"If that's your knife you've got behind your back," that cunt Brighid says, "know that there are three armed soldiers right behind me. You'll be ribbons before you can stand."

I debate calling her bluff and charging her, but I can hear other feet scrabbling near my cell.

"What do you want?" I say, not bothering to move my arm.

"To apologize for the condition of the cell. We're preparing better accommodations for you, but they're not ready yet."

I let go of my knife and pop up to my feet, blood

63

pounding inside my fists. I quickly see she wasn't joking: the three soldiers point their rifles at me. I stay in place, jaw clenched, wanting so bad to just hit something.

"*That* is what you want to apologize for? This cell?" I gesture out, my hands needing something, anything, to occupy them. "What about what happened out there? Beheading your father. Destroying our chance at being free. Ruining all the work we've done the last six months, making all the people who died for us to live freely die for nothing." My voice rises with every word, and despite the soldiers' fingers getting twitchier as I shout at Brighid, I can't get myself to stop. "Hell, what about riding in here like our savior and fighting alongside us when you were lying to us the entire time? How about you apologize for any of that? That's what I'm upset about, not how hard my goddamned mattress is."

Brighid stares at me for a long minute, and with every tick I expect her to give the signal for them to execute me. I could have died a number of times during the uprising but skirted around it at each pass. At least this way it will be quick and painless.

She raises her hand. I close my eyes.

"She's just upset," Brighid says to the soldiers. "Understandably so."

I inhale through my nose, breathe out my lips.

"Lower your weapons," she says.

I open my eyes and no longer have a target on my chest.

"Leave us a minute." She says it without looking at them.

"Ma'am," one of the soldiers starts.

"I said leave."

"Ma'am, she's armed."

Still Brighid won't break eye contact with me.

"She won't use it," she says to them, then to me, "will she?"

I don't give any response, which I guess is a response in itself. The soldiers don't like it, but after a moment they relent and leave us. Brighid steps forward. My fingers curl behind my back, like they're seeking out the knife. It's tempting, but before I could grab it, she would likely jump me and gut me with my own knife or call for the soldiers.

"I do apologize for those things too," Brighid says. "Just so you know."

"You'll understand if your word means shit to me, right? You sold us out. You betrayed us."

"I can see why you feel that way. But you have to understand where I'm coming from."

"Hell?"

She smirks. "It really was a privilege fighting with you. I wasn't lying about that."

"I guess that's the only thing," I spit. "Where is Henraek? Is he alive? Is he safe?"

"He's very alive and very safe. Donael and Cobb are with him."

"Where are they? I need to see them."

"Henraek was needed for important business in Vårgmannskjør."

"In Vårgmannskjør? What business?"

She cocks her head. "The important kind."

"You should've come to Eitan earlier," I tell her.

"You were born to be a politician."

"No, I was born to be a savior, to save Eitan from Daghda," she says, her voice dead serious. "There are so many things you don't understand about my father. I spent years following him, moving from small villages to enormous cities. I've traveled across every continent, through more countries than I can remember. I've seen palaces with rooms people have never even entered, and I've crept through slums where children skewer rats and roast them over the smoldering rubble of a bombed house."

"Why are you telling me this? You think you know tragedy better than we do?"

"Our destinies rode on the wind and took us to whatever political leader, businessman, warlord, or gangster would pay my father the most money to kill someone. If you asked me how many heads I've seen explode from one of his bullets, I couldn't even tell you. I've lost count. And you know what I learned through all that?" She takes a step toward me. "There are only two people my father thinks about."

"Who, you and him?"

"No," she says. "Himself. And Fannae Morrigan."

I'm surprised by the name.

"He never forgave her. After all he did to save Eitan from those vulture resource companies, she tossed him aside, discarded like garbage, the same thing the companies would do to the land once it had been fully harvested. He didn't kill for money, he killed to salve his wounds. The only thing that let him wake up every morning was the possibility of revenge."

"I'd want to kill her too if I was him."

Brighid breathes out something like a laugh. "Not revenge on her. He wanted revenge on Eitan. For abandoning him. For not avenging him." She pulls closer to me. "For forgetting him."

I swallow hard and realize my hands are shaking.

"We were in the far east when he heard there was a defector from the Tathadann meeting with Ødven. We took three boats and traveled for a week to get to Vårgmannskjør so we could meet the defector in person." She shakes her head. "He was creepy, only had one eye."

That description sounds familiar but I can't place it. I wonder if Henraek knows him.

"My father aligned himself with Ragjarøn because they had the firepower and the numbers to crush Eitan. His plan was to return, destroy Fannae and the Tathadann, then burn the city to the ground. Payback for what he saw as slighting him." She throws her hands out to the side. "That was your savior. A weak and petty man."

"So why didn't he?"

"Because Ødven and I stopped him. Ødven's more of a..." She gestures absently. "He's a forward thinker. He sees possibilities where others see restrictions. The way we looked at it, we could draw on the resources and technology in Vårgmannskjør to get Eitan back on its feet. Before Ardu Oéann can be autonomous, we need to be stable. This region is volatile enough. We need a steady hand here, and Ødven's providing that."

"We're supposed to venerate him now?"

"No, just thank him." She gives a smile that could

cut glass. "So yes, I am sorry for the condition of the cell. But no, I'm not the least bit sorry for the patricide."

She turns to leave but I can't help myself.

"I don't care about your daddy issues. You betrayed us," I say. "But I guess I shouldn't be surprised. All the Morrigans do is lie and steal."

She whirls around and stomps toward me, then before I even see her hand move there's a sharp crack and my face is on fire. She whips her hand again and backhands me across the other side of my face. I don't press my hand against it, refusing to give her the satisfaction. I taste blood in my mouth and spit it on the ground.

"Let's get something sorted right now because you will never make that mistake again. I will gut you before you blaspheme me with that name." Her hand shoots out and grapples my throat, tight enough that I feel the blood pound in my temples but not so tight that I can't breathe. "My mother was a Tobeigh. *I* am a Tobeigh. My father's name is a mark of shame but one I will bear witness to. I am not a Morrigan. I am a Tobeigh."

She pushes me to the back of my cell, the imprints of her fingers still throbbing on my neck.

"By the time we're done with our work here, every nation will know the name Tobeigh. They will respect it. And that starts right here," she says, pointing at the ground. "And right now."

7.
HENRAEK

If I were a different sort of person, I would look on this as some kind of dramatic comedy. The one thing we sought for years in Eitan, we are currently surrounded by; yet that one thing is the source of all our pain and suffering.

But, with my fingers curled around the rim of the toilet and my face hovering inches above a fine glaze of bile and coffee floating on the surface of the water, I'm not of a mind to look at this philosophically.

The first few hours passed nicely. Cobb, Donael, and I sat on the bench and stared out the window at the sea, the scenery never quite the same but still never really different. I kept returning to the thought that someone could jump off a dock a few hundred miles from Eitan and create a wave that traveled across the ocean, and that same wave would crash on a beach near a child who has never even heard of Eitan or Westhell or the Tathadann and whose language doesn't even have the sounds to properly enunciate those words. The vastness and simultaneous connectedness fascinated me.

After dinner – light by their standards but on par with what we had at home – Slåtann brought the boys and me up to the bridge so they could steer the ship and look at all the navigation devices. The captain let Cobb pull the rope that unleashed the horn, and I thought he'd sprain his mouth he clicked so hard with glee.

Later, Slåtann showed me how to strap the boys into their bunks so they wouldn't be pitched out in the middle of the night. The trip had been so calm, the sea so placid, that I actually laughed at him.

Then the winds picked up.

The boys were already dead asleep and nothing short of a bomb set off in our enclosed room would wake them, so they hadn't noticed the constant rocking and shifting. I've always thought of myself as pretty resilient after all I'd endured during the Struggle, then my double life under the Tathadann, then the uprising. But this is a sensation unlike anything I've ever felt. It's not even as if we're barreling through gale force winds. Hell, some of the soldiers are standing outside smoking cigarettes and laughing as they hold on to the rails. Meanwhile, I've puked so many times that nothing's coming out anymore. By this point I'm praying for a quick death or at least a large wave to slam my head against the toilet and knock me unconscious for a few hours.

When the sky begins to lighten over the horizon the winds die down, and after an hour I no longer feel like I'm stuck inside a centrifuge. I make my way around the room, creeping along the walls as much for stability as to avoid waking the boys. I ease the door closed and step onto the deck. One of the soldiers rests against the railing, a cigarette perched between his fingers. He glances over at me, gives a slight nod, then returns his gaze to the ocean.

Standing here now, looking at the water shifting between variations of blue, the waves constantly morphing and changing in a way that is never jagged or inorganic like so many things in Eitan, I can see why so many poems have been written about the sea. I am calmer than I should be after getting yanked from my homeland and thrust toward an uncertain future in a distant land.

Which immediately triggers the reptile part of my brain that assesses every situation for possible attack. They could be shipping us out into the ocean only to throw us overboard. But why wouldn't they just have shot us back in Eitan? They could be transporting us up to Vårgmannskjør to torture us or conduct experiments on us. Maybe Doctor Mebeth fled to Vårgmannskjør. But he was also a large part of the Tathadann and I'd be surprised to see Ødven Äsyr overlooking that. And again, they could've just killed us after Daghda.

That leaves Slåtann's assertion that Äsyr needs my counsel, but what on earth could I advise him on? How to lose a revolution? How to destroy a family? How to murder your best friend?

As I'm mulling over the different ways in which I've failed, something flashes in my eyes, so bright it actually hurts. I shield myself with my hand, ducking down by instinct as if it was a sniper's laser. I glance around and catch the soldier looking at me like I'm hallucinating. I move my hand and it catches me again in the side of my eye, but this time not as intense. I squint my eyes and look out over the water.

And sitting on the horizon, casting a yellow sheen over the water, is the sun, rising above the curve of the earth. It's only a yellow ball floating above a blue sea but is more beautiful than I'd ever thought it could be. I wish Emeríann were here to see it with me. Part of me wants to go grab the boys, but I don't think they'd have quite the same appreciation at their age. Then after a second I have to squint and look away, blink hard to remove the pale yellow dots from my vision. I'd always thought the phrase "staring at the sun" was metaphorical. Apparently not.

My vision cleared, I glance over at the soldier, who is again looking at me like I'm insane. He shakes his head then chains another cigarette from the one in his mouth and flicks the old one into the water.

"Do you know how much longer we have?" I say to him.

He shrugs, never looking at me. "Scheduled to dock tomorrow evening. If no storms, maybe tomorrow afternoon. If storms, next day, day after."

"Tomorrow evening?" I feel my stomach get queasy just thinking about another night aboard. "Are you serious?"

Now he looks at me, his pale blue eyes and angular face seemingly designed to cut through another person without touching. "If no storms. If storms, next day, day after."

He flicks his cigarette into the ocean and walks away.

I remain on the deck with my eyes closed, focusing on the feeling of the sun shining on my face. Then I hear Donael say, "Holy shit."

He comes up next to me, but I don't bother to correct his language. This is too nice a feeling.

"I always thought that was a story," he says.

I don't have much response other than to wrap my arm around him, hold him close. We stand on the deck, the boat shifting side to side as it crests over the waves. After a few minutes, his body language changes.

"What's up?" I say.

"Nothing."

"Donael." I look down at him. I have a good idea what it is but am not ready to bring it up first. "What's up?"

"Nothing, I…" He pauses a second, arranging his words. "I still don't get why they did that, back there."

I figured that was it. I let out a long sigh, not really sure how to explain allegiance and duplicity to a kid who has already seen too much.

"Sometimes, it just happens," is all I can muster.

"But you guys – the guys you fought with before – you were all good, right?"

"I'd like to think so."

"So why'd you agree to fight with Brighid and Ødven, if she was so bad? I mean, they destroyed everything we had, Dad. All of our stuff, in the apartment, it's all gone because of them. Why'd you fight with them?"

Heat spreads across my face, through my arms. It's not anger, but an adjacent feeling. I crouch down onto my knee to come eye level with him.

"There are two things you need to understand, son. Number one: in war, people lie. They do what they need to do and tell you what they need to tell you so they can win. That's just how it goes." I set my hands on his shoulders, making sure he's focused solely on me. "But number two, and this is the most important thing: possessions are just things, and they will never destroy our family. Do you understand me? I told you before that I was never going to let something pull us apart, and I would die before that happened again. OK?"

He mutters something noncommittal.

"I need you to say you understand," I say, "and I need you to mean it."

He finally looks me in the eyes. Something about his gaze, it just feels natural, organic. Like it's familiar on a cellular level, because it's like looking at myself.

"I know," he says. "I understand."

"Good."

He bites his lip a second, then says, "But I still hate them for it."

I clap his shoulder, because there's no arguing with that. "I do too, kiddo. I do too."

I guide him back to our room and get him in his bed to sleep a while longer, but he just tosses and turns. After a few minutes, I hear him pad across the room toward my bunk. Without saying a word, I slide over and lift my blanket, and he curls up against me like a long-lost part of my body. Two minutes later, he's snoring softly. I stare at the ceiling, listening to the soft rhythm of his breath, and it's only a matter of moments before it lulls me to sleep as well.

The second night is rougher than the first, but I feel like I handle it well. I only vomit twice, in any case. The boys sleep just as soundly. The winds stick around for much of the morning and afternoon, which the captain says will impede our progress, but it's time that seems to stall. The sun stays perched high above us, in possibly the longest afternoon ever.

After the boys eat their third meal of the day, I go up to the bridge and check the navigation clock. It's after nine. At night. But the sun is still sitting at the three-quarters mark, when we should be squinting to see things in the dark.

I go over to the captain, my head dizzy and my body sloshing with liquid inside, disoriented. "How much longer do we have?"

He nods forward and points with one hand.

Not far in the distance, I can see buildings jutting up against the dimming sky, gleaming and glistening even from this far away.

I head back down to the room and tell the boys, who are already yawning.

"I think I need a nap or something," Donael says. "Maybe I didn't sleep so well."

"Yeah," I say, unsure how else to answer. "Maybe."

Not more than twenty minutes later, the captain tells the crew to prepare for docking. We come out of the room and as the boat slips into the harbor we are greeted by sleek, angular buildings made of glass and polished metal, streets made of cobblestones instead of potholes, cars zipping along the street and citizens flowing along the sidewalks and scenic pathways. The feeling of dizziness and liquidity doubles, and not from the sky that refuses to darken.

Slåtann stifles a yawn as he comes up next to me. "We'll get you right to your accommodations so you can get your boys down to sleep. I know mine become cranky when they stay up too late."

"Yeah," I say, my eyes tracking across an amphitheater and a football stadium near the water's edge. "That sounds good."

The boat judders against the pristine dock.

"Well, Henraek," Slåtann says, gesturing broadly across the city. "Welcome to Vårgmannskjør."

8.
EMERÍANN

The soldier slides open the door to my cell and I don't immediately lash out and cut him. I think I'm getting soft.

"On your feet," he says.

"Suck my dick."

"Excuse me?" He steps forward, hand now resting on the butt of his rifle.

"I thought we were giving arbitrary commands."

He runs his tongue over his teeth and I can almost hear him thinking how much he'd enjoy beating my ass.

"I have orders from Befälhavare Tobeigh to collect you and move you to new accommodations."

"That's what you're calling restraining cells now, accommodations?"

His jaw flexes, nostrils flare as he exhales hard. "If you are unwilling to cooperate, I will be forced to make you comply."

I take a read of him, his body language. He

obviously wants to smash that rifle against my face, but if he wanted to shoot me, he could have already done it.

"Where are these new accommodations?"

We pause by the front desk to Clodhna, opposite of where we entered. Three men pace by the guard, their rifles in hand and ready. The soldier holds up a blanket.

"What the hell is that?"

"A blanket. Put it on."

"Blow me." One of the guards snickers. Another scowls.

The soldier gives me that look again, his patience wearing thin. "Do you want to get shot?"

"You're going to shoot me if I don't get under the blanket?"

"No. But they will." He leans down and points at a monitor on the desk, displaying feeds from multiple security cameras. "When they see our uniforms, do you think they'll recognize your face quick enough to miss you when they start shooting? Are you willing to take that chance?"

On the east side camera, a group of soldiers hunkers down behind clear riot shields as rebels lob bricks and chunks of wood. On the west side, two soldiers drag an unconscious woman across the street by her armpits then toss her on a pile of four other unconscious people. At least, I hope they're unconscious. The south camera is mostly obscured by black smoke, but I'm not sure what's burning.

They're out there brutalizing everyone I fought

with and I'm stuck in here, cuffed and passive, listening to Brighid apologize.

This is bullshit.

I swing my cuffed hands up and wrap them around the soldier's neck then yank backwards, pulling him toward me. In my head I can already see us falling backward on the floor, then me wrapping my legs around him and yanking the cuffs until he chokes, then using his body to shield me as I grab his rifle and mow down the guards.

But he plants his back foot before I can flip us, then latches his thick hands on my forearms and hurls me over his head. I crash against the glass wall and my hip digs into the floor when I land.

Before I can blink away the stars, his rifle muzzle is in my face. His chest is heaving, his face red and eyes wild. I can see his finger twitching on the trigger and expect at any moment for him to unleash a bestial scream and spread my brains all over the lobby. Instead he pitches the blanket at me, slamming my head against the glass.

"I'm walking out the door now," he says, his voice deadpan. "You don't come now, I'll be happy to deal with the consequences of shooting you."

There are scores of rebels and citizens outside, but there are also a shit-ton of Ragjarøn soldiers. If I run, this soldier will gun me down. Or the guards will. Or one of the other soldiers will. Supposedly Brighid wants me alive, and they haven't killed me yet despite a good amount of provocation, so I guess they're not lying about that. And giving in now will give me a little more time to figure my way out of this.

I push myself up to my feet, blanket draped over my arms.

"I'm going to need some guidance," I say to the soldier.

He comes back toward me, says, "That's one word for it," then drapes the blanket over my head and leads me outside.

I recoil immediately at all the commotion. After having been inside the deathly quiet rooms of Clodhna for several days, the noise of the street is damn near deafening. Gunshots. Screaming. Cars backfiring. Cinder blocks tumbling as explosives rock the air. I make my way down the sidewalk by watching his heels just under the edge of the blanket. For a second I lose his trail and end up on a dirt patch, banging my shins against the edge of a water fountain. Figures. I look down and there's a finger lying in the dirt. The soldier calls out for me to stay close and I follow the sound of his voice.

A minute later, he tells me to stop. There's another voice, sounds like a younger soldier. Then a door opens. The younger voice asks for my hand and helps me into the car.

"Keep your head covered, miss. There's some crazy people out here today." He's got a slight twang at the edge of his words. He's definitely not Ragjarøn, and he's not from the hills either, which means he's probably lived in Eitan for a while. Which means Brighid has either secretly recruited people or he was part of a group she arranged to be here. Neither makes me feel better than the other.

I keep the blanket on, partially because I don't want

someone getting a potshot at me and partially because it's cold as balls in here. Must be a commandeered Tathadann vehicle. Light slips in through a small hole in the blanket. It's perfect because, despite knowing that I should stay covered for my safety, I have to know where we're going. The outside passes in flashes and slivers, but what I see is enough to chill me.

Rebels lined up against the wall, hands on the back of their heads, waiting as Ragjarøn soldiers load them onto transport vehicles, taking them who-knows-where.

A butcher shop owned by a rebel sympathizer who let us take over his back room so we could drill through the floor and connect to the underground tunnels and evade the Tathadann, although it ended up being only a small portion – not even a quarter-mile – of the rumored tunnel system.

Piles of bodies. White ones, brown ones. In rags, in Amergi clothing, in Brigu garb. Some of them whole, some of them not.

Our uprising, our chance to be free, gone. Everything we'd fought for over the last six months – and the year before that – erased in a few days.

I slink down in my seat and let my head fall against the blanket.

The car ride barely lasts fifteen minutes. We slow to a stop and the soldier rolls down the window and speaks to someone. Then we pull forward. A checkpoint. I peek through the hole but don't recognize where we are. We continue down a small road, potholes making the car judder and shake enough that the autodriver has trouble navigating and the soldier has to take over. Something that looks like a wall or a store passes by, then a tree. Where the hell are we?

The soldier stops and exits the car. I sit and wait. Outside, I hear him talk to another soldier, something about secured location, sightlines, penetrability. The young soldier gets out of the car and, after receiving the OK, opens my door.

"We're going inside, miss," he says as he takes my arm. "Watch your step."

We head up a staircase that had been cement at one point, before it was overtaken by moss and dirt. Once we're inside, the young soldier tells me I can take my blanket off.

The room is small. I might call it cozy in a different situation. Old wooden floors. A few worn armchairs that look like they'd be comfortable. A kitchen table made of reclaimed wooden planks. Three paintings on the wall, abstract shapes in contrasting colors that smash against one another and seem to vibrate with the way the brushstrokes cross.

"Miss," the young soldier says, "if you could follow me upstairs."

We pass through the dim hallway. There are rectangles on the wall, a few shades lighter than their background. Family pictures from before the house was commandeered.

At the end of the hall is a tight stairwell up to the second floor. This whole place has the feeling of a cabin out in the woods, but we're only a short distance from Clodhna. Still, there's a hush that fills the place, like the people who lived here suffered some tragedy that couldn't be reckoned with so they just decided to never mention it and it absorbed into the house. Or maybe I'm just too inside my head, like Henraek used to say.

Used to? Don't say that, woman.

"This is your room," the younger soldier says, his hand showing me the way.

It's only a little bigger than my former cell, but there's an actual bed with sheets, a freestanding mirror – albeit one that has oxidized and fogged over – and a small dresser, though I don't have any clothes to put in there. A small window, the size of a manhole cover, too small to climb out of and too high up to drop down from. The floor is carpet, which makes me cringe at the thought of all the years of dirt and grime ground into it. I glance outside the window, see a few trees in a small backyard ringed in by a fence, but still no landmarks.

"Miss, you need to eat," he says.

"Eat?"

He points at a night table in the corner, at a plate holding a sandwich stuffed full of meat and cheese with fresh fruit on the side. I pick up the sandwich, sniff it, and my mouth instantly waters.

"Holy shit, is this salami?" He nods yes. "Real salami? Not ground up pigeon with so much spice you can't tell?"

"No, miss. It's real. But you do need to eat quickly."

I'm about to bite into it before I hear what he said. "Quickly?" I say. "Quickly before what?"

"You'll be accompanying Befälhavare Tobeigh on a mission."

"I'm what?" My hand drops, pieces of meat falling out and landing on the carpet. "What kind of mission?"

"That's above my rank, miss. You'll have to ask Befälhavare Tobeigh."

"I will," I say, bringing the sandwich to my mouth. "As soon as I see her."

He clears his throat. "Miss, she's waiting downstairs."

9.
HENRAEK

I had to carry both of the boys into our room, then lasted all of ten minutes before collapsing on the bed and falling asleep.

I wake up what feels like a few hours later – disoriented because of the foreign, magical sunlight streaming through our windows. It's brighter now than it had been on our arrival. I roll over to face Emeríann, and find only an untouched pillow on her side of the bed. Right. I remember now. I wonder where she is, if she's awake or sleeping, if she knows that there are places where the sun actually does shine. I wonder if she's safe, if she broke free of Ragjarøn and is hunkered down with rebels, planning the next phase of the uprising, the war in Eitan that never seems to end, or if she's still under Ragjarøn's control. I wonder if she's thinking about me too.

I struggle to pull myself upright in bed. My mouth is tacky, head filled with cotton. I blink and glance around for a clock but find none. The boys are still snoring, both of them lying on top of the covers with their shoes still on. We have no other clothes to wear, but I must've been really tired if I sloughed them off in their bed without taking off their shoes. I push aside thoughts of all the bacteria that I brought into their sheets as I pad quietly through the room, taking it in. Minimalist décor. Light colored walls with polished metal shelving. Carpet the color of an Eitan summer evening, which strikes me as nostalgic in a strange way. The room next to this is something like a sitting room – couch, two chairs, dinner table, coffee table – that extends into the kitchen, all decorated the same austere way. But the far wall is a window. The entire wall, just glass stretching from floor to ceiling, end to end.

A halo of condensation forms around my hands when I press them on the glass. The whole city unfurls ten stories beneath us, as far out as I can see. The harbor where we came in sits to the far west, a few boats motoring in and out. Trams slip quietly through the streets as people move around them, like water parting around a duck. I glance up and figure there must be at least another twenty stories above us. This building is easily twice as tall as anything in Eitan. Any tall buildings we had were destroyed during one of the wars waged over the last sixty years. The window is so large and immersive, I feel like I'm leaning out over the void, and when I look down I get a rush of vertigo. The wavering feeling could also be cognitive dissonance, because nothing about this city resembles what I've always heard about Vårgmannskjør, not to mention the whole country of Brusandhåv. Hell, the name of the capital means "People of the Wolf," which aptly described the citizens here. Or so I'd thought.

There's a large square in what appears to be the city center, and in the middle of the square sits a statue. It's hard to tell from this distance but it appears to be a two-headed wolf with the body of a man, and the fact that I can determine that from this distance means the statue must be massive.

"Holy shit," Donael says behind me.

"Watch your mouth," I say this time. He's always so quiet. I never hear him enter.

He stands beside me. "Come on. You'd say the same thing. Look at that!"

"OK. Maybe you're right."

"I thought this place was supposed to be terrible," he says, pressing his face against the glass. "Like, people eating each other and stuff."

"Where'd you hear that?"

He shrugs. "School."

"You can't believe what they taught you at school. The Tathadann lies with every breath and their schools are just a center to brainwash the next generation."

He looks at me like he's already bored of what I'm saying. To be fair, I do rail against them a good amount.

"I meant other kids at school. Craesa's dad told her that in war they wear the skin of the people they kill like a mask."

"Donael, that's disgusting." I'd heard the same thing too. Also that they left spare body parts in front of the houses of their conquered for the families to discover.

"What? I didn't say it. They're the ones who are doing it anyway. It does sound kind of badass, though."

"There's nothing badass about war. And we haven't seen anyone wearing skin yet. You know, the Tathadann said a bunch of terrible things about the rebels too, and none of that was true."

"At least we expected the Tathadann to try to kill us." He points outside. "Those soldiers were supposed to help us."

"I told you there's nothing good about war."

He glances up at me for a second, then turns back to the city. "Maybe we just need to learn who to trust."

"You trust me," I say, a little more forcefully than I meant to, annoyed I've had to have this conversation twice. But I'll repeat myself until I'm hoarse if it dissuades him from taking the same path I did. "And you stay as far away from fighting as you can, understand?"

He doesn't look at me but I can tell he's playing out the options in his head.

"I'm talking to you, Donael. This is serious."

"I know, Dad. OK? I know." He sighs hard. "You're talking to me like I don't know what happens."

I don't flinch from his words, but only barely.

"I'm sorry that you've had to see what you have, that I couldn't protect you from it. But I will do everything I can for the rest of my life to make sure you don't have to suffer that again." He leans against me, not very hard but enough to say *OK, I know* without actually having to say it. I'll take the small victories where I can get them.

We're just finishing breakfast when someone knocks on the door. Donael and Cobb freeze, their eyes darting to me, their faces stricken with fear.

"We're OK," I tell them. If they wanted to kill us, they wouldn't put us up in a nice place first. I hope.

My stomach sloshes as I stand, the five glasses of water I drank this morning distending it uncomfortably, and when I open the door I find Slåtann waiting in the hallway.

"Good afternoon," he says.

"Afternoon?" I glance over at the boys, shoveling in the last of their breakfast.

"It's just after midday." He gives a wan smile. "Most visitors have trouble adjusting to the seasons. This far north, we have odd seasons that change quickly. Right now, obviously, we're in the season of light. It dims at night but never gets dark. You'll find it difficult to sleep at first, but trust me, it's much preferable to the season of dark, which will start in about a month."

I nod.

"Now please, make yourselves ready. Härskare Äsyr awaits you."

"We're supposed to be at his beck and call?" I say. "I thought he was still in Eitan."

That smile shifts, as if I'd already answered my own questions.

"We're waiting outside." With that, he turns and walks down the hallway.

I stand in the door, staring at the empty space for a moment, still trying to orient myself to it being afternoon.

"OK, boys, finish up." I close the door and set the dishes in the sink. "Time to see the savages up close."

Donael lays a hand over the fork, as if trying to palm it. He sees my eyes, knows that I watched him do it. He hesitates a second, then pushes it aside. Which makes me glad he made the right decision, but also opens a small crack in my chest, because he thought to bring a weapon in the first place.

Ødven and Slåtann lead us around town, wrapped up in our heavy jackets with puffs of breath bursting from our mouths. They point out various social welfare programs they have implemented. Some of the people in the city wear light jackets, a couple wear mid-weight, and one or two wear no jacket at all, which makes me feel even colder. We walk most of the time, which seems odd to me. Although he is the leader of the country, Ødven still sports short-cropped hair and a trimmed white beard and dresses in military fatigues. He prefers walking along the sidewalks and hopping on and off trams – even paying for them – to being driven around in an ostentatious car like Morrigan and the rest of the Tathadann did. On occasion, he even stops and talks to people passing by, though I have no idea what they're saying. I'm sure he has a security detail – he'd be careless not to, given how freely he walks around – but they blend in so well that I haven't once seen a soldier. Or maybe, it occurs to me, the citizens are just too terrified to move against him.

We stop before a squat square building. A line of people wait to enter, most of them holding canvas or plastic bags. I saw the same thing in Eitan during the Struggle, Tathadann soldiers watching the line with rifles drawn, except the people were rebels and once inside they would be executed.

"This is one of our heating stations," Slåtann says. "There are seventy-seven throughout the city. They run all day long, driven by our self-sustaining power infrastructure."

"Anyone can go in them?"

"Anyone who's cold and has no way to warm themselves," Ødven says. He calls out to a man in his mid-thirties exiting the building, a stack of towels in his hands. "Gaagnir. Gaagnir Nilsson."

The man turns slowly to the sound of his name. He looks like a lagon, and part of me is surprised they have a memory trade up here.

"How many people have you helped today?" Ødven says to Gaagnir Nilsson. When Nilsson responds, his words sound like a combination of English and the native language, but with a strange, swirling affect to them. "More than two hundred already," Ødven translates for me. "That's a slow day."

Slåtann points to the building beside it, a tall thin one with geometric panes of glass patterned through it. "That is one of fifty-eight shelters. Anyone can go in those as well, but they must work in order to stay. Cooking, cleaning, maintenance, checking guests in or out."

"Guests? I thought it was a shelter."

"It is, for those who don't have any place to go," Ødven says. "If I was without a home, I would rather be referred to as the guest of a shelter and keep my dignity than have someone state the obvious and refer to me as homeless. It's a small thing, but it makes a big difference."

Slåtann clears his throat. "Along with the other social programs I told you about – the food reserves, the energy conservation and recycling – we provide everyone without shelter the opportunity to earn it through work. Provided that they either contribute their current skills to the city or learn new skills that are in need, we offer modest housing options. They're not luxurious, but they're not an icy patch of cold sidewalk. Many citizens fulfill their part of the bargain, although some do not. We extend ourselves for anyone willing to do the same, but we will not be taken advantage of and must move those citizens out of housing. Still," he says, gesturing to the line outside the heating station, "even if they won't comply, there's no reason for them to be completely miserable. Some people take longer to learn their lesson than others."

The way he says it makes me wonder if that's directed at Emeríann and myself.

"I think it's incredibly generous what you've done here," I say to Ødven as we continue walking, "providing for your citizens."

"It's only proper," he says, with a pride that belies his tone.

"So, since you've seen fit to colonize Eitan, will that generosity extend to my people as well?" I keep my tone as flat as possible. "Or are you only so kind to the pure-bloods?"

Donael snickers into his hand, then cuts it short when I snap at him. Slåtann doesn't look very amused, but Ødven maintains his magnanimous expression.

"I understand your concern." He gestures toward the people lined up. "Yes, most of them were born in one of Brusandhåv's provinces, but many others have sought refuge here, whether fleeing wars in their home countries or seeking a better life. But as long as they are willing to abide by our social contract, then we are happy to provide for them."

I take this in as a group of people passes us on the sidewalk, most of them upright and briskly walking, though not necessarily like they're annoyed or hurrying. Most even have something like a smile on their faces, though few are talking.

"But I'll warn you only once, Henraek." His smile remains though his voice takes on a sharp edge. "I have treated you with respect and will not tolerate condescension. Nor will I suffer dog-whistle speech. Do you understand me?"

I hold my hands up. "Just looking out for my people."

We continue walking. Cobb points at a building and clicks. A heavyset man with a beard that reaches halfway down his chest bumps into my shoulder. I flinch by instinct, ready for a confrontation, but he holds his hands up in apology, giving a great belly-laugh. The wealth of interpersonal connection and civility is weird.

Some of the people, however, shuffle their way along the sidewalk, their blank stares cast out to some far point. They look like more lagons, but they also look different from lagons. *Wispy* is the best way I can think of to describe them. I try to think back to Nilsson, but the towels obscured most of his body.

"See, Henraek," Ødven says, back in his benevolent ruler demeanor, "what Fannae Morrigan failed to understand – and Daghda, too, for that matter – is that you do not need an iron fist to earn the loyalty of your people. You need to treat them compassionately, but also fairly. You are a father. Think of how you parent your sons."

I wince slightly at the words.

"If one of them steals from a shop, you must correct him, yes? But do you chop off his hand or simply punish him? Chopping off the hand is an effective deterrent, but if he steals again, then what? Chop off his other hand? How will he eat? How will he write? How will he help carry wood? No, what you must do is help him understand that stealing is unacceptable, but also try to help him be a better person. Your hand must be firm, but not iron. Sometimes that calls for sacrifices from yourself – all of these programs come at a great cost to our country's coffers, but we deem it important – but that also means sometimes something sterner is called for. Do you understand?"

I nod, mostly because I have no idea how to respond. This is not the bloodthirsty tyrant I've heard so many stories about. The man who speared his enemies' heads with pikes and posted them in his army's areas to discourage defections. The man who, because two towns were spelled similarly and the scout wasn't sure which one held dissidents, leveled both of them. This man is dangerous, but he is also rational, thoughtful, and I'd dare say wise. The people here have not tried to rob or murder anyone walking down the street, have not followed us or snatched goods from our hands. They smile and say something I assume is *pardon me* when they bump into you. Hell, I even saw someone in a car stop to let an older couple cross before they had even gotten into the street. In Eitan, the driver probably would've sped up to hit them.

So, if all that I have heard about this man and these people is wrong, what else am I wrong about? And, the more disconcerting question: who is the actual savage?

A man in grey fatigues rushes up to us, waving to get Ødven's attention. He's on the shorter side, with eyes that are bluer than the sea we crossed.

"Härskare, Befälhavare, our scouts have apprehended a dissident we believe to be linked to Nyväg. He's being detained near Evivårgen Torg." The man pauses to catch his breath. "What would you like us to do?"

Something passes over Ødven's face, shifting from the pure joy he had shown at introducing me to the humanitarian advances his country has made. I recognize the expression. I have seen it, and I have felt it.

"Hold him. We are coming."

"Absolutely, Härskare." He says something into the comm device on his shoulder and hurries away.

Ødven looks over to Slåtann. "Ibra, call for a car. We can't wait for the tram."

Slåtann nods and takes a comm device from his jacket, starts talking in their native tongue.

"What is Nyväg?" I say to Ødven. I set my hands on Donael's and Cobb's, already feeling their anxiety radiating off them.

"Dissidents. Radicals who are attempting to foment insurrection and destroy everything we have taken so long to build for our people," he says. "You have seen the benefits we've offered, Henraek. Now it is time for you to see the stern hand."

The crowd gathered at the square – the torg, I suppose – parts as we approach, Ødven in the lead with Slåtann following. I hang back from them, keeping the boys near me. Up on the platform, a young man stands with his hands and ankles cuffed, his black hair flung back from his face and his black fatigues flecked with dirt. His back straight and chest puffed out resolutely, he will not be cowed. Yet still, in his eyes, I can see the bone-deep fear of death swirling. Ødven makes his way up the steps with Slåtann in tow and moves to the center of the platform. Behind him looms the statue of the two-headed wolf-man, the stone a deep grey at the top but oxidized near the base. The crowd murmurs in anticipation. The whole scene – the sights, the sounds, the energy – is frighteningly familiar.

I lean over to the man standing beside me, nudge him with my elbow, and point at the statue. "Who's that?"

"Evivårgen, the protector of the land," he says

in accented English. "Legend says his family was attacked by a tribe of Jötun, the ancient giants. Evivårgen felled them all and used their corpses to shelter his family from more attackers." He points to the mountains in the distance. "Vårgmannskjør was built in that space and the mountains have been protecting us ever since. Invading armies. Surveyors looking for resources. Hostile parties. All of them have been driven away."

Images of Belousz and his mother knelt before Berôs, of the Nimah statuettes rebels used to carry during the Struggle, flash through my head. Something pings inside me, that no matter the language or race, everyone is telling the same story.

"People of Vårgmannskjør," Ødven calls out emphatically, "there are traitors hiding within our ranks, dissidents who want to destroy our city, our country. They wish to dismantle the systems that power our lights, our heat. They aim to ransack the pantries that provide food for those who do not have it. Their only goal is to tear apart our people and our way of life. And as Evivårgen did so many years ago, we must defend ourselves against attackers."

"Do people really believe that?" I say to the man.

His expression borders on offense. "You don't?"

"I'm not from here," I say, by way of apology.

"I can tell."

Slåtann approaches Ødven with a knife in hand – not ornate like the one the priest used to baptize Belousz in blood, yet beautiful in its simplicity and fine craft. Still, at the first sight of the knife, I already know where this is going.

"Boys," I start to say.

But before I can tell them to turn away, Ødven yells out, "All Powerful Evivårgen, accept our sacrifice," and slashes the knife through the man's wrist, his hand falling to the ground. The rebel screams "Tillräckligt!" and thrashes as blood squirts from the stump, but Ødven and Slåtann restrain him, point the gushing at the statue and it's only now I realize that the statue isn't oxidized, it's caked in frozen blood. This is not an isolated incident: this is ritual human sacrifice.

I already brought the boys into another conflict, and now I've placed them in close proximity to a man who has no qualms with ritual sacrifice.

Manic clicking behind me. I spin around and Donael is pressing Cobb's head against his chest, trying to soothe him, but his own breath is rushing so hard I worry he'll hyperventilate. I pull them both into me, wrap my arms around them, make sure their eyes are covered, and repeat, "Stay with me, I will not let anyone near you, you are safe with me," over and over and over. Donael's fingers clutch and knead at my back like he's trying to bury himself inside me. I put my lips to his ear and say, "This is what war is. This is what I'm protecting you from."

On the platform, I hear a high-pitched shout quickly turn to gurgles, then a splashing sound as the man's throat opens.

I grip the boys tighter, forming us into a small cell, a circle, one that can never be breeched.

10.
EMERÍANN

We're in a small, open-top vehicle with knobby tires, but I'm not sure if it's supposed to function as an all-terrain vehicle for soldiers to jump in and out of or if the top of the truck was ripped off during one of the uprisings. Two Ragjarøn soldiers I don't recognize sit in the front seats, rifles resting in their laps. More follow in the vehicle behind us. Brighid sits behind me, her eyes closed as the wind whips her hair. She looks like she's enjoying herself, and I don't know if I should admire that, that even in something as catastrophic as this whole new war she can still appreciate something small like the wind in her hair, or if I should punch her in the throat for smiling when the whole city is about to be torn apart again.

She glances over at me and for a minute I'm pretty damn sure she can hear my thoughts.

Blow me, I think extra hard.

"I trust your room is OK?" she says.

"It's fine."

"And the food?"

"I don't know. I never got a chance to eat it before I was yanked out here on some alleged mission."

"We need to move on a piece of intel," she says. "And you weren't missing much anyway. The meat's not very good." She turns her attention back to the road. We take a right at what used to be a market owned by an Amergi woman who provided us food during the uprising. The whole eastern corner is now an angular silhouette, cinder blocks sticking out at assorted angles after the Tathadann bombed it for aiding us. We head down a side street.

"Do you remember taking me down here when I first arrived in Eitan? You and Henraek showed me how to skirt around the back of the Tathadann's barricades. You two always amazed me at how well you worked together, like you could communicate telepathically."

Hearing Henraek's name makes me as sad as it makes me angry, especially with this stupid woman waxing nostalgic after she shipped my only remaining family up to the great white north and ruined everything I'd based my life on. "Did you drag me out here so we could gab and braid each other's hair?"

She glances over at me, then returns to the road. She says something to the driver I can't understand and the car slows, pulling to a stop in front of a boarded-up café.

"This was it," she says. "This was where you entered the tunnels. Henraek was nearly giddy showing them off."

"He does favor the theatric." I remember that ecstatic

look on his face, contrasted with the disappointment when, ten minutes later, we hit the end of the route. He was sure we'd find the rest of the tunnels if we'd only kept searching.

"And showing how smart he is."

"There is that." I don't like agreeing with her but she's not wrong.

"It's not surprising. Both of you are walking reference guides. You both always seem to know who is aligned with whom and where they fight best. It's really impressive. You're natural leaders." She pauses, maybe trying to let the compliments get to my head, which they do, a little. "We met up with Lachlan's squad here, right?"

The engine tries to idle but mostly coughs and rumbles.

"No. Lachlan was positioned in the southeast quarter. Speider held this quarter. Speider Stachae."

"That's right." She nods. "He used to play that little whistle thing all the time."

"Tin whistle." I let out a long breath. "Look, is there some reason we're out here? What the hell are we doing?"

"Do you have someplace you need to be?" she says. "Maybe locked back in your room?"

I glare at her, doing my best to channel Donael's teenage disgust. Pasted to a brick wall across the street is a faded and torn poster from early in the uprising. It's the silhouette of Fannae Morrigan, except there's a skeleton face where her features should be, one of our slogans in block printing underneath. *Better Dead Than A Slave.* Two young kids hurry down the sidewalk on our side. The dirtier one of them carries something beneath his jacket. At first I think it's a loaf of bread, until I see the fabric of his jacket writhe. I look away.

"I heard Speider deserted his squad. No one has seen him in two weeks."

"Speider? No way. He'd never abandon them. He's probably taking care of his mother. She's got cancer or something."

"She's up in Fomora with the rest of them, right?"

I laugh at the thought of Speider in Fomora, dressed in all black with that wide-brimmed hat he's so fond of, walking around with all the Tathadann blue hairs and their pancake makeup. "None of ours can afford Fomora. She's in the north end of Amergin, near the border."

"Right, by that bakery that separates them," she says.

"Sure. I don't know."

The car starts forward, pulling a U-turn in the middle of the street and narrowly avoiding hitting a woman walking down the sidewalk.

We drive for a few minutes, Brighid with her eyes on the road and me staring off to the side, watching buildings pass by. Every other street holds some kind of memory, whether ducking beneath a wall with Henraek and being pinned down by Tathadann fire or stopping at a corner store and picking out candy with my mother. In none of them would I ever have imagined riding in the back of a truck with a woman like Brighid. It makes me second-guess myself, wonder if I should've listened to Henraek and tried to overthrow the Tathadann by ourselves. But something Brighid said the other day keeps picking at me, that there was a Tathadann defector who had already been in contact with Ødven – the mystery man with one eye – that makes me wonder if he was Forgall's source. It might be a stretch, but it wouldn't be a surprise either. It would also mean that this takeover was already in motion while Forgall and I were discussing the uprising.

I turn to Brighid to ask about the one-eyed man and see her point to something up ahead, a bakery on the corner, another all-terrain vehicle like ours parked diagonally across the street. These buildings, the shanties, the lumbering masses crowded on the sidewalk.

"What are we doing in Amergin? They hate the rebels as much as they hate the Tathadann."

But before anyone answers, the car stops. Brighid and one of the soldiers jump out. Three soldiers from the other vehicle join them as they take position in front of a door flaking off red paint, next to the bakery.

And then it crashes down on me. She's showing me how much she knows.

"Brighid, no," I shout; but the sounds of the door splintering and the soldiers shouting spill across the street. A group of children stop and stare at the commotion before their mothers usher them away, tucking them inside their shanties. There's the noise inside the house of chairs and tables flipped, lamps thrown, glasses shattered. Then I hear a man scream, then a gunshot, followed by rifles unloading.

Then the street is silent.

My breath catches in my throat. My arms quiver. Speider and his mother are dead and I couldn't protect them.

A minute later, the window shutters on the second floor open. Grey-sleeved arms poke out then disappear. Then a huge lump flies through the glass, catching on a rope and slamming against the side of the house. Speider's punctured body hangs on display for all the neighborhood to see. A warning to rebels against fighting. A warning to the neighborhood against shielding or conspiring.

Before my brain can process the thought, my legs are moving, vaulting my body up and out of the car. The soldier behind me shouts to stop but my legs don't give a shit. All they want is to put as much distance between me and that car. I glance back and see the soldier raising his rifle. I swerve wildly left and right, waiting for the bullets to chew up my back, then look again and he's lowered it. He shouts for someone to *stop that rebel*. They can't shoot me. Brighid needs me. If I can get far enough away–

My face grates against the asphalt as I tumble across the street. My palms burn. When I roll over, I see a kid who can't be older than Donael. He points at Speider's body and mouths *I'm sorry*, then runs away.

I can't even push myself up before the Ragjarøn soldier is looming over me. "Stupid bitch," he says as he yanks me up by my arm and shoves me back toward the truck. People on the sidewalk pass by as if this is an everyday occurrence, nothing unusual here, but no one will meet my eye.

They heft me back into the car. A tiny smile plays across Brighid's lips.

"That's part of the reason you're such a good warrior," she says. "You never know when it's over."

As we pull away, blood falls from Speider's corpse like rain from a swollen cloud.

When the car arrives back at the house, I have the brief thought of running. But my knees are still sore from eating the asphalt, and the last couple escape attempts have just ended with me getting beat to hell, so I figure maybe it's better if I wait for an opportunity to arise instead of forcing it.

I climb out and feel the soldier's rifle poke against my back, prodding me forward. A dozen other soldiers mill around, some patrolling, some posted up by the doors of the house. It seems like overkill, given that I could easily throw a ball across the property. But what the hell do I know? Regardless, I need to get a message to Henraek.

In all the commotion of executing Speider and my trying to run, they forgot to put the blanket over my head. Or maybe they don't care if I know where we're staying anymore, them being confident enough in their operation. Neither reason matters, though: I still have no idea where the hell we are. Some small neighborhood south of Macha, the center city area that was formerly a Tathadann stronghold. The place doesn't look like Macha, though. Modest is the best word that comes to mind. Houses that could fit a family of four comfortably, if a little tight. Siding that could be replaced but isn't falling apart. Lawns that are various shades of brown – no fancy landscaping here – but several trees dotting the area. I'm curious as to why they chose this house, whether it belonged to someone in particular or was just a house that was easily commandeered. A breeze slips through the yard and shakes the branch of a tree; the positioning of it makes it look like something falling from the window, and I flinch.

One of the soldiers walking a beat turns when I reach the steps and goddamn if I don't recognize him. Younger guy, Melein. He'd been in Lachlan's squad for a while, and I think Lachlan was grooming him to take over his own squad. So, what the hell is he doing here? He catches my eye and a wash of fear passes over his face. He turns away quickly and continues on his loop around the south side of the house. That wasn't fear he'd been found out by us, though; that was fear of them knowing we know each other. I want to chase him down and talk to him but the soldier jabs me in the back. I walk up the steps and inside to my room. They close the door and lock it. They know one small lock couldn't really contain anyone, which is why they have a soldier stationed outside my room.

I wait quietly for a few minutes, letting everyone settle back into their routine, then begin searching the room. The lights flicker then dim, but I get lucky and none of them go out. I don't know that I'd be able to see using only the light from outside. There's nothing in the dresser except a few pieces of clothing they brought for me – which, out of principle, I've ignored so far. Nothing in the night table either, although the tacky floral drawer liner does make me laugh. Maybe this was a grandmother's house. I run my fingers along the edges of the carpet, pricking my finger on a tack nail sticking out of the subfloor. As I suck on my fingertip, I tip the mirror forward, checking the back, but find nothing there either.

There has to be something in here I can use, but aside from pulling up the carpet, there's no place else to look. No closet, no bathroom, no other doors.

Then I think, *of course you can't pull up the carpet but...*

I slide open the drawer in the night table, shake my hand free of blood, then pick at the edge of the drawer liner with my fingernail. It pills at the end, lifts up, but then turns into a sharp tear. I pick at the other side, making a long line of pilling, then as that piece begins to lift, grab it with both hands' fingertips, spreading out the force as much as I can. Little by little the liner pulls free, until, at a hand's length, it rips.

Close enough.

I crouch back down on the floor and run my fingers along the carpet edge until the tack pricks me again, and in the same goddamn spot. I bite my bottom lip to keep myself from making noise. I grab the nail with my other hand and shimmy it back and forth. It takes a few minutes, but eventually it works free. I lean back against the wall and let out a long breath. That was the easy part.

I picture myself now and almost start laughing. I'm living in a city that has made unparalleled technological advances. We can create food from nothing. We have cars that drive themselves. We can reconstruct full memories using only a liquid. Despite all of that, the future of our rebellion, of our city, of our people, all relies on a carpet tack and a strip of drawer liner. Maybe it proves that all our technology is worthless and analogue is the way to go, or maybe it proves that everything is meaningless. Regardless, if that's not a kick in the balls, I don't know what is.

Before I start, I press my ear against the door, making sure no one is coming in. I sit on the bed and lay the drawer liner on the table, the plain bottom facing up. Then I take a deep breath, prick my finger with the nail again, and goddamn if it isn't twice as bad every time I do it. A bead of blood forms on my fingertip, and I roll the tip of the nail in it, then start scratching out a letter on the drawer liner.

Brighid is killing us.

Please help.

I love you all.

When the letter is done and four of my fingertips are throbbing, I prick the last one, smear my blood on my lips, then press them against the liner.

I set the paper beneath the bed, hiding it while it dries.

Someone knocks on the door, announces that he has my dinner. I sit on my bloodied and bruised hand, tell him he can come in.

He sets another sandwich on the night table and leaves without saying anything else. I wait until the lock latches before moving off my hand and grabbing the sandwich. It looks like salami but sure as hell doesn't smell like it, and part of me thinks this is some kind of message from Brighid. Mess with me, I'll mess with you worse. I've survived the last however-many years on food worse than this, but, despite my growling stomach, it's a matter of principle, so I leave the sandwich on its plate.

Forty-five minutes later, I fold the drawer liner into quarters and slip it inside my underwear, then knock on the door.

"I need to use the restroom," I say to the soldier.

I can hear him waffling outside, mumbling to someone else.

"Seriously, I'm ready to burst. You want to squeegee this carpet?" He mutters something. "Then open the damn door."

The lock clicks and doorknob turns. The rifle barrel is the first thing that enters.

"Come on," I say to him. "Don't you know you never point a loaded weapon at a loaded weapon?"

He lowers the rifle, flicks his head. "Go down the steps. It's the second door on the left." I start to totter down the steps when he calls out. "I know you're not going to try anything." He leaves the threat dangling in the air.

I exaggerate my steps as I head downstairs, making it look like I'm within an inch of pissing myself. The soldier on the first floor looks at me. *Really gotta go*, I mouth to him, and he turns away like he's embarrassed. When I hear the front door shut, I stand in place, listening hard. The soldier upstairs is in the same position, and there are no other sounds in the house. Close as I'll ever get.

I pad past the bathroom and into the sitting room, then crouch by one of the chairs in a position that gives me a sightline out the window facing south but keeps me out of view of anyone coming in the front door, silently pleading Melein to walk past. The floor above me creaks and I hold my breath, but it's only the soldier shifting his weight. I move from one foot to the other, keeping the blood flowing through my legs. Outside, I hear a woman with a low, gravelly voice talking to a man with a soft Brigu accent about dinner for that evening. Their voices disappear around the corner.

After what feels like an hour but was probably only a minute, Melein's head appears in the window. I rush over and tap on the glass with my fingernail. He stops in place, looking around to find the noise. I dig my fingers into the old wood frame and crack the window open.

"What the hell are you doing?" he says in a harsh whisper.

"What the hell are *you* doing?" I say back. "What about Lachlan?"

He glances around then shuffles up close to the window. "They raided us. They've been raiding everyone. Any squad that doesn't comply is imprisoned or executed on the spot."

My skin goes cold. "Lachlan is dead?"

"Hell no. He took out a dozen of their soldiers then blew up half a building to create a distraction. Got away with about ten of ours."

That makes me feel a little better. "Why are you here?"

He looks around, visibly more nervous than a minute ago. "They were going to kill me. What else was I supposed to do?"

I purse my lips and nod, commiserating with him the best I can.

He leans in and lowers his voice. "They're using you. She knows where most of the rebel cells are and needs you to confirm the rest."

"I know. She got Speider this afternoon." The mental image of his body careening out the window, the snap at the end of the rope chills me all over again.

"We've all done things we're not proud of," he says.

"Make sure you tell everyone I'm not here by choice. I don't want people to see me next to her, get the wrong idea and start aiming for me instead. I'm not with them."

"No one thinks that. But you need to keep her happy while we figure something out. If that means giving up more cells…"

He lets me fill in the blanks but the thought of more rebels dying at my hands sends blood pounding through my limbs.

"To hell with that. I won't give up my people."

"Emeríann, if you're gone, and Lachlan gets caught, then…" He pauses, either grasping for words or not able to bring himself to speak them. "Then we're done. All of us. What happens then?"

I check behind me to make sure no one's come into the room, then reach into my underwear and pull out the drawer liner.

"Get this to someone who can get it to Henraek." I slip him the paper. He hesitates to take it but I shove it at him. "He's in Vårgmannskjør. Ødven needs him for, I don't know, advising or something. But that means he's alive. Maybe he can talk to Ødven, reason with him."

"How am I supposed to get it to him?"

"You'll find a way." I pull my hand back. "If you don't, then you're right. We're probably done."

Melein glances to the side. Fortunately, he doesn't see the same irony in the situation that I do because he slips the paper into a breast pocket then hurries away without a word. Nahoeg help us all if this doesn't work.

I start to close the window when I hear the front door open, two voices carrying inside. The bathroom is too far away and too exposed for me to make it there. Instead, I hop forward and duck behind the farthest chair, hoping to all hell that they don't look down.

They pass through the room, carrying on the conversation from outside. One of them pauses a second outside the bathroom door and I think my heart stops. He's either listening – in which case he's a pervert – or he's about to knock, in which case I'm going to get my ass beat. Maybe Melein's too. Then the other soldier nudges his arm.

"You know they take forever. Probably fixing her makeup."

"She don't need makeup," he says. "I'd take anything right about now."

My jaw clenches so tight I can feel it in my ear.

Deep breaths, woman. Just relax, and remember his face when the revolution comes.

They move on to what I think is the kitchen. Once they're out of sight, I hurry over to the bathroom. I'm just at the door when the pervert comes out of the kitchen.

I stop short and hold my breath. He cocks his head.

"Sorry," I say, putting on a terrible smile. "Had to fix my makeup."

I start to head back upstairs when I see him reaching for the door. The unflushed toilet, the dry sink, any of that will give me away.

"You might want to steer clear of that a couple minutes." I manage not to smile when I say it. "Something about that sandwich meat didn't sit well." I shake my head, letting him fill in the blanks, and go back to my room.

I flop down on the bed and stare at the ceiling, willing the letter safe delivery to Henraek. Willing safe delivery for Henraek.

11.
HENRAEK

Ødven's headquarters is surprisingly small, given his position. I should really stop saying that: surprisingly. Everything about this city, this country, these people, has been surprising. How clean it is. How welcoming the people are. His office reflects what I've seen in the city. Clean lines. Open space. A lack of ornamentation. Given my interactions here, however few, one could go so far as to say the aesthetic and architecture reflects the temperament of the people. And why shouldn't it? People learn to make do with what they're given.

It's clear to me now that the Tathadann fed us nothing but lies and rumors to stoke a fear of outsiders, keeping us reliant on them for our safety and well-being. It makes me wonder what outsiders – people from farther away than the hills or a few miles past Westhell County – would make of Eitan and its people.

The only thing that hasn't been unexpected was

Ødven performing a ritual human sacrifice, though
the brazenness with which he did it – and how fully
the people embraced it – did take me back. Then
again, after sixty years of near-constant war in Eitan,
I'm not so positive we haven't been performing our
own version.

None of that makes me feel any better about
leaving the boys on their own. The only thing that
gives me comfort here is that the wall separating this
space from the waiting room is glass, so I can keep
a constant eye on them. Sitting on the couch, both
of them look reasonably composed after witnessing
the horror show out on Evivårgen Torg, though Cobb
seems more rattled than Donael. He has always been
the more fragile soul. In some way, I admire Donael's
self-control, the way that he appears wise beyond his
years, because Nahoeg knows the easiest way to be
cracked is to show weakness. But that hard exterior
also disappoints me, because it reflects me. Half of the
reason I've fought so hard for the last twenty years
is so that my children wouldn't have to grow up in
the same conditions as Walleus and I did, where one
flicker of emotion could mean the difference between
being labeled hunter or prey. And the fact that he
easily suppresses emotion means, to some degree,
that my life has been a failure. Then again, there are
numerous other things pointing to that.

"It wasn't always like this."

I startle in my seat on hearing a voice, stuck so
far inside my head while considering the boys. I
turn and see a lithe woman standing by the window
that overlooks Evivårgen Torg, a view probably not

dissimilar from the one in our apartment. Something about her posture exudes regality, someone who doesn't ask for things but merely says them to the air and expects them to manifest before her, someone who has always known the world to be that way. She casts a final glance outside before exhaling hard, her breath condensing on the cold glass. She turns to me and pulls aside a wisp of blonde hair with a thin pinkie finger before tucking it behind her ear.

"What wasn't?" I say.

"This. Everything." She gestures absently toward the city. "All of this concession, keeping everyone happy."

This must be Federijke, Ødven's wife.

"I'm not sure I follow." She lowers herself onto the desk with the grace of a crane, as if she could balance her entire body weight on a single toe and look effortless doing it, and crosses her legs. Her hands find rest in her lap, fingers crossed. It's just now occurring to me that, in her long shimmering dress, she looks much more the part of party leader than her grey-fatigued husband. I'm sure that dress cost more than I'm worth, but it doesn't look like it. As opposed to the Morrigans' ostentatious display of wealth, Federijke Äsyr errs on the side of classy. It's a dress that would look great on Emeríann, though she'd sooner die than be caught in something so expensive.

"Years ago, when we formed Ragjarøn, Ødven didn't feel the need to ask for things. When we united the provinces, we did it because we needed to make one sovereign state. We didn't ask what everyone felt about the prospects. We knew what the people required and acted accordingly."

"If I might say," I wager, somewhat hesitant to contradict her, "your husband just murdered a man in front of hundreds of people. Where I'm from, that doesn't qualify as making concessions."

She dismisses it with a flick of the wrist. "That's only theatre. Something the dumskålles need in order to clap."

"Dumskålles?"

"I don't know how you translate. Those who cannot breathe through their noses, always through their open mouths."

"Ah, right." I glance out into the other room. Cobb is now lying with his head in Donael's lap and, though he looks slightly annoyed, Donael is reading to him from a magazine. Or at least pretending to read, because I'm pretty sure that's a local magazine. I doubt Cobb knows the difference and it's a sweet gesture anyway. "Still, I have to say that it's effective theatre."

"Oh, don't tell him that or I'll never hear the end of it." She holds out her hand, considering her nails, which draws my attention to them, and it's only then that I realize the slit in her dress has crept mightily up her thigh. "I've heard of what you did in Eitan. You, Henraek," she says, conspicuously oblivious to her shifting wardrobe, "you understand what my husband no longer does. That good will is a wonderful idea, but it is merely what we wrap around war to comfort ourselves, convince ourselves that we are doing what is right, not what is just."

I swallow hard, feeling the heat radiating off her. "I'm sorry, but I'm not sure I follow."

"What this city needs," she says, now fixing those eyes on me, so much that I feel the need to lean back in my chair, "is someone with passion. Someone who knows what they want, what they can't live without, so they seek it out, destroy everything that stands between them. Someone who burns with righteous fury."

As she's saying it, I can see in those blazing eyes what she really wants: someone to rule like the Morrigans ruled, with authority and a complete lack of compassion. But I also see – and, maybe, feel – the other ways she's trying to convince me. And in that glint in her eye, I see the duplicity behind her. She wants me, wants me to help her, and wants me out of her way, all wrapped in one messy, volatile emotion.

"Honestly, darling." Ødven's voice booms and I jump again, though Federijke sits unfazed. "How many times have I said it? Sleep with the help if you must, but not our comrades. Some things are more important than your momentary pleasures."

"It can last much longer than a minute, dear." She regards me with one last long, searching look. "Not that he'd know." Then she twists off the desk, making sure that her dress flaps up right at my eye level before leaving the room.

"I see you've met the missus," Ødven says. He reaches into a low bookshelf behind his desk and pulls out a bottle of liquor a shade somewhere between caramel and urine.

"She's… charismatic."

He pauses and regards me for a moment, then proceeds to pour the liquor into two bell-shaped glasses. "You're kind to say that." He hands me a glass and sniffs his own. "Smart, too, because I might kill you if you'd said otherwise."

I hold my glass as I wait for him to say *just kidding*. When it doesn't come, I just swirl the liquor around.

Seemingly satisfied, he lifts his glass up to mine, says, "Gutår," then swallows his whole. I bring mine to my nose then hesitate when I get a full snort of it – it's like a handful of black licorice caught fire atop a pile of pine – but throw it down my throat anyway lest I appear inconsiderate. I manage not to cough or pound my chest and consider that a small victory.

"Ødven, if I may," I push out past the fumes, "what am I doing? Why did you bring us here?"

"What do you mean?" He pours himself another glass and I'm glad I'm still holding mine tight in my hand.

"They said you needed my advisement. Given what happened," I say, gesturing out the window toward the Torg, "I don't think I can be of much help to you. I'm hardly the leader type. More the..." I bobble for the word, as whatever that liquor was sprints straight toward my head.

"You see yourself as the spark. Not the match, not the kindling, but the spark."

I cock my head. "I think that's a fair assessment."

"Yet I think you can be more." He rises from his desk, hands crossed behind his back. "You have been inside many a fire. You understand them. How they start, how they burn, how they spread." He slaps his heels together with military precision. "How they are extinguished."

I flinch slightly at the last comment, although I'm sure that's not how he meant it.

"I need you – and your boys, of course – to travel to Rën, a village near the sea."

"I'm not sure how much you know about Eitan, but we're not well-versed with the sea. Or water of any sort, for that matter."

"The man you saw earlier. The Nyväg man. I wasn't being theatrical, despite what my wife has doubtless told you, when I said that they want to destroy our way of living."

I spin the glass in my fingers, glance out and see both boys are napping on the couch. Good for them. They need it.

"The dissidents are trying to destroy our power systems, those which provide heat, light, water, electricity. The plants are located in smaller villages around the country. Rën holds the largest one."

"If they're so vital, why does Nyväg want to destroy them?" I recognize the irony of the statement as soon as I say it. We knew the water distribution plant was a necessary sacrifice when we went in.

He gestures toward the crowd outside. "Choose your cause. Fourth-generation villagers who resent being brought into the union. Teenage anarchists with nothing else to do. Pigs from another party who don't agree with my vision for the country." He considers his glass, picks it up and swallows the contents before replacing it on the desk. "Their reasons are as varied as their names, but their desire is all the same: destroy a peaceful existence for the majority because of hurt feelings of the minority. I don't think I need to tell you the consequences if they should succeed."

"I think I understand." I slide my glass across his desk. He catches it with a wan smile and refills it.

"Then you'll understand why I need you to help restore order to the village."

And there it is. The real reason. Draw on my rebel past to track down the members of Nyväg and eliminate them. I dump the liquor down my throat, feel the warm, comforting hand spreading through my chest.

"How many people am I supposed to kill to *restore order?*" Initially I'm not sure if he can hear the inflection in my voice, but his flatlined mouth says he gets it.

"To that, I would remind you that your precious Emeríann is very comfortable back in Eitan, and she remains safe because of the word of my ally Brighid, and by her word only."

I swallow hard. "There is no way you would need to remind me of that."

"Then I would remind you that Brighid also beheaded her father but a few days ago." He pours one last glass for himself, savoring this one.

I nod.

"Concern yourself not with the details of the job, but with fulfilling it. Are we clear?"

I run my tongue along my teeth, tell myself to shut up while Emeríann and I are still alive.

"I suppose we'll pack our bags."

"Yes," he says. "I suppose so."

12.
EMERÍANN

I'm staring at the blackened and bruised tip of my finger when the soldier knocks on the door.

"Be dressed and ready to leave in five minutes," he says.

"I'm not going anywhere with you."

Even through the door, I can hear him sigh. "I'm not going through this again."

"Then tell Brighid *she* can suck my dick. I'm not going to be her patsy and let her use me to assassinate all my comrades."

"Your rebel friends are the ones causing the problems, miss," he says, with special emphasis on certain words. "Every time we try to rebuild something, they start firing at us. Meanwhile markets are bare, faucets are dry, and schools are in ruins. If they really want water and electricity like they say, then stop with all the bullshit and let us work."

"I guess one regime is the same as the next, right?"

He doesn't respond, and for a minute I think I've

swayed him.

"Now you have three minutes."

I jump to my feet and press my mouth against the door crack. "I told you. I'm not moving one goddamned foot for you people. You want to get me out of here, you're going to have to shoot my ass and haul my corpse down to the car. And I know that Brighid will have your balls if you hurt me."

"I'm warning you, miss."

"Try me." I lean back, smiling at the little shit. He thinks he can intimidate me? I've seen much tougher bastards in the field.

Then there's a crash and a splintering sound, then a dull smack on the wall behind me. I jump back and duck out of instinct. Wooden shards stick out from a small hole in the wall less than an arm's length from where I was standing.

"You asshole!" I say. "You almost shot me."

"No, I shot sixteen-to-eighteen inches from where your head was." He clears his throat. "And now you have two minutes."

I stand up and set my eye in front of the hole, see his staring back at me. "Don't watch me change, pervert."

His eye disappears and I pull on the grey fatigues they gave me last night. This is a moral compromise, clothing myself in their uniform, but after wearing the same outfit for nearly a week my clothes have become disgustingly stiff with dried sweat and I'm tired of smelling myself. These fatigues make me even more determined to avoid seeing anyone I know, lest they get the wrong idea.

When I'm dressed, I knock on the door, tell him I'm ready.

"Grey's a good color on you," he says with a smirk before he points down the steps.

Brighid is in the sitting room, perched on a chair with a map spread across her lap. She looks up as I enter, running her eyes over the fatigues but choosing not to comment.

"I'm not giving you any more locations," I tell her. "That was some bullshit yesterday."

"Come off it, Emeríann. Speider blew up two of my vehicles with a car bomb – vehicles that were carrying parts to rebuild a generator." She folds the map in half. "He and his people will fight anything I do, just because it's me doing it."

"Maybe you should tell them what you're doing."

She gives me a look that could flay skin. "We can't rebuild the city into something better if we're constantly under the threat of being murdered every time we set foot in the street."

"You murdered Speider's mother. She was senile, for shit's sake!"

"At least she won't suffer like the rest of us," she says. "Stop playing the innocent. You're forgetting who fought with you the last six months. I've seen you committing acts on the battlefield you'd rather not admit later."

I bite the inside of my lip, my hands nearly shaking I'm so angry. "I'm not telling you one more damn thing."

"Fine." She folds the map again, shoves it in a pocket by her knee, then points to the front door. "Then go."

"What?"

"Leave. Go back to your city, the one you love so dearly."

"What, so you can shoot me in the back?"

The chair creaks when she stands and she goes to open the front door.

"I promise no one will shoot you as you're walking out."

My feet start to move, but something about her statement sounds qualifying. "Once I'm off the grounds, I'm a live target."

"For us? No." She motions toward the streets. "But to all of them, those who see you in those fatigues, those who have seen you riding with us?" She shakes her head. "I can't offer you the same assurance with them. You are free to leave here, but you will be hunted by rebels, by Brigus who have seen you cavorting with the Ragjarøn soldiers who murdered one of their own. So, the way I see it, you have two choices." She leaves the door hanging open and strides across the room, pulling up right in front of me. "You can go out there and face your fate alone. Or you can stay here, stop being such a cunt, and start working to make the city whole again."

Our truck pulls to a stop on the side of a street in Macha, the soldiers disembarking with Brighid behind them. I refused to speak the whole ride, no matter her question, but she already had the location of a former Tathadann cantina that's housing two rebels in its basement. I've never been here before, but I recognized the name. Once I heard the location, I considered answering her questions with disinformation, but thought that would be too conspicuous a shift in tactic.

I hate to admit it but she has done a masterful job of using me. The optics of everything are so damning. Contacting Melein was pure luck, but despite what he said, I don't know if I can even go back to my old people. I vouched for Brighid at the start of all this. It was my idea to bring her in. Even if there's no conspiracy theory swirling around about me being a deep-state infiltrator, I'd be gambling that the rebels won't be so blinded with anger and bloodlust that they'll shoot me on sight. And I don't know that I can put my life on that thin a line.

It feels like digging in and hoping to hell Henraek gets my message is my only option. That and look for any opportunity to hamstring her operation. If that's my only option, it's a shitty one.

"I'm not coming with you," I say.

"Hope you're fast on your six, then." She nods at the faces poking from the windows, the glares and the daggers they stare at me. "And I'm not leaving a gun with you, let you shoot me in the back as soon as I turn around."

I take my time getting out of the truck. Only then does she hand me a pistol.

I follow her along the sidewalk, creeping down the same side as the cantina. These streets, once packed with people under the Tathadann's rule, are now largely deserted. Most of the people who lived here either fled during the fighting in the fear of being captured by the rebels or were killed. The cantina appears to be deliberately built to look broken down, that slumdiving aesthetic that had been so popular with the Tathadann people, giving them the illusion of danger without having to risk anything. Then the uprising happened, and the place became genuinely broken down. I heard the owners were hanged and nailed into the front of the building as a warning, but never felt the need to confirm that for myself. Either way, the rebels who took it over are not prone to surrendering.

"What did you mean back at the house?" I say to Brighid.

"You don't understand what a cunt is, or you don't know how to stop being one?"

I cringe at the return of that uneasy banter we'd developed during the uprising. I look at the pistol in my hand – not a rifle like all of those assholes are carrying – and imagine myself lifting it, setting it behind her head, then firing. Imagine what her brains would look like as they flew across the sidewalk. I blink away the image, whisper to myself *Just don't get shot, Emeríann.* You can't kill this goddamned traitor if you've got a hole in your own head. Bide your time and remember that going along with something doesn't mean you're actually going along with it.

"No. I've been around you long enough to know what one is. I meant making the city whole."

There's a clattering sound in the alleyway between here and the cantina. The soldiers hold up their hands, keeping their rifles trained on the opening as they strafe toward it. The lead one waves for the other to flank him as he kneels to cover his compatriot.

The second one goes around, calls out for someone to halt, flicking his muzzle to the side. A disheveled man shuffles out of the alleyway, his eyes empty and staring at something far away, his mouth hanging open.

"Goddamn lagons," I say.

"Everyone has their crutch," she says.

The man totters off, and we keep moving.

"So," I say, "the city?"

"We have the backing of one of the most powerful parties in the hemisphere. Do you know what kind of resources Ødven has access to? Do you know the kinds of technology at our disposal with him as an ally?"

"But he's a savage," I say. "You've met him. You've heard the stories about him."

"Do the stories make the man or does the man make the stories?" She glances back at me. "Is anything he's done worse than executing a girl at point blank range just for doing her job and protecting the water plant?"

"I don't know what you're talking about," I say. But I still see that poor girl's head in the water distribution plant, the way it snapped back after I shot her, the way she begged for help as the atomizers prepared to blow it all to Hell.

"These people wouldn't see her as a necessary sacrifice. They're too enamored of fighting. That's all they know anymore, which is what made them so good for taking down the Tathadann and so bad for trying to rebuild Eitan. Without someone to lead them, to guide them through the rebuilding, they'll start fighting against anything that doesn't meet their vision of revolution," she says. "But you're different. You can see—"

There's a clap, a gunshot. Then one of the soldiers screams as he falls to the ground, his fatigues washing from grey to red. Everyone ducks down, guns at the ready, eyes scanning the sidewalk. Then the cement near my head fractures, shards of it smacking against my cheek. More gunshots, rapid fire, peppering the sidewalk around me.

"It's an ambush," Brighid shouts at me.

"No shit." I point at a car to the right, the wheels long gone. "There."

Staying crouched, I hurry over behind the car, Brighid close behind. I wager a peek through the window. A rusted cab sits in front of the market across the street, boards across the market's windows but no barrels poking out from inside. A small shop sits next to that with a few people inside, but they're all cowering on the ground, covering their heads.

Then up on the roof of the market, a man pops up from behind the ridge along the edge. Three bullets ping the car hood, skipping off and burying themselves in the wall. I pull the trigger without thinking and a red circle blooms in his forehead. He falls forward, crashing on the sidewalk below. Two other voices call out to each other to fall back.

We wait for a moment, listening for any other signs of attackers, but only hear their footfalls retreating down an alley. The soldier creeps out from his cover, rifle drawn, and clears the area. Brighid and I stand cautiously, then I make my way across the street.

There's a splatter of gore on the sidewalk surrounding the man, a shard of pale bone with sinew stuck to it lying in the puddle of blood. I come up to him, nudge him with my toe out of habit. No way he's moving, what with his neck bent at an obscene angle and his eyes somehow examining his own back. That's what he gets for shooting at me. Rule number one, Henraek used to say: don't shoot at someone if you don't want to get shot at.

I step over his body and when I crouch down the breath rushes out of my lungs.

I scramble backward, slamming into the wall, pressing my hands against my temples.

Nael's eyes avert mine. Nael, our bombmaker. Nael, who helped engineer the Gallery bombing. Nael, who fought with Henraek for many years during the Struggle.

And I just shot him in the goddamned face.

I didn't mean to shoot. It was instinct. I'd never hit a shot like that again even if I tried.

I just saved Brighid and killed Nael. I killed one of my own. I'm one of them now.

No, you're not. You're just trying to stay alive so you can continue the fight.

And part of me believes that, but another part keeps saying, *You just killed one of your own.*

"Hey," Brighid says, her tone like it wasn't the first time. "They're not inside. Come on, let's go."

When I don't move immediately, she rushes over and grabs me by the arm, hefting me up.

"I have no idea who else is here and don't want to get in another firefight. Move it."

I shove her hands off me, cock back my fist, ready to punch her, but for some reason don't. Maybe because, after seeing Nael's face, his eyes, the thought of more violence just nauseates me. Instead I walk around her and climb back into the truck, sink down into the seat, then close my eyes and wait for this to end.

"I'm not hungry," I shout at the door when the soldier knocks. The doorknob jiggles, then the lock turns. "Are you goddamned deaf?"

Brighid walks in through the door. Wonderful. Best day ever. Then I see her holding a bowl in her hands. Steam rises from the bowl, and as soon as I smell the aroma, my stomach unleashes an unholy growl. I don't remember the last time I ate a full meal. Still, I press my hands against my stomach, trying to stifle the noise.

"I thought you might need something to eat," she says as she sets it on the night table. "Those sandwiches get old after a while, but we have to ration food, and it's better than squirrel."

"I've eaten a lot of squirrel. Worse than that too."

"I'm sure you have." She nods at the bowl. "A little taste of home. You're from the lowlands, right? The bogs?"

"Yeah." I lean over and check out the food. Big chunks of golden potatoes sit in a creamy base, with chopped kale or spinach mixed in. A sizeable hunk of dark brown crusty bread torn from a loaf. I can feel my mouth watering, smelling all the garlic and yeast. There are even a few pieces of pink meat that are definitely from a farm, not a park. I reach for the food, then stop.

"How do I know there's not poison in this?"

"I guess you can't know for sure," she says. "But I could've killed you a dozen times already. Wouldn't make much sense for me to waste perfectly good food to do that." She shrugs. "I appreciate the dramatic flair, though."

She has a point, and I'm starving. So I dig in. After almost a week with little food – and months and months surviving on scraps – the flavors are so intense I'm briefly afraid they'll overwhelm my brain circuitry and make me pass out. Then I shovel more into my mouth and stop worrying.

Brighid smiles, watching me eat. I must look like a pig at a trough, but at this moment I don't care.

I only pause when the lights blink out, darkness settling over the room.

"Is this part of your grand plan for the city?" I say. "Teach us to navigate by echo?"

"We're working on it." Her voice sounds different in the dark. Less guarded. Maybe I'm projecting. "That's part of the reason we're trying to get the rebels under control. The last thing I need is to have someone like Speider blow up our new power systems just because they weren't the ones who thought of it."

"That's not–" The lights flash back on and I can see my food clearly. I decide against arguing and continue eating.

"I really am sorry about today," she says. "Grateful, but sorry."

I ignore her and keep eating.

"Who was he, the man you shot?"

I chew on a piece of meat, concentrating on the flavor and texture. For some reason, it brings an image of my mother to mind, of her washing our clothes in the sink to conserve water.

"Nael was his name. He was a bombmaker during the Struggle. Organized the Gallery bombing." I shovel more in my mouth. "Him and Henraek were pretty good friends."

"You don't ask about Henraek very often." She rests against the edge of the dresser. "Why not?"

I spoon more food into my mouth to avoid giving an answer.

"You don't want to seem vulnerable? Constantly asking me about him would mean I could lord something over you, so you sit there, suffering in silence?"

"If you're so sure you know already, why are you asking me?" I dunk the bread into the cream, letting it soak up the sauce and get heavy.

She looks over at the window, the branches lashing against the sky.

"I killed my first boyfriend," she says.

I inhale a piece of bread, start coughing until my eyes water. Eventually I eke out a response. "Why doesn't that surprise me."

This makes her smile slightly.

"Salamaar was his name. He was from," she taps her chin, thinking, "I don't remember what country we were in. It was hot. There was a lot of sand. Lots of flowing robes.

"Anyway, I met him in one of the big open-air

markets they had there. I was wandering around the city while Daghda was doing whatever it was he was doing. I was starving, but didn't have any money, so I stole two pieces of fruit from a stand. To this day, I don't know why I did it, because I stood out so much already. Daghda and I were about the only pale people there. Salamaar saw me do it. It was his father's stand. His father was arguing with some of the other men, but he happened to turn right as I was stuffing the fruit inside my pocket, just one of those random things. Over there, the penalty for stealing was having a hand chopped off. The whole thing sounds ridiculous looking back on it, because with a penalty so severe, why would you even try it? But at that age, you never expect anything bad to happen to you."

I swallow my bite of food. "How old were you?"

"Twelve, I think. Maybe eleven. Anyway, his father turns and almost catches me, except Salamaar yanks on his robe and distracts him long enough for me to hide the fruit. His father rapped him on the head for interrupting the men, then went back to arguing.

"A little bit later, I'm sitting on the sidewalk, eating the second piece of fruit, when Salamaar comes up. He keeps his eyes down, even when he's standing in front of me, and holds out two more pieces of fruit. I take one of them then scoot over so he has a place to sit. We did that for about a week, every day, same place, same time. One of the last days, he finally worked up the nerve to lean over and kiss me. I kissed him back. His lips were really soft and his mouth tasted sweet." She crosses her arms and leans back, eyes dancing far away in the past. "I remember thinking that kissing was pretty great and that this was how they would all be. It made sense at that age, you know?"

I nod that I do. I was a little older the first time Riab and I kissed – fourteen, I think – but I remember thinking the same thing.

"The next day, Daghda assassinated one of the most outspoken tribal leaders in the region. Everyone went insane, people fighting in the streets. From the little I understood, the conflict was between two factions of the same tribe. I guess they had a tenuous peace agreement, until Daghda went and blew it all to hell."

I gesture, indicating the city. "He seems to have a habit of doing that."

Brighid barks out a laugh despite herself, and I think that's the only time in six months I've ever heard her laugh.

"I headed back to the market to meet Salamaar that afternoon – because, of course, that's the most logical thing to do when a civil war is breaking out. Young love, I guess. But as I get over there, I hear someone scream my name. I look up and Salamaar is standing there, his robe covered in dust and flecked with blood. His face was just… unholy. I don't know if I've ever seen anyone as betrayed and hurt and scared as he was right then. I can still see him if I close my eyes. He was holding a long tent stake in his hand. Apparently word had traveled quickly about the pale assassin, so I was immediately pegged as his conspirator. But what I didn't know until later was that Salamaar's father had been the tribal leader Daghda was hired to kill. He was probably organizing something with the other men while his son was stealing his fruit for his pale-faced girlfriend."

I realize that I've stopped eating as I'm listening to her story, and as delicious as this food is, I've sort of lost my appetite.

"And then Salamaar charged at me. He was sprinting, the tent stake pointed at me, and all I could think was *I'll pay for the fruit.* But when he was a couple feet away from me it all registered, what was happening, and I reached down and grabbed a big rock from the sidewalk and swung it at Salamaar. Hit him right here." She taps her temple. "One shot, and he was down. Died right there." She pauses for a long minute. The only sounds in the room are our breathing. Somewhere outside, rifle shots echo. "I threw the rock into an alcove, and then I turned and ran. There was so much commotion going on that no one noticed me. No one noticed that poor boy lying dead in the street."

I want to say something, to console her, to share my own story, but in the same turn I also want to ridicule her for thinking a story could wipe away the fact that she shipped my family to a far-off land and has been holding me hostage for days and turned me into a traitor against my own people. But seeing her sitting there, her warrior-woman mask slipping ever so slightly, it makes me feel bad for her. And what could I possibly say anyway that would mean anything?

"Anyway," she says abruptly, standing, "I'm going

to rest. We have a mission tomorrow morning and can't be tired. Intel gave us something we need to look into."

And my body deflates, all sympathy and connection draining out. "After everything you just told me, we're still going to go on these missions?"

She looks at me like I'm insane. "Nothing has changed. Our objective is still the same. We're trying to rebuild Eitan." She walks to the door. "But before we go, I'm going to take you somewhere. I think it will help you understand."

She leaves without another word, the door closing as loud as a rifle shot.

The room is quiet except for a sucking sound inside my chest. It takes a few minutes for me to process that swirling and roiling, but eventually I can identify it. It's realizing that I can't remember the last time I had a real conversation with another woman.

It's the sound of loneliness.

13.
HENRAEK

The ride out to Rën is much shorter than it seems it should be, owing largely to the massive transformation in landscape, but that also could be because of the hyper-fast train that runs on magnetic levitation, not the old rails like the ones in Eitan used to. Where Vårgmannskjør was largely flat, with great mountains far in the distance and tall evergreen trees scraping against the sky, as we traveled west the land began rupturing, the frozen plains cracking at first before splintering into giant fissures that butt up against massive, jagged ridges. I want to call them fjords but don't think that's quite accurate. As we approach Rën's central station, those ridges creep higher and higher on the north side, then drop away dramatically as they crash into the sea on the western side of the continent.

As the outside whisks past us, Donael leans over.

"Dad? Are you really doing this?"

I don't know what he's talking about, but at the

same time I already knew he'd ask. I manage not to sigh hard.

"Do what, Donael." It should be a question but I can't quite make it into one.

"Find all the Nyväg people."

"We're just out here as observers. Just like I said."

"You mean, like Ødven said to say."

"Same difference."

Donael shakes his head. "They're just like you, you know."

"Who, Ødven?"

"No. Duh, Nyväg. They're fighting Ødven like you fought the Tathadann."

The announcement comes that we're about to stop, which I use as a reason to end the conversation.

"I'm just saying." He pauses for dramatics as he checks his seatbelt, and goddamn if he isn't my kid. "That's like killing your friends because Fannae Morrigan asked you to. And I know you'd never do that."

I don't give him any response.

In an engineering miracle, the train hushes to a stop at the platform with barely any jostling. I grab our bags from the overhead racks and toss them to the boys. I figure they're old enough to carry their own stuff. I check the map displayed near the station's entrance to find our housing. Ødven arranged for us to stay in a small lodge, which is supposed to be a five-minute walk from the power center. But judging by the map – which consists of about ten streets branching off the main one – it doesn't look like anything is more than a five-minute walk from anything else.

We step out into the street, and the first thing I notice is that there are no sidewalks. There aren't many cars either. In fact, I think as the wind picks up, blowing in from the sea through short, stumpy evergreens, there isn't much of anything. I pull my hood up and motion for the boys to do the same, but they're twelve and therefore impervious to both discomfort and advice.

"Our lodging is down this street, on the left," I tell the boys, then set off.

"You don't have anything to say?" Donael says to me as we walk.

"I've said everything I need to, son. You just need to listen."

Though it's a small town, most of the buildings are connected to each other, probably to break the wind and retain warmth. Each has a façade of dark wooden planks, likely to absorb whatever heat they can from the sun. Some have white trim, some green, some red. On the top of each house is a tall, sharply pitched roof with an inclined gulley in the valley between properties, presumably to drain snowmelt during the winters. Given that there's no snow on the ground now, just frozen scrabbled land, I conclude this is what passes for autumn up here, and the realization that their winters are even colder than this turns my blood to slush.

Walking down the main street in town we see two restaurants, a bar, a market, and a general store. There are less than a dozen people out. One woman chases her three kids down the street then herds them into the general store, past a man wearing all black who stands in the doorway. The man stays put a moment longer, glancing across the street to a gigantic man leaning in the doorway of the bar, then heading inside to help the woman. I get the creeping feeling we're being tracked. A younger lagon man ambles along, the woman beside him holding a baby wrapped in blankets. That woman must be pretty brave, because I wouldn't leave my kid around a lagon. A heavyset lagon shambles down the street with a huge bag flung over his shoulder. As he turns to enter the market I catch a glimpse of his long beard. He looks familiar. It takes a minute before it clicks: the man who bumped into me in Vårgmannskjør. His beard was a good hand-length longer, though. And that was back in the city, not here. They must be relatives. Still, it's strange.

"Are we going to start another riot?"

I stop in place, my shoulders slumping. "What are you talking about?"

"I'm not saying it like it's a bad thing. It's just, you know," Donael fumbles for words, "it seems like that's a lot of what you do."

"That's not why we're here."

"Maybe it should be."

I take a deep breath, tasting the cold, crisp air, then glance around to make sure no one's moving in on us. "There's more to revolution than just blowing shit up."

"Like what?"

"Like self-determination, freedom of choice, being able to chart your own..." I pause, realizing what he's trying to do, then shift course, eager to get off the street. "Know what, that isn't important right now. Right now, we just need to appreciate that we're all together."

"For shit's sake—"

"Hey, watch your mouth."

"What?" he says, and he actually seemed surprised. "Emeríann says it all the time."

"Well," I say, knowing that she does, "she's a grown up. When you're a grown up, you can say whatever you want."

He mutters *that's bullshit* but it's quiet enough that I can pretend I didn't hear rather than get in another argument.

Besides, we're already at our place. It's a house used for members of Ragjarøn when they visit Rën. The exterior is made of dark wood planks in the same style as the rest of town, layered atop one another with some kind of caulking to keep the heat in. As we step up onto the porch, the house senses the proximity beacon in my pocket and the door unlocks.

The interior is what I anticipated from the outside, an old house from centuries ago but with the modern technology of today. It's a lot of dark wood, a nice fireplace in the center, some woven rugs in what I assume are traditional patterns scattered around the floor; then there are several voice-activated control boxes on the walls, handling everything from temperature to music to the window shades. I've seen ones like these in Tathadann houses, but never had the opportunity to use them. I'm not sure if I should be impressed by the ease of use or worried they'll become self-aware and annihilate us in our sleep. The boys dump their bags just inside the door and bound toward the couch, Donael jumping and doing a half-pike before crashing into the cushions while Cobb just runs smack into it and smashes his body against Donael's. At least Donael seems to have lost his revolutionary ambitions for a minute. I carry our bags into our rooms, which are made out in much the same fashion.

The kitchen, however, is the polar opposite of the rest of the house. Every appliance – some of which I can't identify – is gleaming metal, with blue tile floors and white walls. I stand in the middle of it, thinking how happy Emeríann would be to have a kitchen like this. Even the refrigerator and cabinets are stocked, enough that we won't have to go to the market for a couple days. Whether or not I can recognize any of the items is a different question.

I wrangle the boys and take them out, ostensibly to explore the town but really because I want to go back to the man at the general store. I want him to know immediately that I'm aware he's watching. The man stands behind the counter, conspicuously not looking at us as we peruse the shelves filled with fishing rods and cooking utensils and an assortment of what appears to be jerky. I can still feel his eyes on us. We used the same techniques during the Struggle. At the end of the aisle, I find the clothing and pick out boots and gloves for the three of us, then some balaclavas and goggles in case we end up here for a while. I return to the fishing rod section and scan the shelves. There's not much of a selection of knives – nothing like I had at home – but I grab a six-inch hunting knife with a serrated blade. That'll do for now.

I carry our gear up to the counter, and it's not until I set it down that I realize I have no wallet and no way to pay.

"I'm going to leave this here a second," I tell him. "I left my wallet–"

"You're the new delegation, from the city?" he says. His accent makes his words come out cold.

"Why? Is there an account I can charge this to?"

"Never been here, have you?" He takes our gear from the counter and sets it in a paper sack.

"No, obviously."

"I can tell." He says it like he's divined something from the larger mysteries of the universe, and not because we look different from most people here and are the only ones constantly shivering asking questions. "You're staying down the street?" He shakes his head as if returning to a fond memory.

"Just a day or two." I have no idea how long we'll be here but this man radiates something that's just off and I don't want him knowing more about me than he has to.

"Just bring me payment when you can." The man slides the bag across the counter. "I can trust you, yes?"

"We appreciate it," I say, then feel an icy splinter in me realizing I just willingly aligned myself with Ødven. "The boys and I appreciate it. We're still getting used to the cold."

The man says, "Cold?" then coughs out a laugh. "Just you wait, bröder."

We drop our things inside the door then continue to walk around town. If I'm supposed to help restore order, I should at least get an idea of what disorder looks like. Judging by the bit we've seen, I'm of the mind that Ødven and I have very different conceptions of it.

We head west, away from the station, toward the sea. The boys spend most of the time picking up any pebble or rock they see lying around and chucking them as far as they can. I have half a mind to stop them and point out the cliffs nearby, tell them that the pebbles they're throwing were likely part of those dramatic outcroppings at one point, same as the small rocky beach that makes up the border of town. Then I realize they'd probably be bored to all hell by my circle of life observations, so I warn them not to hit anyone, including each other.

Before long, the street dead-ends. Fifty feet of rugged grasses give way to the beach, which tapers off into the frigid waters of the sea. The boys come up beside me. I lay my arms across their shoulders, the wind pressing against us as we stand at the edge of the world.

"If you squint hard, you can see Ardu Oéann from here," I say.

Cobb clicks twice.

"No, he's just joking." Donael pauses. "You are joking, aren't you?"

Inland, to the left, sits what looks like a small

cemetery. Beyond the cemetery is a squat metal dome, maybe thirty feet in diameter and with ten small metal domes arranged around it, all of them completely incongruous with the rest of the town. It looks like an ancient burial ground, but the fencing that runs around it, and signs warning people to stay away mean it's probably not, which means I automatically want to investigate. It's too far for me to go now, especially with the boys, so I'll have to have a look later.

Donael chases Cobb into the cemetery, both of them hopping over the tombstones – in Cobb's case, setting his hands on top and pretending to jump then running around them. My eyes dance across the names, a habit I picked up in Eitan. I think it's a part of my brain looking for men I'd fought with over the years, though few of them would have been buried in a cemetery. Their bodies were more likely burned by the Tathadann or interred in mass graves after being collected from the battlefield.

I'm walking through a row when a name catches my eye: Gaagnir Nilsson.

That one sounds familiar, where none of these others do. I continue down the row, searching for the name in my memory when it finally hits me: the man with the towels in Vårgmannskjør, the one Ødven called out to in order to show me how many people they were helping. It must be a coincidence, albeit a weird one. Perhaps it's a common name in the north.

"Who are you?" Donael says.

"I am the alpha and the omega. Who are you?" I look up, wondering what he's talking about, and see he's looking over my shoulder. I turn and see three people standing behind us, a man and two women.

The man is now wearing a thin black jacket that looks quasi-military but I immediately recognize him as the man from the general store.

"You need something?" I say, squaring up my chest.

"I thought that was you." He smiles and shakes his head, his dark brown chin-length hair brushing against his skin. "You're finally here."

"Excuse me?" I reach for my hip by instinct, then realize I didn't have my pistol on me when they grabbed me from Eitan, and I left the hunting knife in the bag with our gear. Stupid, Henraek. But judging by the man's appearance – tall and wiry – I'd guess I could beat him in hand-to-hand.

"Henraek Laersen, leader of the Struggle in Eitan City. Helped overthrow the Tathadann party with your partner Emeríann Daele." He steps toward me and I clench my muscles. "We've heard all about you."

"Who the hell is *we*?" I step to my left, putting myself between these people and the boys. I'm just now getting a good look at the women. Twins, it seems, though one appears to be a lagon. But now that I'm closer, I can see that she doesn't actually look like a lagon. She doesn't look… right… either. Wispy is one way to describe her. Like her membranes are barely holding on. And when a car passes along the street behind us, I can see something like that shadow of the car on her. No, not on her – through her.

"I'm Dyvik." He holds out his hand, a broad smile

making his cheeks even gaunter. He gestures to the woman next to him. "This is my wife, Lyxzä."

Then he points at the woman next to her, the one who is perpetually receding into the light. "And this is Lyxzä's ghost."

14.
EMERÍANN

Brighid gathers me before I can even finish my breakfast. Just like last night, my meal this morning saw a serious uptick in terms of quality from what I'd been given before. Part of me thinks she's still thanking me for saving her ass during the ambush yesterday. Another part thinks she's trying to cushion the blow that comes after killing one of your close friends. A deeper, darker part of me thinks she's trying to lull me into complacency before flipping the tables.

We climb into a car – a real car, with a roof and everything – and head north. It's just the two of us this time, which is a little strange and, in some way I'm not ready to acknowledge yet, kind of nice.

Winding through the city, I'm overwhelmed seeing, all at once, the changes the last six months wrought on the city's landscape. It started with the Gallery and the water distribution plant. After those two fell, it was like they sent shockwaves through the city, destabilizing everything else. Two of the commercial centers north of Macha were completely destroyed by Tathadann forces, and those took out two more when they tipped over. Eitan's silhouette is flatter now, but also more contrasted, the buildings taller than three stories sticking up like skyscrapers. It makes me wonder about the future, whether the structures will ever be rebuilt as tall as they had been or if people will keep everything small – harder to knock over, and quicker to rebuild if another revolution comes.

"What's important enough for us to drive all the way up here?" I say to Brighid.

She nods out the front window in place of an answer. The mountains sit a bit back in the distance, a group of block buildings rising up before them.

"High-rises?" I say. "You looking to invest in real estate? You might've been gone a while, but you know only amadans do that here, right?"

"It's not the buildings I'm interested in," she says as the car pulls to a stop. "It's the people inside."

She grabs a set of binoculars from the back seat and hops out of the car, then climbs up the side of a brick wall that had once been part of a home. I scramble up behind her. She looks through the binoculars a minute, then hands them to me.

"What do you see?"

I scan the building but don't see much. Once or twice it looks like somebody passes by a window, but otherwise the building appears deserted.

"A couple lagons, maybe. Nothing really."

"Turn on the thermal imaging."

I do, and the screen lights up. Where before it

looked like there were only three or four people, now I can see dozens milling around across three floors. Positioned at the perimeter are armed guards, rifles resting against their shoulders. Some people inside hold what look like pots and skewered animals. A burst of light shoots up where flames flare after someone lights a fire. I yank the binoculars from my eyes, blink at the change in color.

"What the hell is that?"

"Do you know who those people are?"

I let out a sigh. "I'm guessing you're going to tell me."

"These are rebels who had commandeered the building. Obstructionists. We surrounded them and captured them. Then we started using it as a holding center. Some are your friends. People you probably fought with, drank with, conspired with. So I understand that this is not going to be easy to hear." She looks at me for a measured beat. "These people are the problem, the reason Eitan is being held back."

"Oh, go to hell," I say, but she holds her hand up, and there's something incredibly composed about her that makes me fall silent.

"This isn't a Tathadann screed. This isn't *death to all rebels* or any of that authoritarian decree masking as liberation frequency. This is me, talking to you."

Her voice is different from how it normally is, graver. More sincere. More human.

"These rebels are within their rights to protest, but you have to ask yourself what they're protesting."

"Um, the slaughter of their friends and comrades?"

She gives me a look that nearly makes me laugh.

"They're protesting anything that's not them, just like I said last night," she says. "That's why we captured and detained them."

"Who's in there?"

"The most influential one we can identify is a man called Cantonae. Perre Cantonae."

I recognize the name immediately. He led the charge for that whole cadre of insurgents, the ones who thought Henraek and I weren't going far enough after taking down the Tathadann. He's a real asshole.

"But what we want to do…" Brighid pauses a minute, collecting her thoughts. "To best benefit everyone, we want to raze that whole complex."

"You're going to destroy all that housing on a whim?" Even as I say it, I recognize the irony. But that was in service of a larger good. This is just destruction.

"Have you been inside there? You know there's a reason the old and infirmed party members are shipped up there, right? If there was still a functioning government, they would be brought up on war crimes for letting people live there."

I start to reply but figure it's better to stay quiet, let her say her piece.

"Twenty years ago, those places were beautiful. Fit for Tathadann elders. But no one's touched them since they were built. Those places are falling apart now. The electricity pulses when it's actually working. The floors are tilted. There's black mold in most of the *kitchens*, where they cook. Once the new detention facility is complete, we'll raze the buildings," she quickens her pace, not giving me a chance to interrupt, "so that we can build new housing. Housing *anyone* is eligible for. Housing that is current and affordable and more efficient than those giant units they built. We'll fit four families for every two they had. Can you imagine what we could do for people here, what we could provide, with Ragjarøn's technology and resources?"

"You're insane to partner with him."

"You only know what lies the Tathadann told you," she says. "You have no idea what we could accomplish in this city with their help. We'll tear down the vestiges of the Tathadann, including their architecture, and build something that reflects this city. The whole city.

"But all of this would require the remaining rebels – the ones, I'm sorry, that you've been helpful in identifying – to concede, and join us."

"There are rebels and there are insurgents. The insurgents, Perre's people, they won't listen because they're only content with chaos. And the rebels, my people? They'll never lay down their weapons. Not for someone who beheaded their savior."

"They are all fighting against us, so they are all rebels. They're all fighting against Eitan," she says. "Do you know why, out of all the abandoned buildings in the city, the rebels chose those high-rises to take over?"

"Why?"

"Because, with a good enough rifle, they'll have a clear shot on us." She points toward the mountains, down at the foothills. "That's where the new power station is going. The one that will bring Eitan back online, provide water and electricity to everyone. Free, consistent water and electricity."

"If the power station is such a good thing for the city, why would they try to take it out?"

"You already answered that," she says. "I'm the one who beheaded their savior. They'll never listen to me, even if they don't know what Daghda was really like."

"What if I pitched it? They might listen to me."

Brighid nods for what seems like forever. "I wouldn't count on that. Between you being seen with us, and Henraek's contentious status…" She trails off a minute. "It only takes one bullet, and that bullet doesn't care about mislaid patriotism. I understand where those people are coming from, all that idealism and principle. I've seen it exposed for what it really is a hundred times over in my travels, but I still understand it."

"But?"

"But you have to clear the brush before you plant the field," she says.

"That's someone's sister out there. That's someone's son," I say.

"So are the dead. They're sisters, sons, fathers, mothers," she says. "So if people have to die – or, like these rebels, fight against any leader who isn't the amorphous *the people* – then they have to die. I'd rather them join us and I would gladly welcome them in, but they're trying to kill us while we're trying to help Eitan. And I'm sorry, but the whole must come before the individual."

"Morrigan said the same thing to us."

"What would you have us do, Emeríann?" she says, more aggressive than I like. "What's your grand plan to unite Eitan? Should we let the rebels go? Should we let loose ten angry people so that they can gun down thirty of my people who are trying to provide electricity and water for two hundred more? Just because they're on the 'wrong side'?"

I stare through her a moment. "I don't know what the answer is."

"It's easy to tear down what's wrong. It's much harder to build up what's right. I'm not saying we're doing a perfect job, and I don't know what the right answer is, but when I say *the whole*, I mean everyone."

"Except for those who stand against you."

"No. Except for those who try to kill us." She points out beyond the mountains. "The city. The counties. Anyone willing to work to better our home is welcome. But we can't let an angry handful ruin it for everyone else."

"What are you worried about? You've got all the guns and shit of Ragjarøn behind you. Ødven eats out of your palm."

She snorts. "Ødven Äsyr is helpful right now, but the day will come when we need to survive on our own. If we can all pull together and work as one, we will stand. If we don't, if we continue with in-fighting and cutting down one another at the knees with ideological purity, then we will fall. But whatever our fate, it will be *our* fate."

I look out over the city, at groups of prisoners huddled around a fire – a fire lit inside a goddamned building – and think about what she said. The possibilities of it. What if this city was actually rebooted with real people in mind? With something that resembled inclusion, equality, someone who gave as many shits about the Brigus as the bankers. Could she actually be telling me the truth?

Maybe it's because I watched this woman chop off her own father's head, but some part of me still calls bullshit on the whole people's revolution thing. Maybe it's Henraek's spirit, traveling alongside me.

"Why should anyone believe you?" I say to her. "What makes you different from any other party mouthpiece, or the Morrigans – who, you know, many people will see you as an extension of?"

And then she turns to me, almost smiling from incredulity.

"You know how I grew up. Do you know how many cities I've seen ripped apart? How many countries I've seen thrown into civil war? How many acts I've borne witness to that started those wars? If there's anyone who understands the dynamics of mass populations, who can predict reasonably well which actions will incite bloodshed and which will spurn it, I think I'm the prime-goddamn-candidate."

I hold up my hands, partially to calm her down and partially so that if she's angry enough to charge me, at least I'm ready. "I'm not saying you don't, but you understand how you're viewed around here."

"I do. Unfortunately." She inhales a long time, then lets out a breath that seems to drain her of everything. "Is moving twenty families into pre-fab housing the best choice? Maybe not, but it's better than four families taking that space and the others living on the street. Should they all be able to voice their opinion on that housing? Sure, probably. But while they're arguing about who gets which unit, how many are still sleeping beneath a tarp in an alleyway." She exhales again, her shoulders sagging. "We're not a perfect system, Emeríann, but we're trying."

She looks out over the city, rests down on her haunches, picks at the remnants of whatever this building once was.

"Eitan's tired. There's been nothing but war and oppression for the last sixty years. Running from building to building. Walking hunched over. Jumping at every bang. Rationing water down to the sip. That's just – that's no way to live. Especially not if there's the possibility of something creating better."

And the way she gazes over the land, with that deep longing in her eye and the sadness of a revolutionary who has been in the field for far too long, it's easy to think that she really means it. I can see where she's coming from at least. She's some combination of Forgall and Henraek. A dangerous mix of optimism and victimization. Being cast as the aggressor in her own country, while still fighting for the advancement of said country. It's enough of a contradiction to make Henraek's head explode.

Brighid looks over to me. "If you have better suggestions, please, tell me."

I wish I could give her something but I can't, because she's right: tearing down is easy, but rebuilding is much harder.

This is not even remotely the woman who I'd pegged

her to be. This is someone who cares. Someone who will fight. Someone, who, as we said at the beginning of the uprising, can actually win.

When we get back to the house later, I bid Brighid good night and head up to my room. I sit on the bed for a little while, letting everything process. Brighid might be batshit insane and have zero fear of death, but after everything she said, I'm not so sure she's the Morrigan I took her to be. I can hear the Tobeigh in her, echoes of similar conversations I had with Forgall. So similar that, despite how much it kills me to say it, I have to reconsider my position on her.

I kneel before the nightstand and pull out the drawer, then pause. Am I really going to do this again, send another letter? I don't even know if Henraek got the first one, if Melein was able to get it out or was caught in the process of smuggling. If whoever he gave it to was able to get it to Henraek. If Henraek got it and immediately left for Eitan and will miss the second letter.

I'm struck again by how much technology we have at our fingertips yet how far away all of that is for me right now.

Whatever. I can second-guess myself all day, but all that will do is put Henraek one step closer on a collision course with Brighid, put him in a position where he has to make a decision that might be impulsive and will probably be self-destructive. If it's our destiny to lead this rebellion, to finally liberate Eitan, then I'll have to trust that Nahoeg will safely guide the letter to Henraek. And if Nahoeg fails us, Henraek and I will just do it ourselves.

I start picking at the rest of the drawer liner. It comes out easy this time.

I was wrong.
She might be what we've been looking for.
We're going to rebuild Eitan.

I miss you.

15.
HENRAEK

"That's where they extract them," Dyvik says, pointing to the metal dome behind the fencing. "Then there's some kind of processing in those domes before they're able to come out into the world. Otherwise they would just evaporate when they touch air. I don't fully understand how Ødven's people do it, but that's what our people inside have found."

I'm still having a hard time comprehending what Dyvik is telling me, which is saying something for a man who used to make a living by stealing and selling memories.

"Is Gaagnir Nilsson a common name here?" I say.

Dyvik looks puzzled. "Not at all."

Lyxzä speaks up. "He was a farmer who lived just outside town. If you took the main road a mile or so south, you'd find his place. He raised sheep."

"I saw a man with that name in Vårgmannskjør, two days ago."

Lyxzä shakes her head. "Gaagnir died ten years ago."

"But Ødven called out that name and spoke to someone."

Dyvik nods. "You saw his ände."

"Ände?"

"That's what we call them," Dyvik says. "It's more like a ghost or spirit than a soul. We believe in a world beyond this one, but *soul* implies a benevolent god, which we don't do up here.

"Anyway," he continues, "two years after they extracted Gaagnir's ände, he tied a cinderblock to his waist and walked into the sea. He couldn't deal with the separation anymore."

"It can drag you down if you don't fight against the feeling," Lyxzä says. "It's not uncommon to find bodies floating in the harbor."

I shudder at imagining how cold that water must be.

"Some people can't handle the feeling of separation," Lyxzä continues, "like a piece of you that is always missing. When your ände leaves, it takes part of you with it. It's like the volume is turned down. Things aren't quite as bright, not quite as sharp. Sometimes it's more, sometimes less, depending on how spirited the person is."

I wonder if that was supposed to be a joke or if it's just something lost in translation.

"Your ände is still part of you. It can feel things, physically and mentally. It just doesn't have your – what do you call it, volition? Some people even say they can feel what the ände is feeling, like a cord that's not completely cut, and they can't tell when they're feeling something themselves or when the ände is feeling it. After a while, it can drive you insane."

I hear clicking behind me, and when I turn around I see Cobb creeping toward Lyxzä's ände, his hand out as if he wants to touch it but is scared. I snap my fingers at him and he pulls back like he's been bitten.

"Watch your brother," I say to Donael, who looks annoyed that I'm keeping him from hearing more. He's too close already, and I couldn't handle losing him again.

"Let me get this straight," I say to Dyvik, trying to understand why this is so urgent for them. "On the winter solstice of their thirty-fifth year, every citizen of Brusandhåv is required by Ragjarøn to commit their soul–"

"Their ände."

"They're required to commit their ände to the party, who extracts them and then... conditions them... in a labor farm. And then those ändes are shipped out to do all of the menial work in Vårgmannskjør? Am I following you correctly?"

"And that's just a side benefit. When the ände is harvested, energy is released. That dome collects the energy, which is then used to power the capital for a good period of time. Then the next wave of people commit and the grid gets more power and the businesses get more workers, and so on and so on. In the end they get our ändes and our energy," Dyvik says.

The way he describes it, the process sounds not dissimilar to the stripping used by the Tathadann, except it doesn't kill them and it produces energy.

"That sounds awful," I say to them. "But without

being rude, you all still have it much better than we did in Eitan. You have running water. There are no bodies in the streets." I gesture up at the sky. "You can see the sun. Do you know how long I went without seeing the sun? Years and years."

"Yes, we have those things. We're lucky to have them." Lyxzä takes a step closer to me. "But at what cost?"

Something occurs to me. "If people keep committing, won't all the jobs eventually be taken? And then they can stop committing?"

"They send the older ändes to other countries and get resources in return," Dyvik says.

"Exploiting us in this life is bad enough," Lyxzä says. "But according to our belief, without our ände we are doomed to wander the Great Beyond as only half of ourselves. We spend eternity wanting while our ände spends it working."

"Lyxzä committed two years ago," Dyvik says. "She understands that wanting."

"And you haven't?" I ask Dyvik.

"He turned thirty-five two months ago. Magnus, a week later," Lyxzä says. "Many of Nyväg will be thirty-five this year, and the solstice is not far away. It is very hard to fight without your ände."

Which is why they are so determined to do this now.

"It's not just one camp, either." Dyvik nods to the one beyond the graveyard. "That's the one for this region. Ours was the first they built, so it's the largest. But there are more than a dozen around the country. Many are outside Vårgmannskjør, where there is the greatest demand, but they reach from here out past Skaö, deep in the Jötun Mountains."

"They give you no choice in whether to do it or not?" I say it a little more forcefully than I'd meant. "They just strip your souls – your ändes, whatever – without your permission and leave you feeling muted for eternity. Just for electricity. That's horrible."

Dyvik comes closer, puts his hand on my shoulder. "And that is why we need your help to stop it."

"And your group, Nyväg, you're trying to, what, destroy the machines to stop them from committing any more?"

"Hey," Donael says, butting in. "Wasn't that guy in Vargman-whatever Nyväg? The one they, um…"

"Yes, Donael." I put a little steel in my voice, trying to keep him out of this conversation. A chill runs up my spine, remembering the sound of the man's throat opening. "The one who was murdered."

"They do that to anyone caught dissenting," Lyxzä says. "No matter which of the provinces they're captured in, they're brought to Vårgmannskjør and sacrificed before Evivårgen."

"But we continue fighting. That is the kind of dedication we have in Nyväg," Dyvik says. "We know that you've been sent out here by Ødven to monitor us."

"His words were 'restore order.'"

Lyxzä breathes out a laugh. "And how many people does he expect you to kill in order to do that?"

"I asked the same thing."

"I told you they were horrible." Donael shakes his head, an expression on his face that is equally familiar and terrifying. The expression of bone-deep disgust. I remember it well, on Walleus's face, and in the mirror, years ago.

"That's why I'm telling you to stay away from it," I say to Donael. I mean for it to come out strong and authoritative, but there's a waver in my voice I can't keep out. Like it can sense Donael's interest and is fighting to get through, or that my own voice senses my hypocrisy and is betraying me.

"We're asking for your help." Dyvik clears his throat, then continues. "Ragjarøn has ruled over us for too long," he says. "The Äsyrs simply take whatever they want and expect everyone in Brusandhåv to accept it as what's best for us. This country was formed by stealing native lands, combining communities with no relation to one another, without any input from our people. Who are they to decide what we need, what path we should take? We have no voice, no path of recourse when we've been wronged, no arena to air our grievances. There's no congress, no courts, no parliament, no group of common people brought on as advisors. Just those two tyrants and their oändlig insikt, their supposed ability to somehow see inside the hearts of the people. We want our land back, to be our own rulers again, to answer only to ourselves and our people."

I understand what it's like to ache for self-rule, to define yourself for yourself and be beholden to no one, especially as tyrannical as the ruling parties could be. If I'm being honest with myself though – I'm just tired. I lost my wife. I lost my son for too many years. I lost my best friend – who was very nearly my only friend. I've lost my girlfriend. I don't want to lose any more.

But at the same time, that familiar tingling spreads through my body, starting in the center of my chest and radiating out like a star gone supernova. The thrill of possibility, of free breath, of an unrestrained tongue and an unshackled mind. Of a better future for my boys, and all the other young ones like them.

"OK," I say finally. "I'll do what I can to help. But I can't do anything that will endanger the boys. I won't."

They both smile, relief settling over their faces as quickly as the optimism bubbles. We all shake hands, then Dyvik brushes it away and pulls me in for a hug.

As quickly as those revolutionary feelings returned, they dissipate even faster when I look over Dyvik's shoulder and see the look on Donael's face. I remember feeling that too, when I'd first heard about the villages taking up arms against the Tathadann, the feeling that I was about to become part of something bigger than myself.

And right now he's feeling that same thing, only it's for some villagers he doesn't know, next to his hypocrite father.

Would you have done this, Walleus? Or would you have kept him away?

16.
EMERÍANN

I stretch out my legs beneath the table in the kitchen, not necessarily because I slept wrong and they're cramping but because I *can*. After more than two weeks stuck in shoeboxes disguised as living quarters, I've earned enough trust to be allowed to roam the house, though I'm still under lock and key at night. At first I was insulted, thinking I was being treated like a dog that was only partially housebroken. Then I decided I would enjoy it for what it is and look around.

I wash my dishes in the sink then pour myself another cup of coffee, wrapping my hands around the mug and letting the steam drift over my face.

There's not much to the house that I hadn't seen in my few trips in and out, but everything has taken on a different quality now, being able to wander of my own free will. The wallpaper seems more vivid, the chairs softer, the color of the wood deeper than it had been, despite the scuff marks I left while digging my boots into the floor, trying to stop them from restraining me. Henraek would say my head is about to float off my neck, but he takes everything too seriously to allow himself any flights of fancy.

Since that first night, Brighid has come into my room a few times more. Always with food, always something that reminds me of home, like she somehow found my mother's recipe book, learning how to make delicious food from scraps. As the week's progressed, she's worked her way from the dresser, to the bed, until we were both sitting on the floor, leaning against the bed with our legs flung out. It was how I always imagined women – *girls* – acted, but I never had many girl friends when I was growing up. Possibly because none of them were particularly keen to clomp around the bogs and shoot things. Or because most of them were cunts.

These conversations have not only humanized her more, but also reinforced that she genuinely wants to improve Eitan. Do I agree with everything she says? Absolutely not, beginning with murdering Speider. But, in some perverse way, I understand. I shot the young woman in the water distribution plant because she was in my way. Would she have shot me? By the way her hand shook I'd say no, probably not. Brighid is confronting what Henraek and I would've had to deal with, were he still here: what do we do once the Tathadann is gone?

Though we had discussed it a couple times, neither of us had a good answer.

I take a big swing of coffee, forgetting it's hot, and burn the everloving shit out of my mouth. I hurry

to the bathroom and turn on the faucet. It sputters,
only a small stream of water coming out. I take a sip
and hold it in my mouth. It's more than I'd get at the
apartment but still doesn't help.

The front door closes. A woman's and a man's voice
come down the hallway. I recognize the woman's
gravelly tone and the man's soft Brigu accent. They
were outside when I was waiting for Melein. I'm
about to step out of the bathroom when I hear the
woman say, "If you don't get them in line, we're
going to miss our opportunity. We're never going to
make this work if we don't do this now."

I ease the door mostly closed, press my ear against
the crack.

"I told you they would comply and they will," the
man says. "Don't question me again."

"Then don't make me have to." The woman reins
her voice in. "We're only going to get this chance
once. I don't want to miss it."

"I still don't understand why that space is so
important. It's a shitty old building."

"It's not the building." She lowers her voice
conspiratorially. "It's the power. You have the land,
you can see the right things. You can see them, you
can get the power."

"What are you going to do once you get the
power?"

I can practically hear her smile. "What do you
think? Get more."

The man barks out a laugh so harsh and abrupt
that it startles me. My hand jumps back and clips the
edge of the coffee cup, knocking it off the sink. It

shatters against the tile floor. The man's laugh dies immediately. I hold my breath. I'm trapped. I don't know who they are. I don't know what they're planning. I don't know who else is out there. I don't know what weapons they have.

I flush the toilet and close the door, the click buried under the rushing water. Outside the door, I hear their footsteps receding. I crack the door and peer through the sliver to outside. Only their backs are visible. A tall and gangly man, his bald head with close-cut ginger hair that looks like rust. Medium-height woman with long brown hair pulled into a ponytail, as generic as can be. They hurry out the door without looking back.

As I scoop up the broken pieces of ceramic, I wonder who they are. It sounds like they're going to do something with the high-rises, but I don't know what and I don't know when. And to Brighid, me not having those details could make all the difference.

Every time Brighid looks at me, I can feel her eyes worming under my skin. Every glance seems accusatory and every look away feels dismissive. I'm probably being ridiculous, but that's the weight of uncertainty, as Henraek would say. But what am I supposed to say? *Hey, I overheard some people – Who? – I dunno who, but they were planning on doing something – What? – Dunno that either, but they want to take over a building – Which one? – I think the high-rises, not sure about that either, but it's definitely to seize power.*

That last part is the most dangerous. *To seize power.* It's a direct threat to Brighid – to all of us, according to her – but the source is unknown. If I tell her there is some vague threat, I can easily see her thinking I'm sinking back to my rebel ways, eroding the foundation of her group with disinformation, making people question one another.

And the worst part is, I don't know if I'm more worried about being labeled a rebel or walking into an ambush. Because either will result in a bullet in my head.

The road crests the hill that overlooks Fomora, near the spot where Brighid took me last week. I close my eyes for a second and concentrate on the air passing over my face, glad once again to be out in the open. Our truck passes by the high-rises where the insurgents are detained and winds into a more residential area near the edge of the city.

The houses are small but well kept, or as much as anyone can manage these days. Small rectangles of yard, waist-high fences keeping people out. Cars sit in some of the driveways, and most of them look to be autodrivers. Could be that the people are older and can't drive themselves anymore or could be that they're largely former Tathadann people and can afford that kind of stuff. Some of the yards have small plaster statues of frogs and elves, and many of the others have children's toys strewn around, probably for the grandkids. One house has a granite statue of a woman's torso on a serpent's body. I recognize it as one of the old gods from farther north, not quite as far as Brusandhåv but just as illegal. Or used to be. One of the many things that's changed since the uprising. Still, I wouldn't let the boys play there if that person was our neighbor.

I lean over to Brighid. "You sure your intel is up to date on this one?" I nod at the various topiaries. The urge to tell her about the saboteurs rises along with my anxiety of being caught off-guard. "This doesn't strike me as a hotbed for insurgent activity."

Brighid doesn't bother to look back at me. "Which is why it's the perfect place to hide."

I lean back in my seat and worry the bottom of my shirt. She has a point, but it'd be pretty shitty for them to use their grandmothers as human shields. Then again, part of the reason the Tathadann was so effective was because they would stoop to levels we wouldn't. If these insurgents are so dead set on taking down Ragjarøn, they could adopt Tathadann practices. The two saboteurs in the house seemed pretty set on taking over the space at any–

Something flickers in the corner of my eye, some small movement near the edge of a house. I squint, trying to figure out what it is, when something jumps up in the yard. A snake.

A snake?

Then I see the points. Not a snake. A chain, with three-inch metal spikes.

And it's lying across the road.

"Stop!" I scream.

The driver stands on the brake, slamming me and Brighid into the seats in front of us. The truck skids to a stop, and then the trailing vehicle crashes into us and pushes our truck over the spikes. The front wheels explode. I jump out of the truck, pistol in hand, and tell Brighid to take the other side of the street. I point behind us, tell the trailing soldiers to clear those houses and the soldiers in our truck to stay where they are and give us cover. I duck behind an ornately trimmed bush and clear the yard before strafing across to the next one.

"How many?" Brighid yells over to me.

"Don't know." I pause, hear a rustling beside the house. Probably the person who was holding one end of the chain, which means there's someone in a parallel position on the house side.

I chirp a quick whistle. Brighid turns to me and I mime going around the house, rounding them up and pushing them into the street where the soldiers are waiting with their rifles. She gives the go sign and we move.

The side of the yard looks largely like the front, though with no topiaries. I feel exposed out here with nothing to hide behind and keep my back against the wall, checking in front of me then behind, then scanning the yard across from me. Several of the soldiers yell out *clear* as they check the nearby houses. As I pass the halfway point, I catch movement in the neighbor's window. I whip my pistol up and train it on the glass. An old woman freezes, teapot in one hand, a ceramic mug slipping out of the other. It shatters on the floor. I flick my pistol, telling her to take cover, then continue.

At the edge of the house, I take a breath to ready myself, then glance around the corner. Small backyard. Self-propelled lawnmower – though not an automated one – sitting in the yard, unused. A small shed in the back corner, ringed by tiny red and orange flowers, meticulously planted. But no attackers. I hurry across the backyard, pausing by the back door, though there is no one peeking out the window.

I haven't heard any of the soldiers yelling anything other than *clear*, so the attacker is still on the side of the house. I glance around the corner and see an exterior ventilation unit. These bastards have it all up here. Henraek and I were lucky to have a fan. And right beside the unit, I see someone's back, crouched down and hiding.

I creep around the corner, stepping lightly with my pistol held before me. He keeps peeking out, looking for a good angle to get off a shot. Even from a distance, I can tell by the hair it's the tall man from earlier.

When I'm a short distance away, but not so close that he could reach me, I call out to him. "Stand up."

His body goes rigid, ready to jump up then thinking better of it.

"Drop your weapon and stand up," I tell him again, creeping a little closer. "I don't want to shoot you but I will."

"That was you in the bathroom, wasn't it?"

My face burns. "Bathroom? No, I don't hang out at those kinds of bars anymore." Past him, I can see the soldiers moving in, providing backup. Brighid yells something across the street and the man winces.

"You've no idea what you're doing, Emeríann," the man says, finally standing but not dropping the handgun as I'd told him. "She's not what you think she is."

"Drop it," I say as firmly as I can, ignoring the crawling sensation beneath my skin at him saying my name. My finger tenses on the trigger.

He turns around to face me. His face is long and angular and rests well above my own. It makes me uncomfortable, having to look up to see his eyes. "You've got your mouth open like a fish, and all her plans are the hook set inside you."

"Drop your weapon." I say every word individually, readying myself to shoot if I have to.

"But you don't know it because all her talk, her lies, that's the worm wrapped around the hook. You can't taste the metal, and you don't know you're being brought up into the air."

I raise my pistol higher, pointing it right at his face. I can feel my hands tremble slightly and tell myself to stop acting like a pussy. "I will not tell you again."

Behind him, Brighid is leading two insurgents into the street, one of the soldiers providing cover. She hands them off and looks up at the tall man and me.

"Just remember what I said when you finally break the water and find out you can't breathe the air. See if *your* soul can handle it." The man smiles. His teeth are surprisingly white. "Hořte v pekel."

"What are you–"

Before I can finish, he whips his handgun up. I start to squeeze my finger but he's faster and there's a great boom, one that reverberates deep inside my bones, ricocheting off my rib cage, settling into the pit of my stomach. His body collapses, breath evaporating as the top of his head flies off, bloody scalp and hair landing behind him. It seems to take his body a second to realize it's dead, his handgun still resting inside his mouth, now covered with rushing blood. Then it tumbles to the ground and I gasp like I'd been held underwater.

I sink down into a crouch, press my hand against the lawn to give myself some grounding.

Brighid rushes over, yelling, "What the hell was that?"

I've seen people die before. I've shot people before. But something about the way he did it, the calm way he spoke to me while knowing what he was going to do the whole time, was chilling. *See if* my *soul can handle it?*

"What the hell?" Brighid's hands grab my arms and pull me up. "Are you OK?"

I nod, shake her off. "I'm fine. Nothing hit me."

She looks down at the man's body, nudging his arm with her foot. "Dumb sons of bitches. They'd rather die than work with us."

"He was with us, before," I say. She gives me an odd look. "He knew my name."

I crouch down. Blood flows from the hole in his head and the sound of effluvia sloshing almost makes me puke. His eyes are still open, staring at me. Judging me.

"Shit," Brighid says.

"What?" I say. "You know him?"

She nods. "Joined up with us recently. Maybe two weeks ago?"

"He had a friend too. They were planning this."

Her head whips toward me. "What are you talking about?"

I swallow hard, looking at the dead man's eyes. "I overheard him and some woman in the house this morning."

"What did she look like?"

"Medium height. Brown hair in a ponytail."

"So me or any of the other thousand women who match that description."

"I was hiding in the bathroom so they wouldn't see me. I only recognized him by the height and hair. They were talking about taking over a shitty building and the space letting them see the right things, giving them power." I shrug. "It was all really vague. I wasn't sure what it meant."

"But you felt it. When we were driving."

I look back to her, not following.

"You yelled for us to stop, right before we hit the road spikes. You felt something was off."

"I saw the chain jump in the yard. That's why I yelled."

"No one else saw it. You did." She lays her arm across my shoulders and leads me back to the street. "I think both of us could use someone watching their back all the time now."

"Sure. Whatever."

"But you hear something again and don't tell me immediately, we are going to have some very big problems."

Five insurgents are gathered in the middle of the street, kept on their knees with their hands restrained behind their backs while the soldiers cover them with their rifles. Two are women, but one is a Brigu and the other is blonde. I don't recognize any of them and wonder if they were recruited from another country specifically to fight.

"Neither of them?" Brighid says to me. I shake my head.

She steps in front of one of the men. "What building are you taking?"

He doesn't respond. She moves to the blonde woman, asks the same question. Same response. She whips out her pistol and points it at the first man's head. He flinches for a second then regains his composure, but the throbbing vein in his forehead says he's not so calm inside.

"You'd rather let your friend die than help Eitan heal itself?" she says to the woman. "That sounds more like selfishness than civic pride."

The woman swallows hard before opening her mouth. But instead of naming a building, she starts singing. Her voice is accented, but not from Ardu Oéann or Brusandhåv. "Down near the river where our brothers bled–"

They're from the eastern part of the continent, brought in by Cantonae and his cadre. They're co-opting our revolution.

And somewhere deep inside me, I hear something snap. I smash the butt of my pistol on the bridge of her nose. She grunts as blood pours out, smearing over the front of her shirt.

I crouch before the woman, making sure she's looking right into my eyes. My breath comes in ragged waves and it's about all I can do to keep myself from smashing in this amadan's face with my gun. "You do not get to sing that song. What you are doing now is the antithesis of our rebellion. You are the Tathadann, standing between the people and a better life. I should gut you for even thinking you were the same."

I sink my boot into her stomach, knocking all the wind out of her. She doubles over, gasping for breath on the inhale and unleashing a stream of vomit on the exhale.

"Stop," one of the men shouts. "Stop, OK?"

Brighid stands over him. "Which one?"

The other men whisper harsh threats at him, some in tongues I don't understand, but he keeps his eyes on Brighid.

"There's a rec center four blocks north of here. Kids used to play indoor football there."

One man shouts at him to shut up. A soldier hits him with the butt of his rifle.

"That's been condemned for years. There's nothing in the space."

"It's not what's in the space," he says, and as he tries to continue the thought, an insurgent brings himself onto his feet to launch himself at the man, trying to silence him. He nearly has the man until a rifle shot crackles the air and the insurgent's body slumps against the ground.

The blonde woman cowers and the men lower their heads, but the Brigu woman – now splattered with the insurgent's blood – remains resolute, though I can see the corners of her lips trembling. She is definitely from here.

"It's not what's in the space, it's what's under the space," she says, taking over for the man, who has lost the nerve to speak. "The building is the center point of the tunnel system."

Brighid cocks her head. "Why would a football pitch be the center of the tunnels?"

"It used to be a facilities maintenance plant. There were chutes that went down into the sewer system. When the people seized the plant from the resource companies, they dug tunnels off the sewer lines to evade the fighting and shuttle food to the areas that needed it. Then after the Tathadann shut down the plant, one of the residents – he built the two factories that made the autodriving cars – remade it as a football pitch." The woman shrugs. "His kids loved playing and he didn't want them to get shot during the fighting."

Seeing the right things, I think to myself. It's good I didn't say anything to Brighid because it would've been about the high-rises, not the rec center. And I would have a bullet in my head right now.

Brighid examines the woman for a long minute, then motions to the soldiers. "Get them up and take them to the high-rises." She points at the woman. "See that she gets something to eat and clean clothes."

The soldiers haul them into the trailing truck and head back toward the city center, while the other two start fixing the flat tires on our truck.

Brighid stands in the middle of the street, bottom lip pinched between her thumb and index finger, staring off into the distance. I come up next to her, nod toward the indoor pitch.

"That's some story," I say.

She says, *Mmmhh*, and continues to knead her

bottom lip.

"Henraek always used to talk about those. He said he sent a bunch of rebels looking for them during the Struggle but no one could ever find them." I look at her from the corner of my eye, trying to get a read on her train of thought. "Want to go check it out? They could be useful to have."

Her hand drops like an anchor, her expression with it.

"There are no tunnels."

"But we found them. Beneath the butcher's shop."

"Those were dug during the Struggle. That's why there were so few of them."

"No," I say. "Henraek heard about them. And we found part of them."

"They don't exist," she says, an edge to her voice. "It's a rumor, disinformation, something to keep the people looking for the thing that would save them but never let them find it."

"What? Why? How do you know that?"

She looks at me and for a flash I see something like sadness in her eyes.

"Because Daghda told me. He's the one who started it."

I come back into the house after the long-ass day and go straight to the kitchen area, scouring the cabinets for food or booze. Between the bar and Henraek and his bourbon, I'm used to relaxing with a drink. Now, cut off from most other people and unable to go walk around town, I'd murder someone for a tumbler of liquor.

I settle for a few sips of mostly clear water and head up to my room. Since Brighid now wants me by her side at all times, I was told I'd soon have better accommodations – specifically ones that don't require a lock and key – but they'll take a day or so to get in order. I've gotten used to this tiny room, so another night won't kill me.

I push open my door, ready to collapse on my bed and stare at the ceiling until I pass out.

But when I flick on the light, I stop in my tracks. My pillow is covered in blood, with something black sitting in the middle of it. My eyes scan the room. Nothing disturbed, nothing taken, no blood anywhere else. I step back outside, scanning up and down the hallway, but find nothing suspicious, so I come back in my room and make my way to the bed.

The black lump, I see when I get close, is a pigeon, lying on its back with its wings extended as if it died in mid-flight. But its eyes have been carved out, tiny black holes in its tiny grey head. Sticking out of its chest is a curved, white ceramic piece with a sharp point at one end. When I pull it out, I know immediately what it is.

It's a coffee cup handle. The same one I broke this morning.

This is from the brown-haired woman. The one whose plan I ruined.

This is her warning me not to get any closer. But who the hell is she?

17.
HENRAEK

We take Dyvik's car east, heading up the road into the ridges and tracing the jagged edge. He handles the vehicle well, but every time we come upon a tight turn I hold the back door handle and take a deep breath, reconciling myself with dying. Dyvik's right hand, Magnus, the barman whose name is as awe-inspiring as his barrel chest and arms, glances back at me from the front passenger seat, amused by my anxiety.

We're headed to a nearby town, just under an hour away, to get a better look at a labor farm. Rën would probably be the worst place to be seen poking around a farm with two known members of Nyväg. This one is also one of the newer ones, which Dyvik tells me is important. As we drive, I try to memorize as many details as possible in order to give Ødven enough information to remain credible while still keeping Dyvik and his people safe. It's farther than I'd like to go when the boys aren't with me – Lyxzä is watching them and Magnus's boys, Axel and Edvin, though I get the feeling his boys can fend for themselves and it's more a show of solidarity – but the next closest one is at least three hours.

Eventually, the trees begin to thin, likely unable to weather the harsh winds that must whip through here during the winter. We top a crest, where a small outcropping of houses sits off to the right of the valley. A river slips through the center of the area. The beauty of it all, combined with the reason for our visit, is nearly overwhelming.

Dyvik pulls the car into a small copse of trees, half a mile outside of the village.

"Why are we stopping here?" I say to him.

"Don't want them to know we're coming." He says it like it should be obvious.

"I thought Nyväg was here."

Dyvik climbs out of the car, leaving Magnus and me.

"There are Nyväg wherever there are labor farms," Magnus explains. "But not all Nyväg is same Nyväg."

It takes a minute, but I get what he's saying. "These people are amadans."

He arches an eyebrow.

"Idiots. Morons. Can't tell an arse from an elbow."

"Yes, like that." He climbs out, motions for me to follow. We hurry to catch up to Dyvik, who points to the right of the village.

"That's it."

I squint, but can only see the central dome and several small ones. "It looks the same to me."

Then he hands me the binoculars.

I pause a second to look. I now see that the fencing that surrounds the domes isn't just to keep people out, as two dozen wispy figures dodder around the enclosure I realise it's to keep the ändes in.

"Holy shit," I whisper. "They just leave them out there to freeze?"

"They're not really alive to be able to freeze."

"But they can feel the cold?"

Magnus nods. "In their own way."

I lower the binoculars, let them hang around my neck.

"What are you thinking?" Dyvik says.

"How many Ragjarøn troops are in the village?"

Magnus says, "The small villages are not heavily guarded. One or two, if any."

"Then let's blow it up," I say. It occurs to me that seems to be my answer for everything.

Magnus grins, but Dyvik shakes his head. "Too risky. It takes preparation to do that, and as soon as we do one farm, security on all farms will be raised."

Shit. "Well, we can't leave them there. That just... doesn't seem right."

Magnus purses his lips and says something in their tongue.

"Is that a good idea?" Dyvik says.

"What did he say?"

Magnus clears his throat. "At times, water gets inside the locks on the fences. The water, it freezes and bursts the lock."

I finish his thought. "And the gate swings open."

"These ändes, they never know to leave because they are not told," he says. "But we could move them along."

"Can they rejoin their... um..." I stammer, not sure what the right term is and not wanting to insult them by saying host as though they're a parasite.

"Their host?" Magnus says. Figures. "Not physically. But being close is good many times. Like Lyxzä and hers."

I whisper, "Then once they're loose, their hosts can find them. And Ragjarøn can't."

I'm moving down the countryside before anyone else can speak. They hurry down the hill to catch up.

We creep along the fence at the labor farm, checking constantly to make sure there's no one around, but the village remains quiet. When we get to the gate, I pause. If we pick the lock, it won't look like it busted. Hitting it with a rock would look like... it was hit by a rock.

"How are we–"

Magnus steps forward as if he could read my mind. He pulls on the lock to test it, taps his fingers against the face.

"What are you doing?" I say.

He shoves his fingers between the top and bottom parts of the lock and yanks hard. The whole thing splits. He shakes his hand, wipes his finger across his pants.

"Now we are good," he says to me, then turns to the ändes and shouts something in their language, *Låt oss gå*. Then I recognize a word. *Tillräckligt*. It's the same thing the Nyväg man yelled before he was sacrificed. None of the ändes stop their listless doddering, but they change direction and come toward us. They amble through the gate, some headed toward the village and some into the valley.

"What happens when Ragjarøn finds out about this?" I say. "Will they kill them?"

"They are eternal and cannot die," Magnus says.

"What about their hosts? Will Ragjarøn threaten them?"

"Shouldn't you have asked that before you ran down the hill to free them?" I can't quite read his tone but it does make me feel like a dick. "But no, they probably won't, because they'll assume it was Nyväg."

"And Ragjarøn will have to catch them all before putting them back to work," Magnus says.

A few alarmed voices call out as the first ändes enter the village.

"Come," Magnus says. "We must go."

Back at his house, Dyvik unrolls a map and spreads it over the kitchen table. We gather around it. Donael and Cobb make a racket in the next room with Axel and Edvin, but I can feel Donael gravitating toward us, casting looks in our direction, waiting to be invited in. I hate to break it to him, but it's not going to happen.

I've heard stories about Brusandhåv for years, about the frigid cold and the rocky, rugged, unforgiving terrain, but have never seen a map of it. It's larger than I would have thought. In a car, it would probably take a good twelve hours to cross, if the roads in the mountains aren't too winding. On the map, the village we visited looks almost next door.

"We're right here." Dyvik points to the westernmost point, a jagged outcropping that juts into the sea, then slides his finger to a point in the south, tucked into a harbor. "Vårgmannskjør is all the way over here. And all of these red lines are transportation tracks."

"Why do you rely on trains so heavily? Why not transport vehicles like everyone else?"

"Those worked fine for today." He gestures outside. "It's light most of the time, the weather's still nice for autumn."

I suppress a laugh.

"But the seasons change quickly here," he says. "In a few weeks the cold and dark will set in. You won't be able to see any of the roads. And then there's the snow and ice and high winds. It's terrible. So they stick with trains, mostly. You can move more at a time too."

I point at a dozen green circles. "These are the other camps?"

He nods. Though the camps are spread throughout Brusandhåv, half of them are within five kilometers of Vårgmannskjør city limits. The others are dotted incrementally around the periphery of the country. All of them are located a short distance from the rail line – to make it easier to transport the people to the extraction centers, according to Dyvik, and then move the ändes to where they're needed – but nothing else seems to connect them.

"If you're going to strike a blow against Ragjarøn, you need to do more than just let a couple ändes loose. I'd say you'd need to destroy all of the labor farms."

"I thought you were staying out of it?" Dyvik says.

I take a deep breath. "If Ødven falls, Brighid will fall soon after, and Eitan can be free once again." That familiar electricity thrums through my arms. I realize that I feel more comfortable in my own skin right now than I have in weeks, and part of me wonders if I'm doing this for the liberation of Eitan or because I don't know who I am if I'm not fighting.

"So," I say, "is there a common power source?"

They both shake their head.

"What about a central computing system? Something that runs the extraction process?"

"There is much distance between the centers," Magnus says. "We don't have cables that will conduct so far, and wireless transmission can't penetrate the winters."

I run my fingers over the map, as if absorbing something through my skin that will allow me to divine the answer.

"Is there anything special about the one in Rën? As in, if this one goes, all of them go?"

"Other than being the first one, no," Dyvik says.

"And it's too close to home to hit."

Dyvik stretches his hands over his head. "That depends." He gestures between himself and Magnus. "We both live here. Our families are here. Our homes are here. We'll have to leave town immediately after, so if we are going to attack, it must be worth it. We must know we'll succeed."

Lyxzä calls out from the kitchen in their native tongue. Dyvik answers, then looks at me. "She's asking if we're moving."

I nod. She and Emeríann would get on well. "Where is Nyväg centered?"

Dyvik smiles, glances at Magnus. "You're looking at it."

"How many members do you have in total?"

"Thirty or so."

"That's it?" I wasn't expecting an army but I was hoping for more than this.

"We had thirty-eight until last month. A house was raided in Vårgmannskjør. And you know what happens then. There used to be more, up to a hundred, until Ødven started hunting us. Six of us are here now, in town, or just outside. The others are spread out, hiding." He points to two villages outside Vårgmannskjør, a small swathe in the east of the country, then a small dot in the Jötun Mountains. "But we're growing. Last year we started a youth brigade – the ungdømstrüpper – in Skaö, tucked into the mountains. It's a nasty place to live, but no one goes out there. The young ones are protected. And after living in Skaö for a few years, being outnumbered eight-to-one in a fight doesn't seem so bad anymore. Magnus's sons went through the training."

Magnus nods. "They learned much. Came back stronger, smarter, more disciplined." He smiles a little. "They listen better, to me and their mother."

"Wouldn't that be something," I say as much to myself as to them.

I understand where Dyvik and Nyväg's drive to be free comes from. I dedicated my life to it. Donael's words echo in my skull, that the Tathadann and

Ødven aren't much different. The worst part of it is knowing that I've spent a long time trying to become someone my son would be proud of, maybe even idolize, and the one thing that would make him idolize me most – being an agent of liberation – is the one thing that I swore I'd keep away from.

Something brushes against my leg. I spin around, startled after being inside my head, and see Donael hovering behind us.

"What are you doing?"

"What?" He puts on his innocent tone while holding up a football, like it just happened to roll over to this very spot, but he's looking right at the youth brigade center in Skaö. I step in front of him, blocking his view, though if he's anything like me he's a quick study. The other room has gone mostly quiet, Magnus's boys saying something in their language, showing Cobb how to break out of a chokehold. Cobb clicks along, pretending that he understands.

"You guys go outside and play," I say to Donael. "And I mean football, not murder each other or whatever you're doing in there."

He holds his hands up, saying *what are you talking about?*

"You heard me. Look." I point out a window at two kids in the street, an older girl and younger boy. "Go make some friends."

"Make some friends? When have you ever told us to make friends? You always said to stay away from kids unless you knew their parents so we wouldn't end up held captive by some Tathadann nutcase."

I don't remember saying that, but it sounds accurate. And also, hearing it repeated to me, it sounds tragic. What kind of parent tells their children not to make friends? *Were you so paranoid about your every choice, Walleus, convinced that picking the wrong one once would send them careening down a path they'll never recover from?*

"We're not in Eitan anymore so I'm telling you something different."

Donael glances out the window. "How do we know their parents aren't dangerous? That we're not going to end up lashed to a pole and have our skin peeled off?"

"Donael, that's an awful thing to say."

"You're the one who said it!"

I glance at Dyvik and Magnus, feeling an embarrassed flush spread over my face. It's an odd sensation because it makes me feel like a normal parent. For their part, the men don't react. I take a deep breath and tell myself that my graphic descriptions come from a place of love, of wanting them to stay safe.

"I know those two," Dyvik says, gesturing to the kids outside. "Their parents own the restaurant up the street, next to Magnus's bar. Good kids, but a little too much energy."

"That boy is risky," Magnus says. He looks up at Dyvik, who says something. "Shifty. Right. You must watch him in your house."

I turn to Donael, say, "There you have it," then nudge him along. "Now go. Don't get arrested."

Donael gives me an insolent look, squaring up for

a face-off. I stand a little taller, trying to forestall an argument I don't want to have right here. Magnus barks something at his kids before Donael can say anything. They respond with what sounds like acquiescence and come gather Donael, though he makes it known he's only going because they're going, not because I want him to.

"I told them to get their football," Magnus tell me. "Many of the children in village play on the local youth team. Your boys do?"

"Donael does." I pause. "Or he used to a lot. We played in the park back home. Cobb, well…" I shrug. They both nod. I tell myself football isn't too bad, that it's hard to indoctrinate for the revolution while slide-tackling each other. I push away the blooming images of our platoon at Hoeps matches back in Eitan during the Struggle. I cross my arms and return to the map. There has to be a way to do this. There is always a way.

"What about the people?" I say. "Is there popular support?"

"Most people support our cause," Dyvik says. "They want to be free but they are either scared of Ødven and Ragjarøn or they don't know where to turn. But the people of Brusandhåv have been exploited for many years, had their land seized in the name of Ragjarøn. They will support us once they know there is someone brave enough to stand up to the Äsyrs and Ragjarøn. They only need to see it."

I guess we'll have to do it the old-fashioned way. I'd hoped that Nyväg's technology was better than ours in Eitan and we could coordinate something remotely, compensate for our smaller numbers, the same way we used passion over arms during the Struggle, but I don't know this country. And with the solstice approaching, we don't have the time to spend a year laying the groundwork for a revolution.

"Let's be real. We don't have the numbers to take on Ragjarøn." I pause. "And you can't count on the public being inspired by watching you die heroically. So, if you're going to do this, you need to be smart, you need to be quick, and you need to be precise."

"What do you have in mind?" Dyvik says.

I exhale a long breath. The edge of the map flutters. "You should hit all of the camps at the same time."

"At the exact same time?" Magnus says.

I nod.

"That's nearly impossible," Dyvik says. "We'll have two, maybe three men per camp. We can't take down a camp with so few."

I hold out my hands. "Then you'll get slaughtered. So we don't do it."

"But we must," Magnus says. "Many of us are expected to commit our ändes this year and we will not be able to fight in that condition."

"Then don't commit. Isn't that the definition of being a rebel?"

"The punishment for not committing is the same as rebelling," Dyvik says. "We paint Evivårgen's feet with our blood."

"I think something's getting lost in translation. You asked for my help, and as I see it, this is only way. Understand?"

They both stare at the map a long moment, then exchange a glance. I can't quite tell what passes between them, but I also don't exactly care. The odds are already stacked against the three of us in this situation.

Through the window, I see Donael pass the ball to Magnus's oldest, Cobb trailing behind them, sucking wind. The way Ødven rules Brusandhåv is the way he will rule Eitan, and I cannot let that happen.

"Say we can do this," Magnus says.

"Magnus, we can't. It's too dangerous. That's not enough people."

"You either do it all the way or don't do it at all. You can't have half a revolution," I say again, getting more annoyed as the minutes slip by. "Is six fighters enough to take down a camp?"

"Yes, definitely," Dyvik says.

Magnus cuts him off. "Then we leave half the camps untouched. They are alerted and they will kill us all when we attack."

I cluck my tongue and point at Magnus.

"There you go."

Magnus crosses his massive arms, considering everything I've said. His biceps are bigger than my goddamned thighs.

"Dyvik," he says, then rattles off something in their tongue. Whatever it is, it doesn't seem to inspire much confidence in Dyvik, who shouts back. They exchange a few contested points while I stand there like an awkward child caught between arguing parents.

I glance out the window and see the kids are no

longer playing, but are standing in two lines facing each other, squared off. My skin tightens. Then the smaller boy, the shifty one according to Magnus, says something and Donael swings, catching the kid right in the nose. The kid stumbles back, cupping his hand against his face.

"Ah, shit," I say, hurrying toward the front door, leaving them to argue behind me.

I rush outside and the cold hits me like a fist. In my hurry, I forgot to put on my damn jacket.

"Donael," I call out, but he stands there with his chest heaving and ignores me. Cobb stands beside him, staring at the ground. Magnus's boys stand behind him, their hands at their sides but their fists balled. "What the hell?"

The boy pulls his hand back to expose a red smear on his face and palm. His sister straightens up, as if she's ready to throw in on hearing the word.

"Donael," I say as I get up to them. "What happened?"

He points at the boy. "This amadan was saying shit about Cobb."

"What did he say?"

Donael's jaw throbs beneath his skin, the same way it did when he was young and would grind his teeth as he slept. "I couldn't understand it, but I know it was bad."

My body sinks. A couple days in town and my son is already beating up the locals. This will do well for us trying to keep a low profile. I look at Magnus's boys. "What did he say?"

They exchange a glance and say something to

each other, then shake their heads and look at me. "We can't tell you," the older one says.

"Can't tell me?"

The younger says something to the older. "Can't say it, he means. It's not respectful."

Then Magnus's voice booms out behind us. All of the local kids startle, but mine stay motionless, Donael's stare still boring a hole through the boy's forehead. Good boys, them. Magnus asks his boys something and they respond.

"They said something about your boy?" he says to me.

"Yeah." I think that's the first time I've actively acknowledged Cobb as my boy, rather than just grouping him into *Donael and Cobb* or *the boys*. And it's true, I've been warming to him in the last week. Funny what a civil war and being ripped from your homeland will do to you. "But they said it's disrespectful to say it."

He asks his boys what it was, then pulls his head back when he hears their answer. He turns to the other two. "You are very lucky this is a compassionate man." He speaks in English, for my benefit I assume, and points at me. "I do not want to offend him with violence. But if my children said something like that," he draws in close, looming over the other kids. "I would make sure they would never say it again. Do you understand?"

The two kids nod. Magnus says something else to them and they turn around and head back to the store, the girl glancing over her shoulder with contempt raging on her face. At first I think it's directed toward Magnus for dressing them down in front of their friends. But when I look closer, I see she's actually staring at Donael.

"Are you OK?" I say to Cobb. He clicks a couple times, hollow and sullen, and I pull him in against me. I look at Donael, whose anger has subsided but is still there. "You?"

Without looking at me, he says, "Yeah. I'm fine." I lay my other hand on his shoulder but he still stares daggers at the boy. He definitely has his father's tendency to hold a grudge.

"You did well, Donael," Magnus says. "It is necessary here to defend your family."

Donael finally turns, his face lighting up when he sees Magnus's giant paw extended. Donael shakes, his hand enveloped in the big man's, and nods a couple times. "Thanks," he says. "Thanks."

And while I'm happy that Donael has stood up for his brother, I'm a little hurt that he turned to acknowledge Magnus, but not me.

"Come, boys," Magnus says to his sons. They slap hands with Donael and Cobb like young boys do, then head back to the house. Magnus turns to me, offers me that big slab of meat. He pulls me in and slaps my back, a gesture that's probably supposed to be nice but would be a little invasive in Eitan. "We will speak soon, bröder," he says. "We have many good things ahead."

He jogs to catch up to his boys, resting his arms on their shoulder, their silhouette like a miniature Jötun range.

"Let's head home, boys," I say, wrapping my arms

around them in turn. Cobb nestles into me without any prompting. Donael doesn't move away, but I swear I can still feel him pulling.

I stab the last bit of dinner with my fork and shove it in my mouth, chew it and swallow. Music plays throughout the house, lively guitars dancing and weaving through percussive clapping, music from the Zoreños in the far south that is drastically opposite the country we're currently in but does something to soothe my jangled nerves. The boys' plates are still full with smoked fish, boiled potatoes, cheese, and two pieces of thin crispbread with some kind of sweet jam on the side. And it's not because the food isn't good, although I had to walk over to Dyvik's and ask him and Lyxzä what to do with all of this. The Eitan diet of park-meat and root vegetables prepared me to dress things up to cover their origins. Cooking with actual food is something I'm not familiar with.

No, the reason they haven't eaten is because they keep talking about this afternoon. Cobb's shock and embarrassment wore off pretty quickly after we got home, and since then they've done nothing but chatter and reenact the earlier events. They haven't even complained about the music, which doesn't do anything to make me feel better. If it was just Donael punching the kid in the face, I could handle it. But they keep talking about how Magnus banished the two kids to the other side of town and *maybe they'll have to leave Rën now because how could they even stay here?*

"Boys," I say, cutting off Cobb in the middle of one of his wild gesticulations. "Please eat up so I can do the dishes."

They both sigh and start picking at their food like I've suddenly become the household fascist, so instead of antagonizing them I pick up my dishes and take them into the kitchen. While I'm washing, I stare out the window, listening to a woman sing a pained melody that grates against the guitar. The edges of the houses seem fuzzy, unfocused, and I wonder if it's condensation on the windows or if the constant light is finally getting to me. We'll be going to bed in a few hours and the sky looks the same as it did when we ate lunch.

The world, though, the world looks a little different from this afternoon.

I rinse off my plate and set it in the drying rack then go back to the table. They're still jabbering away, though I'm glad to see they ate most of their food in the meantime.

"So what do you make of everything?" I say to Donael.

He pauses a minute, fork wavering before his mouth, confused. "Everything what?"

"This." I motion toward the windows, the house, every invisible thing that is inferred. "Nyväg. Their plans. Their goals."

His eyes narrow slightly he cocks his head, as if he thinks I'm trying to set him up.

"I know you were listening this afternoon," I say.

"No I wasn't." He shoves food in his mouth.

"Do you really think I could've survived this long

without knowing what was happening behind me? I'm not stupid." I knit my fingers together, set them before me. "Come on, Donael. Be real. Talk to me."

He chews while considering me. Weighing his options, it seems. Finally he swallows and sets his fork down with a tink. Cobb regards us both hesitantly.

"I think they're brave, doing what they're doing. Especially after seeing what Ødven did to that guy in the city. I hope they don't get caught."

"I do, too."

"I think they're going to have to fight pretty hard. It won't be easy. It'll probably take a long time too."

I nod that I agree. "But?"

"But what?"

"What they want to do. Their goals. Liberating the people," I say. "All that."

"What do you think of it?"

"I'm asking you."

He sighs hard. "I think it's wrong that Ødven can make their ändes into slaves and make them work for the rest of their lives. I mean, that's messed up, right? Who does that?" He shifts in his seat, adjusting his position, and I can tell from his mannerisms – because Emeríann has pointed out that I do the same thing – he's about to get going. "Who is Ødven to tell everyone what they should do, you know? If someone wants to, I don't know, wash dishes or fold laundry or whatever, then OK, that's cool. But what if they don't want to? What if they want to, like, build things? Buildings and stuff. Why should they have to do all that dumb stuff when they could do something cool and better?"

"Who says they can't build something?"

"Um, Dyvik?"

"He never said that."

"Dad, I know what menial labor means. I'm not stupid," he says, pretending to be me. He does a fair impression.

"So it's understandable that they want to helm their own destiny, that it's a basic human right to be able to dictate your own course in life?"

He glances down at his plate. "Um, yeah, I never really thought about it but I guess so. I mean, it just seems right, right? That you should decide for yourself what you do."

"I agree." I clear my throat. "But is it worth killing for?"

He looks up from his plate, his eyes meeting mine but, surprisingly, not turning away. He holds my look long enough that I'm not sure if he's making some deep connection or if he's daring me to look away. Where is the line between love and antagonism? Cobb sits beside us, in my periphery, and clicks twice. Hesitant, searching. It's beginning to become awkward when Donael finally looks away.

"Why would you ask me that?" His voice is quiet.

"Because that's what's going to happen. You don't love a revolution into happening. You don't overthrow your oppressors by talking it out. You do it by killing. Revolutions are violent things done by violent men, and–"

"I know that, Dad. OK?" He almost shouts it. "You weren't the only one who suffered during the fighting, you know. I lost both of my parents in a day. And you were gone most of the time before that anyway. I saw Walleus dead on his floor and Lady Morrigan with half her head gone. I remember being little and watching you and Mom carry a body from your car into the garage so you could, I don't know, do whatever it was you were going to do with it." The vein on the side of his neck throbs. His voice wobbles. "I know what fighting looks like, from both sides. Really well."

"Then you understand why I'm asking." My voice remains measured, calm. I hate seeing him so upset, especially because that wasn't my intention. After seeing his interest in Nyväg, I only want to make sure he really understands what revolution entails. Killing as an idea and killing as an action are two wholly different things, something you never understand until it's too late.

I start to respond to him when the phone rings. It startles all of us, but I don't look away from him. I don't even know where the phone is.

"Are you going to answer that?" Donael says.

"It's not for me. No one knows I'm here."

"One person does."

Without him saying it, I know he's not talking about Magnus or Dyvik. I slowly go to the phone.

"Henraek," Ødven says. "How are things?"

"Fine. We're finishing dinner at the moment."

"What do you have on Nyväg?"

He gets to the point quickly. I turn my back away from the boys, as if it would dampen my voice a bit. "Things are quiet. I haven't heard anything."

"That is not what you were sent out to do, is it?" His tone changes noticeably within those few words. "You were sent to restore order."

"There's not a whole lot of disorder that I have to contend with." I keep my voice level, thinking anger will tip him off as misdirection. "This is a quiet town. These are quiet people."

"If that is the case, then I have no use for you," he says. "And neither does Brighid have use for Emeríann."

"You leave her out of this."

"We had reports that a group of ändes were set loose in a village one hour north of you. There are no known operatives there. What do you make of that?"

"I don't know. Maybe someone forgot to lock the gate."

"Or ripped the lock open."

"Or that. Sure."

"Then I will ask you again, and for the last time." He pauses, making sure I understand the situation. "What do you have on Nyväg?"

I hear Dyvik and Lyxzä's words in my ears, see the ändes inside my head, feel the rush of freeing them pounding through my veins. But I also hear Emeríann's voice, see the look on Donael's face while running free across the grass, feel the roughness of Cobb's skin.

"Nothing yet, Ødven," I say. "But I'm listening."

"You do not want to disappoint me."

"I understand that, but you've set me up in a place I know nothing about to surveil a group I know nothing about who speaks a language I don't speak, so when I say I'm trying–"

The quality on the other end of the line changes, and I realize he hung up after he said his piece. Asshole.

I hang up the phone and return to the table. Donael jumps on me as soon as I sit.

"Is it right that Ødven is basically killing these people? For what, towels folded into fish shapes or something?"

"He's not killing them." I try not to sound too exasperated, trying to keep the balance in my head, somewhere between supporting Nyväg and their call for freedom, making sure Ødven is happy, and keeping Donael from joining a revolution, without sounding like I'm favoring one faction over the other. "Exploiting them, yes, but not killing them."

Donael leans forward, his head drooping though his eyes not leaving me. "Are you defending him?"

"No, I'm not defending him, but I am aware that people here have a much higher standard of living than we did in Eitan." Donael starts to speak but I hold up my hand to stop him. "And I don't know what it was like for you two at Walleus's. He never brought me into his place for reasons that are now obvious. But I can damn well guarantee that the rest of Eitan did not live like you all did. Emeríann did wonders to our apartment to even make it that nice for you."

"It wasn't that nice," he says, in a tone somewhere between reassuring and a cheap shot.

"Exactly. Even we had it better than a lot of

people. And look around here? Look at this house, at everything we saw in Vårgmannskjør. For shit's sake, Donael, they have places to warm up and places to sleep if you're homeless. And they don't even call them homeless, they call them goddamned guests." I take a breath to rein in my voice, realizing I'm getting angrier the more I talk. "You know what they call homeless people in Eitan?"

"Homeless?"

"Target practice."

"Are you jealous because you're not in charge?" he says.

My shoulders slump, mouth actually hangs open. The singer yelps, her voice swirling in wild circles. "Are you serious?"

"It's a real question. I've heard stories about you during the Struggle. People in school used to talk about you, tell us stories their parents told them. I know you and Emeríann started the uprising that took out the Tathadann." His eyes examine me for a moment. "So are you jealous of Magnus?"

I force myself to take three breaths, concentrating on the air coming in, the air flowing out, letting the anger out with it because my arms are nearly trembling. If this were Walleus, if this were Dyvik, if this were anyone else other than my son, I would punch them in the throat.

"No. I am not jealous." I let the words out slowly, carefully, then clear my throat and tell the music to turn off. It doesn't listen, mocking me. "And Dyvik was the one who came to me asking for help, not Magnus. I didn't ask to be involved, but I will sure as hell help them, because that's what I've spent my life doing: fighting for people who need it. That includes Eitan and that includes you two."

"We can take care of ourselves."

"Not yet, you can't. And that's my job as a parent, to look out for you and let you fall as far as you need so you can learn how to take care of yourself completely."

"Then why are you arguing with me? You act like I did something wrong."

"I never said that, Donael." I shout at the music to turn off again. It doesn't.

"Then why are you arguing with me?"

"Because I don't want you to become me!"

I don't realize I shouted it until I see the look on Cobb's face. But Donael, he's impassive, a piece of stone. I see a flash of Forgall, which gives me a different kind of chill. So many ghosts trapped inside my head. How do I say that to him? How do I explain that every person you kill, every time you watch someone die, some part of you dies with them? I've seen whole neighborhoods obliterated. I've held scores of friends and fellow rebels as their eyes closed one last time. I've trained a pistol on my best friend and watched his forehead absorb my bullet. And each time I've gone into the moment as one person and emerged a slightly different one, slightly less a person.

How the hell can I explain that to a twelve year-old who gets doe-eyed at the talk of armed insurrection?

But before I can even attempt to parse it, Donael stands from the kitchen table and pushes his chair underneath. I think he's going to stomp off to his room, throw a fit because Daddy won't let him join the revolution, but instead he comes around the table and behind me, wraps his arms around my chest. I feel my eyes water involuntarily and wonder where that came from. I lay my hands on his forearms, larger and more muscular than I remember; and when the hell did he start becoming such a young man? I press hard on them, keeping him near to me, holding him close where he can't get hurt, where I can protect him. He rests his cheek against the back of my head and I close my eyes, try to memorize every contour of this moment.

After a few beats, he clears his throat.

"I understand that, Dad, and I appreciate it," he says. "But I'm not you."

He squeezes me tight then lets go and walks down the hallway to his room, leaving Cobb and me at the table. Cobb's head is tilted down but his eyes flit between the fork in his hand and my face.

"It's OK," I tell him. "You can go."

He clicks a few times and gets out of his seat, then pauses as he's turning toward the room. He scrabbles over to me and slams his body against mine, squeezes me once in his version of a hug, then hurries down the hallway to their room.

I sit at the table in the empty room, the air vibrating with jagged guitars and manic clapping, a woman excoriating herself musically, the sunlight streaming through the windows suddenly oppressive. I could be in Brusandhåv. I could be in Eitan. I could be anywhere in the world or I could be nowhere.

Donael doesn't want me to watch out for him, I understand. It's as inevitable a part of him becoming a man as me fretting about everything is part of being a parent. At points I wonder if I'm overcompensating, if I'm trying to make up for the years we were separated – or the years I chose to be in the field instead of in our house – by cramming all that parenting into the last six months. If my father had been around, would he have tried to stop me from speaking out against the Tathadann? Would he have warned me against fomenting insurrection? Or would he have joined in? Hell, part of the reason I began was because I thought he had been killed. I'm still here, yet Donael still wants to fight. Is it just in our blood? Maybe me constantly warning him away from fighting is only pushing him harder toward it. Maybe sitting back and letting him make his own decision is the best way to keep him from harm. Because when it comes down to it, I can't force him to do anything. If he wants to go bad enough, he'll find a way. The same way I did.

A thump pulls me from the depths of my skull. I look around, the sunlight disorienting me for a moment. Someone knocks on the door again.

There's a young man, twenty or so, standing in front of our lodging. But in normal clothing, not the grey fatigues of Ragjarøn or the severe black wear of Nyväg.

"Are you Henraek Laersen?" he says.

"Why? Who's asking?" My fingers twitch, flexing for the knife at my waist.

"I have a message for Henraek Laersen," the

young man says. "Are you him?"

"Message from who?" Ødven just rang. There's no reason for him to send a message.

"I don't know. It was smuggled onto the boat that arrived yesterday. I'm just supposed to deliver." He hands me a thin plastic tube. "All I know is it came from Ardu Oéann."

I snatch it away from the young man and close the door. It's from home. It's from Emeríann. She's OK, she's alive, she's written to me. I try to pry off the end but it's sealed with glue. I rear it back to smash the plastic, then realize I might accidentally rip the message, so I wedge the edge of my knife against the lip of the lid and tap until the seal breaks. I turn it up and a small piece of paper slides out.

Standing in the light near the window, I unfold the paper carefully. One side is slightly tacky, the edges pilled up. Looks like the paper Aífe used to line our cabinets, which I always thought was the most useless invention.

The paper unfolded, I flip it over and see Emeríann's scrawled handwriting. Letters tracked out in dark brown, smudges all over. Blood. Her own blood.

Then I read what she's written and all the breath rushes from my lungs. My legs disappear and my hands are autonomous hunks of meat. Everything I just said to Dyvik, to Ødven, to Donael, it all comes rushing back.

They're in trouble. I have to go back to Eitan.

But how? Do Dyvik or Magnus know smugglers? Do they have ships capable of getting us there? What will they do about the labor farms? What will I tell the boys?

I pace the kitchen for what feels like hours, my eyes running over the letter again and again, hoping to glean something more if I look at it from the right angle.

Dyvik and Magnus talked about pamphlets, a network of revolutionaries. I'm sure they know someone who can take me. And if they don't, they'll find one.

I'll help them overthrow Ragjarøn and retake Brusandhåv, but they're going to help me save Eitan first.

18.
EMERÍANN

I have to admit that I'm starting to regret threatening to gut Brighid and strew her innards across the pilings for rats to eat while she watches, because she's really coming through with this whole rooming thing.

I snuggle back under the sheets and take in the sensation of my body sinking into a real mattress, not a sack stuffed with old cloths and rags and blankets. This is a different house, the one that Brighid and her top soldiers are living in, but I'm not sure if the house was commandeered or if the owners fled during the uprising. Although it's still modest, it's a step up from the last house, and that was miles beyond what I'm used to. This one has one of those hologram televisions I've always heard about but could never afford. You can talk to the oven and tell it how to cook your food and it does – and doesn't even burn it. Hell, even the water feels cleaner. Aside from the hole in the wall in one of the kids' room and the manacles one of the soldiers found in the main closet, this house is pretty damn sweet.

It makes me think about Henraek and wonder how he and the boys are doing. If he's doing OK, if Donael and Cobb are managing, if he's managing with Cobb. If he's lying in bed somewhere thinking about me. To be honest, most things make me think of him. Shit, even seeing that dead pigeon on my pillow upset me because it made me think of Silas. I never expected myself to get sentimental about that disgusting little bastard.

I wish that there were some way to track the letters I sent Henraek, to ensure that he gets the second one – or instead, ensure he doesn't get the first. He needs to know that my initial read of Brighid wasn't correct, lest he go full-Henraek, freak out, and launch himself into one of his white-knight escapades. I'm hoping now that there are few rebels remaining who are trying to destroy everything, things will calm down and Henraek will be able to return to Eitan. Assuming he's done with whatever "advising" he was supposed to do in Brusandhåv.

Outside my window, I hear soldiers discussing something. I half-expect it to be Brighid planning our next mission with them, given that she's always up earlier than anyone. But instead, I hear a different woman's voice – a distinctive, gravelly one.

I roll out of bed and set my face beside the window, edging back the curtain with my fingertips. The woman faces away from me, her hair twisted up into a bun now, but I'd recognize that voice anywhere. She gestures wildly with her hands but I can't hear what she's saying. She definitely looks pissed, though.

I press my fingertips against the ledge of the window and hold my breath as I slide it open slowly, willing it to be silent. Mercifully, it complies.

"That cunt thinks she can do whatever she wants," the woman says, "like she's got a mandate from Nahoeg that her word is command because she had a hand in a couple battles. She doesn't know what we're capable of."

She's still pissed about Brighid, but I wonder if she knows that I'm the one who caught her friend. I also wonder who these two soldiers are. I've never seen them before, but I've only been at this location a short time, short enough that the traitor probably doesn't even know I'm staying here. Does Brighid know about them?

"Then she thinks she can suck up to Brighid and get a bump in her position, have a nice, soft bed and not feel any peas under the mattress. Thinks she's Queen of the Struggle."

And apparently she's talking about me, not Brighid.

"So we're going to show her – show both of them – they're not as bulletproof as they think. We've got more reinforcements coming from the east, ready to help us show Eitan how things should really be, not that horseshit Laersen and Daele dealt out."

"What's the deal?" one of the soldiers says.

"This afternoon, they're raiding a prism-flower shop in the Straits where some of our people are camped. Lookouts for the armory in that fountain warehouse." The woman glances around. I move my fingers slightly, enough to keep them from sight but not so much that the whole curtain flutters and draws attention to myself. Seemingly satisfied, she continues. "When the convoy is on the way, someone will crash their car into one parked on the side of the road. The convoy will have to stop, either to help or to move the accident out of the way. Doesn't matter which."

"Because we'll be right behind them with an arsenal."

The woman clucks her tongue and points at the soldier. "They'll pay for Augie. He was brave and sacrificed himself to protect us. But they'll pay for him."

The soldiers nod and she claps them on the shoulder before striding away.

I ease the curtain down and sink to my heels, my back against the wall.

Shit. Shitting shit. What is it going to take to make them stop? Nothing, probably, since they see themselves as carrying on the tradition of the Struggle, but with some massively perverted message that will only end in chaos. And I don't even know how many members of this faction there are.

But they are not going to win. No goddamned way.

I pull on my clothes and head to Brighid's room. She needs to hear now so we have time to plan accordingly, and so she doesn't try to murder me. But halfway down the hallway, I pause. They were close enough to my window that I could hear them without being seen. Did they know I was listening? Did they position themselves there for my benefit, letting me hear their plans so I'd report them to Brighid and, when we acted on the ambush, they'd ambush us in a different way? I waver in the hallway, not sure which way to turn. It's like the thing about someone who lies and someone who always tells the truth. When they say the same thing, how do you know whom to believe?

No, I need to tell Brighid. Give her the whole picture and we can decide what to do from there. Last time we were lucky we got away unhurt. But I'm not counting on our luck lasting.

"I'll cut her tongue out." Brighid paces across the middle of her room, fatigues already on and drinking her third cup of coffee. I'm not sure this woman ever sleeps. "No, I'll yank it out and tie it to a light pole and leave her for the foerges to pick over."

"You could do that," I say, "and you would make a point. But we could also handle this carefully and take out the rest of the people who are trying to kill us. If they actually are trying to ambush us."

"Explain yourself."

"Assuming that they were telling the truth, and they didn't know I was listening, how many of them remain out there?"

"Their numbers are small, I know that."

"Which means this armory is incredibly important to them, right? You might call it essential?"

She pauses, works her bottom lip between her thumb and index finger a minute, then crosses her arms over her chest. "You're saying we forego the prism-flower shop today."

"Not forego, just postpone. Hit the armory first. Take what we can, because you can never have too many RPGs, then hit the flower shop afterward."

"Which might end up being the last target we have to hit."

I shrug. "If this armory is as stacked as she said it was, then yes, maybe it is. Unless they're telling us this to catch us off-guard some other way. A double feint."

She considers this for a minute, then nods. Decision made. "Alert the troops. We move in an hour. Get them early, before the rebels are ready."

Ninety minutes later, we're approaching the prism-flower shop, two trucks filled with soldiers trailing us. Everyone's on high alert after the tire chain incident. My stomach folds in on itself, my head continually scanning the road for anyone watching us too closely, or conspicuously not watching us. The soldiers in the rear truck post up with their rifles at the ready, scanning the cramped neighborhood as we pass through. Looking for cars that seem primed to crash. Evaluating each person on the sidewalk for anyone hanging around too long. My pulse slams against the inside of my skull, anticipating an attack at any second, and after a few minutes I start to develop a tension headache.

Despite the artillery we carry, the civilians don't seem very cowed. Kids play in tiny front yards, kicking a football back and forth or riding bikes on the cement parking pads. In another life they could easily be Donael and Cobb. Some people hunch over the hoods of their cars, while others paint their house or lean back against their front stoop with a drink in hand. I want to yell at them to get inside before someone catches a stray bullet. I can only hope that we are nearing the end of this.

We pass by the shop without incident, which makes my pulse race even more. Not attacking on the approach to the prism-flower shop means they were double-feinting, and the real ambush will come at any moment. We slow down two blocks from the warehouse, parking behind a large truck to provide a bit of cover. This way, we can creep up to the site on foot and avoid the spectacle of a caravan.

Brighid hops out and I follow. Seven of the soldiers fall in line behind us while the other three stand watch by the vehicles. We hurry down the sidewalk, staying low and inconspicuous, rifles strafing each of the surrounding buildings. Someone steps on a bottle and I jump at the crunch, nearly firing. *Calm down, woman. You're going to kill someone like that.* I take a deep breath and continue following our line, consciously willing the blood to stop thrumming through my forearms.

Anyone who is walking by would know we're about to hit something, but they remain quiet, which is kind of sad. They know it's better to keep their head down and ignore whatever's about to happen rather than risk getting involved and getting killed. *Let them work and they'll let you live,* is the thinking.

Except it doesn't always happen like that.

We're two buildings down when a couple kids run along the street, chasing each other. Then they suddenly pause. I see them and freeze, feeling my heartbeat in my throat. I can hear insurgents racking bullets into chambers, a hideous echo inside my head.

No. No no no no. Do not let them get caught in any crossfire.

Then one of the kids cups his hands around his mouth and screams, "They're coming!" The other one punches him in the arm then takes off, the screamer sprinting behind them. My heart jackhammers against my ribs: they just alerted the insurgents.

"Go," I tell Brighid. "Go now. Move."

We sprint along the sidewalk, readying our weapons as we approach the warehouse. When we get to the place, two of the soldiers slam their metal battering ram into the front door, splintering the wood into large, pointed pieces. They kick the frame twice to clear out the rest of it then we all pour in, rifles barrels scouring the interior.

The inside is dim, bars of light leaking in through cracks between the plywood nailed against the window. I can taste dust in the air. Scores of massive shapes rise in the darkness, the Tathadann fountains the woman spoke of. No insurgents come rushing at us, but that doesn't mean they're not here, lying in wait, because the ruse about the prism-flower shop was obviously a tactic to draw us here. We might not have them outgunned, but everyone aside from me was trained to do this.

We strafe along the edge of the front room, moving as a semicircle with our backs facing one another, covering all angles as we clear the areas behind the fountains. With nothing to be found here, we move to the next room, pausing at the doorway to listen for any sounds of scurrying feet or hushed directives to attack. There's nothing, so Brighid signals to advance.

The second room looks almost the same as the first, though it's five times as long. I had no idea there was this much water in Eitan, enough that they could ever see the need for thousands of fountains. But sitting a couple hundred feet in front of us, off to the right, is a large tarp covering a mound of something I'm guessing is the armory. I nudge Brighid's elbow and wordlessly point to it. Brighid motions for us to split up into three groups, her leading one, me leading another, and the lead soldier with the third. We spread out, covering more of the warehouse area, moving carefully between fountains as we watch at every turn for the insurgents who should be guarding these weapons. I haven't seen any evidence of massive movements of people, pallets of weapons or buckets of ammo, which is no surprise, but I also haven't seen any footprints of the insurgents getting into place to ambush us. Most of the dust and dirt on the floor seems untouched, though it's hard to tell much of anything in the low light. Maybe there's an entrance on the back side of the warehouse we didn't see, or they moved across the metal beams above us. I don't see anyone but–

Then there's a shuffling sound about a hundred feet in front of us, near the tarp-covered pile. The soldier leads his group over while Brighid and I bring ours forward, checking for other insurgents on the sides who might be trying to outflank us. We move as quickly as we can while remaining silent. Fifty feet away.

I swear that my heartbeat is echoing through the building.

There's a scraping noise coming from behind a row of fountains. It sounds like a piece of wood on the cement floor, probably speckled with nails. Someone gearing up to protect themselves. I would've thought they'd have a better choice of weapon, considering there's a goddamned army's-worth cache literally at their fingertips. I guess if they were smart, they wouldn't be fighting against us.

Brighid holds her hand up for the soldier to wait while her group clears the far side of the room. I bring my people up through the center, looking to head off the attackers. Neither of us find any. The distinct lack of people is unnerving. Where are the other insurgents who are supposed to be guarding the armory, who are supposed to ambush us? Is this a triple feint? I don't even know how that would work. I tip my head up, scanning the open rafters, half-expecting to see an insurgent wave *hello* just before splitting me in half with gunfire. But on each side, there's still nothing. Not even a nest for pigeons. What the hell?

Something's not right here. We need to get out, and carefully. Shit, I never even thought to look for tripwires that could be linked to bombs.

I keep at a low crouch and head toward Brighid to voice my concerns and get her read on the situation when we hear footsteps approaching. I turn toward them just as an insurgent appears from behind a fountain, charging at us with a board raised above his head.

Brighid yells for him to stop where he is right as the young soldier rattles off a few shots. The insurgent shakes and twitches as the bullets thump into his chest, like he's being pulled by invisible ropes. He stumbles forward two steps then collapses on the floor, five feet in front of us. There's more scrabbling back behind the row of fountains.

"Got him, ma'am."

Brighid points at the area, says, "Find the others," to the soldiers.

The soldiers advance to capture the rest of the insurgents.

"Search him," Brighid says to me. "See if he has a comm link or anything."

I kneel down and run my hands over the insurgent's back, searching for anything. His coat is rough against my fingers, but it's not because it's military-grade fabric. It's from the stitching – the sinew that's holding the animal pelts together. His jacket isn't even made of goddamned fabric. This is what we're fighting against now? This is their future for Eitan? I crouch down and heft him over, revealing a thick scraggly beard and dirt sunken into the furrows on his face. Shit. I don't run my hands over his front because I don't need to. There's no comm device. There won't even be any weapon. Because even in the low light I can tell that this man is sure as hell not an insurgent or a mercenary: he's a squatter.

But when I jump up to tell Brighid, I see the soldiers rounding the fountains with their rifles raised. Someone yells and I scream for them to stop but it's all lost under the racket of rifle fire, the flashes from the muzzles casting the soldiers' faces in a sickly pall. The echoing of bullets bounces off the metal walls and shatters, embedding itself in my skin and leeching into my blood. I can feel my body sinking away from me, receding from the warehouse. How did we end up like this?

The shooting ends as quickly as it began, the only sounds in the warehouse the cracking and crumbling of the ceramic fountains, the soft pulsing of blood rushing out onto the cement floor. I feel a sucking sensation inside my body, like it's trying to collapse on itself. Someone weeps softly then a single pistol shot crackles through the air, and it's enough to make my knees give out from beneath me.

"God damn it," I yell at the soldiers, crawling across the floor toward them.

They rush forward to secure the armory, but when they yank back the tarp covering it, they find not stacks of guns and bombs and ammunition cases, but sacks. Sacks filled with discarded clothes, with blankets to soften the cement floor, with scraps of food held in airtight containers to keep the rats out. This is a makeshift apartment, not a massive armory.

And in the middle of the apartment, five punctured bodies. I recognize one who fought with us during the uprising. But I'm barely able to say that to Brighid before my breath evaporates. Because lying among the bodies is one tiny girl. Her pigtails are braided, one held with a rubber band wrapped round a dozen times, the other with a chipped yellow flower hairclip. Her eyes are focused on a point a thousand miles beyond the ceiling. I cough out a wail, choke it back, then it comes barreling back. I bite my hand until I taste metal to keep myself from screaming. One of the soldiers slips his hands beneath my armpits and hefts me to my feet.

"Miss," he says, "you need to pull yourself together."

"Fuck you," I scream at him.

Brighid paces behind them, her breath rushing in and out of her nostrils, cursing to herself. I wipe my face dry then start toward her but stop. What am I supposed to say? This was my fault. I should have verified the location with intelligence before bringing it to Brighid, but I was overeager, trying to keep us from getting ambushed again, and now that little girl is dead because of me. That woman, the mole, the one who left a dead pigeon on my pillow, she knew I was listening. She fed me misinformation and I gobbled it down like a starving woman. She orchestrated this perfectly because now we've done something that will fit in with their portraying anyone who isn't them as the new tyrants of Eitan. We gave them more fodder for their cause.

I have to take responsibility for this, for the girl. Yes, the mole was the one who lied, but I'm the one who believed it. Wiggling away is what the Tathadann would do, believing in their own infallibility. Whatever it costs me, I have to fall on my sword.

"Brighid," I say, approaching her with my back straight and my voice as calm as I can keep it.

But before I can get another word out, she spins on her heels and whips out her pistol. I feel the bullet pressing against my skull, the bone giving way and the grey matter liquefying before it splashes out the back, and I'm actually relieved by the whole sensation. Then I snap to and watch Brighid set her pistol behind the young soldier's head before pulling the trigger. A splash of blood and hair bursts from his forehead, then he falls forward, landing on top of the squatters.

"Brighid," I say again, quieter this time, but she ignores me.

"You see this man." She points at the dead soldier at her feet, addressing the others. "He did not possess the temperament necessary to be part of us. He was too easily excited, let his nerves get the best of him and cloud his judgment."

"Befälhavare," the lead soldier says. He stops short when Brighid trains her pistol on him.

"Brighid," I say again. "Let him talk."

Jaw set tight, breath rolling in and out of her nostrils, she looks the soldier in the eyes for some long seconds before finally lowering her pistol.

"Say your piece."

"This wasn't his fault. He didn't plan this."

I can't tell if that's a defense of him or an accusation of me.

"He could not control himself," Brighid says. "If he had restrained the man, we could have defused the situation. He didn't, and now five innocents are dead. And for what? For one rebel?"

She looks down at the pile of bodies and says something that sounds like a curse in a language I don't speak. The warehouse thrums with silence, the normal city noises from outside somehow unable to penetrate. Or maybe my ears are still ringing from the gunfire, keeping the real world out.

She points at three soldiers. "Canvas the surrounding

area. See what people heard. Let them know there were dangerous dissidents who attacked us, the same ones who are trying to undermine Eitan's liberation with Perre Cantonae." They nod in assent. She motions to the rest of the soldiers. "You lot," she says, swallowing like she's got a hitch in her throat, "make these bodies disappear, but save the rebel's. No one can hear about this." The soldiers nod, though their faces are grave.

"They're citizens of Eitan," I say. "We have to give them a proper burial."

"And risk anyone seeing what just happened? We just murdered five innocents."

"All the Tathadann did was lie and manipulate reality to save face. We were supposed to be the antidote to that."

"Well, you're doing a shitty job of it." She gestures toward the soldiers. "Burn the bodies. Leave no trace."

I feel my body rush out through my feet as I realize we're turning into everything we hated.

"Follow me," she says without pausing.

When I start to talk, she shushes me and waits until we're out of earshot before speaking.

"I know she set us up," Brighid says with enough force to make me lean back. I know she could be saying it to get me to relax, lower my guard. I don't hold it against her, though. I'd do the same thing. "That cunt. I know she did it."

"How do you know it wasn't my mistake?" It's a question I don't particularly like asking but the way she answers it will tell me whether I should expect a bullet in the head. Brighid, she glances up at me, still walking through the warehouse toward the trucks. "It was. But you're good at what you do."

I hook my chin back behind us, indicating the bodies. "Those people are dead because of me."

"Everyone has their moments." She steps through the front door into the outside, the sudden light making me squint and washing out all the color. We both blink a few times. "I understand you wanting to do right by those people, but this is war, and war is no time to stumble over feelings."

"They should still be alive."

"And you should've checked with intel first." She spits on the ground. "But here we are."

I nod, biting the inside of my cheek. "Here we are."

"Next time you'll check, and we won't have to deal with this again."

I nod, more out of reflex than conscious thought.

"Because if we do," she says, "I'll have to kill you."

I stop chewing on my cheek, keep my expression as blank as possible while staring at her. I nod that I understand, and she nods in return before jumping into a truck and heading back home.

I watch her drive off, listening to the engine fade as the sounds of the neighborhood filter in. My new mission in life is to hunt down the goddamned woman who got these squatters and this poor little girl killed and is trying to kill us, to – once again – burn down all that we've fought for. That's already happened once and I sure as hell will not let it happen again.

Still, all I can think as Brighid's truck disappears around a corner is, *You can't kill me if I kill you first.*

19.
HENRAEK

As soon as the clock reaches a socially acceptable time, I'm standing in front of Dyvik's house, pounding on his door. The couple on the other side of the street stare at me like I'm insane, and I suppose what would pass for normal in Eitan doesn't always here. Still, I need Dyvik and I need him now, so I bang on his door again. The script in Emeríann's letter has been flowing through my head, unraveling throughout my sleepless night.

Brighid is killing us.

Please help.

I love you all.

I raise my hand to pound again when the door flies open, revealing Lyxzä in trousers and an old long-sleeved shirt, a shotgun in her hand. The neck of her shirt hangs low, and I can see a semicircle of scarring in the middle of her chest, disappearing below her shirt.

"What the hell?" she says, lowering the gun when

she sees my face. "Are you trying to get killed?"

"Where's Dyvik? I need to talk to him. Immediately."

"At work, obviously. What happened?"

"Brighid," I say. "Brighid happened."

She steps past me to get a look outside, scans the area with shotgun in hand, then hooks her chin down the street. "He's at the store, meeting with Magnus." I start to turn away when she grabs my arm. "He's all I have left."

"I know that."

"Nothing can happen to him. He can't be captured."

"You understand that I will be sacrificed before a crowd if Ødven hears even a hint about what I'm doing out here, right? My boys will be orphaned."

"I do," she says, "but betrayal is never anyone's style until it's necessary. Then it's just another compromise you had to make along the way."

I hold her stare for a long minute before turning and breaking away. I head up the street.

Magnus jumps upright when I burst through the front door of the general store, his fists cocked back and ready to obliterate me.

"Henraek?" Dyvik says, standing behind the counter. "What's wrong?"

"We need to get back to Eitan."

Dyvik's shoulders slump. Magnus's jaw clenches.

"You need to repeat that," Magnus says.

"It's important. Incredibly important. I need to get back now. Me and the boys. I can't leave them alone."

"We're supposed to hit the labor farms next week." Dyvik rests his hands on the counter, lets his head hang low. "We've put plans in motion. Our people are already moving to the towns we discussed. We can't get ahold of them now."

"And more important," Magnus says, his voice dropping nearly a full octave into a terrifying range, "you said you were with us."

"And I am," I tell them both. "I helped you free those ändes, and I helped you plan the offensive."

"We need you involved," Dyvik shouts. "We're already dangerously short. You have seen this, Henraek. We have discussed this. We need people with experience, and all three of them are in the store right now."

"I understand that," I say, measuring all of my words, "but I need to get back to Eitan. Immediately."

"What happened?" Magnus says.

I pinch the bridge of my nose. How am I supposed to explain years of sociopolitical warfare to them in two minutes – or less, because I need to get the hell out of here? Then I remember that they've been studying our country, our city, our war, for nearly as long.

"You know who Brighid Tobeigh is?"

They nod.

"You know how she rode in with her father, Daghda, and everyone thought she was going to be our savior?"

Again, they nod.

"Emeríann had a letter smuggled to me. It turns out, making Eitan a satellite of Brusandhåv wasn't enough. She and her troops have been systematically wiping out the remaining rebels. I don't know how they're doing it, I don't know what their end goal is,

I don't know how much if anything Ødven knows about this. But I need to get back and help my people. Taking down Ødven will do nothing for Eitan if Eitan is already destroyed. So, please," I say, "I need your help."

Dyvik and Magnus exchange glances, then look back to me.

"There's no way out of Rën," Dyvik says. "Not anything quick."

"Define quick."

"There are ships that come in and out of the harbor in Vårgmannskjør each day," Magnus says. "But the only ones you can sneak on to are cargo ships. And those are guarded heavily."

"Pack me into the cargo. I can wait two days like that. I've done worse."

"What about your boys?" Magnus says.

I cringe internally, telling myself not to get overzealous. Though they may be tough for their age, there's no way they'd be able to handle that.

Dyvik shakes his head. "They run heat-scanners across everything that goes on or comes off the ships."

"They're checking for people sneaking in?"

"No. Mostly watching for defectors." Dyvik thinks a minute. "The only way to do it is to pay a smuggler. But I don't know anyone who operates out of Vårgmannskjør. Do you?" he says to Magnus, who shakes his head no.

"Then how the hell are we going to get back?" I fight to keep my voice under control. "We got into this goddamned country and now we can't get out?"

"I warned you," Dyvik says.

"The only thing I can think of," Magnus says, "is the freighter that Andrei pilots."

"You're not serious," Dyvik says.

"What are you talking about?"

"Who else has a ship and will come out here?" Magnus says. "We don't have a safe harbor like those ynkedoms in Vårgmannskjør."

"What are you talking about?" I say it again louder.

"But that man is insane. And he's a drunkard. He is not someone who should be trusted with any type of cargo we want to remain intact and–"

"Oi!" I yell it this time. They both fall silent. The refrigeration units hum quietly. "I am not cargo, and I cannot stand by idly while my people are slaughtered. Now, I don't give a shit whether this guy likes to gargle with bourbon. We need to get back and if he's the one who can take us without us dying, that's who we're going with. Now, are you going to raise him or what?"

Dyvik mumbles something I can't understand.

Magnus looks at me. "Things are different in Brusandhåv than they are in Eitan. When we pledge ourselves to something, we do it fully. Even if the penalty is death. Maybe that is why your revolution in Eitan failed." He clears his throat. "Both times."

Before I can respond to the amadan, the front door swings open and two Ragjarøn soldiers in grey fatigues enter the store. Magnus visibly stiffens, though Dyvik says something under his breath that I assume is supposed to calm him.

Dyvik nods at the soldiers, says, "När du går."

They respond, but keep their eyes on me. Did

Ødven send them? Are they here to check on me or to tell me my services are no longer needed and assassinate me?

"Local unit. You're OK," Dyvik whispers to me, as if he could read my mind. "For now."

The soldiers pass behind us, headed to the cooler where sandwiches are stored. I can hear Magnus grinding his teeth.

"Good club this year," I say to no one in particular. "Axel's looking strong as a striker. This could be a good year for our Höjden."

"I've been on him a lot. Pushing him hard." Magnus's mouth says words but his brain is someplace far away. "If he keeps his knee over the ball, he will score with more power."

"Yeah, definitely," I say.

Sandwiches in hand, the soldiers come to the counter. Magnus and I step aside. The taller soldier makes extended eye contact with me, as if he's trying to send me a message or gauge my level of involvement with two known Nyväg members.

"I've seen them play in the field. They are good. Your boy especially," the soldier says to me in English. My muscles tighten. Is that a warning? Is he threatening my boys? "When is the next match?"

"Two weeks," Dyvik says, cutting in. He holds out his hand, palm up, asking them for money for their sandwiches.

The other soldier hands Dyvik a few bills.

"Maybe we will see them," the soldier says. "It's been a while since we saw a match."

"We'll keep an eye out," Dyvik says to them, not

backing down a bit.

The taller soldier gives me a long look before nodding and heading out of the store. I listen to myself breathe, watching them until they disappear down the street. Once I'm sure they've gone, I look to Dyvik.

"What the hell was that?"

"They're fine," he says. "They're locals here. It's nothing to worry about."

"That didn't seem like nothing. He mentioned my son. Specifically. How does he know who he is?"

"He's local. Your boys are not. They stand out," Dyvik says.

"And you were sent here by Ødven himself," Magnus says. "Every local soldier knows your face. They think you are embedding yourself with us in order to... what did you call it, restore order?"

He does have a point. But it doesn't make me feel any better about them mentioning Donael.

"Which reinforces my point. You cannot leave now," Magnus says. "It will raise too much suspicion."

"You have three choices." I step closer to him, and god damn is he huge. He and Forgall could've taken out half the soldiers themselves. "You can do it without me, or you can wait until I'm done in Eitan and can return."

"When's that?" Dyvik says.

"When I'm done and can return." I fix my stare on Magnus, his big chest quivering with anger. "Or the third choice, I can shoot you in the face because you won't help me, and you can try to launch your revolution without a face. Now," I say to both of them, "who's going to raise this Andrei?"

The store hums with silence, quieter than I would have thought it could be. After a minute, Magnus moves toward the front door.

"I'll raise him now."

He lets the door close behind him, leaving Dyvik and me alone in his store.

Dyvik starts to talk but I cut him off. "I'm not trying to be dismissive of your plight. I understand what you're feeling and I understand your situation. But you also have to understand where I'm coming from."

"I do." He nods. "Really, I do. But you've already seen what we've sacrificed, what we go through every day. So when you say you're coming back, I have to know that you actually are. We can hold our attack, but not for long. If Ragjarøn gets wind of people showing up in small towns strategically located near labor farms, they're going to raid us. They'll round us up, they'll ship us to Vårgmannskjør, and they'll sacrifice us while the whole city watches." He leans across the counter toward me. "And all that blood will be on your hands."

I straighten up in front of him.

"I said I would come back here, so I will. And yours would not be the only blood I have on my hands. I doubt it will be the last either." I turn and walk toward the door, pausing for a second with my hand on the knob. "Of all people here, you should know that." I step through it, leaving him alone.

After being inside for a little while, the outside is damn near blinding. I squint my eyes so hard I can barely see, most of the street washed out by the sunlight. Funny that we missed it for so long and now I'm cursing it and calling for clouds. My, but how things change.

I hear shouting at the end of the street, in the field past our lodge, and assume that's where the boys are. My eyes finally begin to adjust by the time I get down there. Donael and Cobb run around the grass, playing pick-up football with Magnus's sons and other local kids. They're using oil barrel trashcans for goals, with no keepers. Even the boy who Donael punched is playing and, surprisingly, it looks like they're on the same team. Keep your friends close and enemies closer. I laugh as I think that he'd be a good general, then shake the thought away.

Donael tips the ball away from one of the kids and takes it down the pitch, passing it to Magnus's older boy then making a slanting run. Magnus's son chips it up over the defender and Donael stretches out his leg, trying to pull it in, but he's not quite quick enough and the ball skips away. Everyone yells in various languages as the ball rolls toward the seawall, Donael and one of the other boys sprinting after it.

Neither of them is fast enough.

Everyone's shoulders slump and I can feel the mood change in that moment. Donael and the boy stand at the seawall, looking down. I think it's a good four-foot drop, depending on the tide. Not too far but farther than either of them can reach. It'd be too far for me as well. Then Donael calls for Axel and Cobb, who does his closest approximation to rocketing across the field, just happy to be involved.

When they get there, Donael says something to Cobb. He doesn't look very enthused, but eventually relents because Donael is his big brother. And it's in that moment that I realize what their plan is. I start to hurry across the field, shouting for them to stop, but I'm too far away and before I make much progress at all, Donael and Axel have already grabbed Cobb by the ankles and flipped him over, lowering him down to the water. I stop running, stop yelling too, because the last thing I want to do is startle either of the boys and have them drop Cobb into the water. I can feel my chest tighten, equal parts anxious that something will go wrong and frightened by how cold that water must be. They hold him there for what feels like ages, until they both crouch down and grab onto his waist, pulling him up with the ball in hand. All the kids cheer as Cobb holds the ball over his head like a trophy, the sun catching water droplets that fall and making them sparkle like crystals. I don't know that I've ever seen Cobb radiate joy like he is in this moment. And for a second, I wonder if Walleus can see him.

Then he tries to boot the ball into midfield but it squirts behind him, rolling to the edge of the water. Everyone yells again and it's only a quick hand from Donael, standing a couple feet away, that keeps it from getting waterlogged again. Donael tosses the ball back to the other players and pats Cobb on the back, encouraging him to keep playing.

Donael jogs back into the match, but when he comes up to the edge of the fray, two of the neighborhood kids stop before him and make a fist, thump it against their chest then set the back of their palm next to their forehead. Donael stops running and does the same thing. Then all three of them whip their hands away, huge smiles spread across their faces. They all go back to playing, and I feel the blood draining from my head. I don't know what that meant, but I recognize a salute when I see one.

Donael, what have you done?

I turn around, suddenly glad that I was too far away for them to see me, and hurry away from the pitch and back to our lodging, as if I'd never even been there.

I head straight to Donael's room. It's about the same size as the one he and Cobb shared back home, but here they have their own space. They also have very little in the way of personal possessions, so the rooms look gigantic. A wash of agoraphobia rolls over me. Maybe it's just all the sun. Maybe it's my son.

I search through the few things in here, starting with the bedside table. Looking for pamphlets, chapbooks, flyers, the same types of things we would hand out at the dawn of the Struggle to spread awareness of our cause in the hopes of recruiting new fighters. Nothing.

I move to his dresser, my worry of him knowing I was looking slipping away as quickly as my panic sets in. He only has a few shirts and a few pairs of pants. Nothing in any of them. I rap my knuckles on the bottoms of the drawers, on the sides, then on the top, looking for false bottoms, safe compartments to hide things. Still nothing.

I fall back against his wall, sinking down onto my haunches. Maybe I'm just overreacting. It's the sun. All the light is getting to me, making me see things that aren't there, read situations and body language in ways I shouldn't. I don't even know what I saw, really. They were just kids, doing stupid kid things. This isn't Eitan. This isn't the authoritarian, repressive, murderous governance of the Tathadann. Ødven is a bastard and the Nyväg fighters are rightfully sick of him, but they don't understand what it's like to truly be oppressed. Not like we were in Eitan. And Donael has seen that, to some degree with Walleus, and every day with me. Not to mention that we've already talked about this. A couple times. It's just in my head, I tell myself again as I push myself up to my knees. I should probably lie down and get some sleep, maybe push on some of the walls here to see if Ragjarøn put any secret rooms in which no sun will shine.

As I stand up, I see his jacket hanging on the back of the door. He really should be wearing it, despite kids being impervious to the cold, but he's also running around. He'll get cold when he stops.

I take it off the door and something flashes in the light.

A pin on the left breast of his jacket.

A shiny black pin, in what I now know is the shape of Brusandhåv. In the center is a bold, red star with the black letters UNV inside them. Ungdømstrüpper Nyväg. The Nyväg Youth Brigade.

I drop the jacket in the middle of the floor.

He did it. He joined. He's part of them.

I startle as someone starts pounding on the door. Donael's back. They've finished their match. I scramble around the room, straighten his clothes and rehang his jacket on the back of the door because I don't want him to know that I know, mostly because I don't know what to do about it yet. I want time to think about it instead of a confrontation from the jump. And Emeríann says I never learn anything.

When everything in the room looks normal, I head to the front door, calling out, "OK, OK, I heard you, calm down."

But when the door swings open it's not Donael but Magnus, his bulk obscuring most of the light creeping in.

"I reached Andrei. You have passage for one person on–"

"One?" I try not to shout, or to whine. "You heard what I said. I need three."

"You have passage for one, two days from now," he repeats, putting extra emphasis on each word, ensuring that I know this is the last time he'll say this. "It leaves from docks on western port, near football pitch. You be there when he docks, because he doesn't wait. That is best I can do."

I can't leave Donael and Cobb alone. We barely know any of these people. I've taught Donael well enough that they should be able to fend for themselves if I don't return, which is a real possibility. We're fighting against organized people who have spent the last six months fighting with us, learning everything about us. For all I know, I'll be walking into a firing squad. But I can't let Eitan be destroyed without trying to help save it.

Could I really leave the boys here? They'd have a better life. The thought of separating the family again after so much time apart and so little time together tears at the inside of my chest. But so does the thought of marching them into a suicide mission.

I would sacrifice my life for my boys, without a second thought. And I would gladly leave them in a place where I know they would have a better life when I don't come back from a mission.

But I can't do it in this town, because I no longer trust Donael around these kids, around these people. Not after seeing what I saw on his jacket. And I feel like the biggest hypocrite for saying it, especially after giving Dyvik a rack of shit for questioning my commitment to liberating oppressed people. But, as a father, I don't want Donael within pissing distance of Nyväg. I know how revolutions tend to go. I want my son in school, or in a trade, or somewhere living a quiet, contented life that doesn't involve roadside bombs and artillery shelling and determining which type of bullet tore your friend's scalp free of his head.

In a disgusting twist of fate, the only thing I can think of in this moment is someone I never in a thousand moons thought I would agree with: Belousz, in the alley outside his mother's apartment. *It's easy to make decisions during peace. But we're about to start a war.*

All of this passes through my head in a flash, the world outside slowing down to a microscopic pace. But now I know what I have to do.

"Make the arrangements," I tell Magnus. "And tell him not to leave without me."

As quickly as he came, Magnus leaves without a word. He pauses for a second when he reaches the street, as if he's about to say something cutting to finally make his point, then decides I'm not worth it and walks away, muttering to himself.

I close the door quietly; I need the silence. Yes, I know what I need to do. But it does not entail getting on that boat.

20.
EMERÍANN

Brighid bangs on my door at some ungodly hour. I don't know how I know it's her, but somehow I can tell. Every rap of the knuckle is another rifle shot, another twitch and flail of the squatters in the warehouse. When I drag my hand across my forehead, the sweat comes back clear, but it feels like blood.

After an exorbitant amount of effort, I roll my body out of bed and plod across the floor to the door and pull it open.

As expected, she's in full fatigues, unslept as ever. She looks me up and down.

"You look like hell."

"I didn't sleep well."

She nods, as if she totally understands. I'm not sure she's ever understood.

"Get dressed. We've got a big day ahead of us."

By the time I drag myself downstairs, she and her usual two soldiers are tossing their dishes in the sink and checking their weapons to head out.

"Can I at least eat something first?"

Brighid nods at the counter, at a sandwich wrapped in foil sitting next to a travel cup of coffee. It's so domestic it makes me want to puke. I grab the food and follow them out to the trucks. The soldiers toss some extra ammo in the back then jump in, and we take off. Brighid leans back in her seat, enjoying the wind whipping her hair around.

In some perverse way, I admire her ability to distance herself from the fighting, from the bodies, from the blood. It's probably better for her mental wellbeing. Not that I have had trouble forgetting about the bodies during the uprising, or even the few I saw during the Struggle. But those felt different. They were warranted, and the people knew what kind of agreement they were entering when they picked up a gun. *You're going to try to kill me, and I'm going to try to kill you first.* Even the young woman in the water distribution plant felt acceptable to me, though her face does flash through my head at times. So what makes the squatter special? They were just in the wrong place at the wrong time? So were all the people who died after Henraek and I blew up the water distribution plant. The man died defending his friends, his family, whatever they were. So did a lot of people after the uprising started. That little girl could've easily grown up into the girl at the water plant. I have more blood on my hands than I want to admit. I know that I should just let this one go, that people die for no reason all the time, but for some reason I can't.

Is it because I'm just tired of being the harbinger of death? All I've wanted to do was help create something better.

"Emeríann," Brighid says, nudging me. I'm dully aware that she's done it before.

I look around and we're near the foothills, but not too far from the city. In the distance, I can see the shape of the high-rises where the insurgents are detained. Above us, giant boulders rest on the mountainside, balanced like the moss growing on them is the only thing keeping them from rolling down the hill and crashing into our cars like bowling balls. Water drilling rigs poke out at odd angles along the ridge, between the evergreen trees. Spread out in front of us is a field fallow that has become overgrown. On the far side is a thresher, a giant machine to scalp the tall grasses.

Brighid hops out of the truck and trots toward the field with a small hologram machine in hand, the soldiers falling in line behind her. I jump out and jog to catch up.

"This was once Tobeigh land," she says, gesturing out over the field. "My great-great-aunt raised six children here and grew crops large enough that she could give some to her neighbors when they experienced blight. Her daughter took over when she died, and my great aunt continued to work the land, raising five kids of her own. Like her mother, she helped those around her when they needed it, and they helped her. Before the resource companies came in and seized the land, forcing my great aunt's family to flee for the mountains and seek shelter with my family, the people who lived here were a community in the truest sense of the word, sharing what they had, relying on help when it was needed. No one was better than anyone else and no one was scorned or turned away.

"That is what Eitan City used to be like. One large community, a set of neighborhoods interconnected and interdependent on one another. That is what it can be again. We can rebuild what the Tathadann has destroyed, and capitalize on what they never could: our spirit." She looks over at me, some dreamy look on her face. "Despite decades of war and oppression, they have never been able to break the spirit of the people. We can use that to prosper again, together. To create something bigger than Ardu Oéann has ever dreamed and give us a seat on the world's stage."

She turns on the hologram machine. It clicks and whirs a moment as the internal systems boot up, then projects a schematic. She holds it up so that the schematic is superimposed across the field.

"This is our new power system. The one I told you about. It is self-sustaining and has zero impact on the land around us. With this new structure, we can get energy to every neighborhood, without any of the fluctuations we have now. We can run water purification plants, as well as the synthesizers that will create more water. No longer will we have to rely on condensers to draw tainted water from rotten air or generators to give us electricity. We – everyone – can have real, pure water. And it's all free."

"That's insane." I didn't mean to say it out loud, but it's what I'm thinking.

Brighid glances over at me, her expression unfazed by my outburst. "It is insane. It's insane to think we – you all – have been living under such wretched conditions for so long that you've accepted it as normal. It's insane that the city hasn't torn itself apart just trying to live. Frankly, it's insane we didn't hear about the revolution sooner."

"But," I sputter, "how? How are we supposed to do this?"

She smiles even larger, if that's possible. "That, my friend, is where you come in." She hands me the projection device. "All of the schematics are in here. Now you need to figure out how to make it as quick as possible."

I hold the device in my hand like a dead fish that fell from the sky. "I can't build this, this reactor or whatever the hell it is. I don't know the first thing about engineering."

"You don't need to."

I just stare at her because I don't have the slightest idea what to say.

"How long did you run Johnstone's for?" she says.

"A couple years."

"You told me it was eight."

I shrug. "OK. Eight."

"Was the bar doing better after you took over?"

"It's impossible for a bar to fail in Eitan."

"But did you make it run better?"

It sounds strange to say it, like I'm bragging, but yes, the bar was much better off after I took it over.

"During the uprising, what was your role?" she says.

I look at her like her head is floating away from her shoulders. "You were with us for most of it, you saw. I did everything."

She points at me. "Exactly. You fought the Tathadann, you organized your fighters, you delegated, you planned offensives, you prioritized sites." She holds her arms out like she holds the answer to everything. "That is what we need, what Eitan needs, for this system to become possible. That is why I want you on this."

My chest begins to swell at the thought of all the positive things this energy system could provide but I tamp it down, tell myself not to get too outrageous yet.

"Is this because of yesterday? You're trying to, what, boost my confidence? Keep me away from intelligence so more people aren't murdered?"

"Yesterday was unfortunate, yes, definitely. But I've had you in mind for this since Ødven offered their technology. You're perfect for this, Emeríann." She leans in closer to me. "And I think you know that, too. Take a couple minutes, look at the field, look at the holograms, let your mind run wild with all the possibilities this project could present. Think about how grateful the people of Eitan will be once this is built, how they'll sing out your name in praise."

My shoulders sink slightly. "I don't care about praise. That was never why I did any of this."

Her smile returns. "I know. Which is why you'd be so good for this."

I stare out at the expanse, letting my eyes flit between the hologram and the field. Beyond it too, imagining what Eitan would look like without the wires looping across alleyways from building to building, the windows adorned with flowerboxes or found-art pieces instead of moisture condensers, the narrow passageways filled with the sounds of kids running around instead of humming generators that cough more smoke and fumes into the already-clogged sky. Creating something better. I imagine Cobb and Donael tearing into the apartment after playing in the park and filling a large glass of water from the tap then draining it and filling up another, instead of splitting one glass between the two of them because it's all we have left in our supply bottle. I imagine Henraek and me eating a whole meal without the power flickering, or just going dark all together.

"OK," I say to Brighid. "I'm game. I'll do it."

Across the field I see four large trucks weaving along the road, coming in our direction. Trails of dust follow them. Two have flat beds in the back that carry large metal pieces. The other two are large transport vehicles, each carrying about fifty people.

"What the hell is all that?" I point at the trucks. "And who the hell are they?"

"That's your crew," she says.

"My crew?" I look around, confused for a moment. "The crew for the power system? But I only said yes five seconds ago."

"Emeríann," she says with something like a laugh. "I knew you were going to do it before I even asked.

And I needed to make sure they got here early."

"Why?"

"Because we need this done yesterday."

21.
HENRAEK

After being in the countryside for a bit – if that's what you can call Rën – the city is nearly overwhelming. Everything seems to loom over me, menacing and oppressive. The sun glints off windows like gnashing teeth. The metal bars stretch like tendons of a great monster. Even the smiles of passersby feel like a veiled threat. *Don't think we don't know what you're doing*, they say. *Don't think they won't find out*. I sneer at a woman passing me. Her face curls up like she's just smelled sour milk and she turns away. I keep my head down to avoid causing any scenes and hurry along.

Life in Ragjarøn headquarters shushes along with the same quiet efficiency as the last time I was here. Ødven's secretary sits behind her desk, earpiece illuminated while she jots something down on a pad of paper. I keep throwing glances her way, as if it would somehow hurry Ødven through whatever he's doing and get him in here so I can get back home.

She continues to go about her job, conspicuously ignoring me. At least Federijke hasn't come in to seduce me in hopes of getting me to agree to help assassinate her husband or facilitate a coup.

For as independent as the boys like to tell me they are, they sure as hell took forever to get out of the house this morning. I know they can fend for themselves in Rën for a few hours while I'm here but, given the new pin on Donael's jacket, I'd prefer to get this done quickly and not to be away from them for longer than I have to. I told Donael I had to do some work and deferred any of his questions, which led him to believe it's regarding Nyväg. That's not a lie, even if it's not specifically true. Still, he went away happy.

For now.

With nothing else to do, I lean my head back and stare at the ceiling.

The door whooshes open and I snap upright, fists clenched and ready to counterattack. The room goes hazy a moment as blood rushes away from my head. Ødven laughs to himself.

"The life of a revolutionary, always on guard," he says. "I'll bet you sleep with a knife under your pillow."

"No," I lie.

"It's OK," he says. "I have since I was sixteen. Only now it's for the woman who shares my bed, not my enemies; though sometimes it's hard to tell the difference between the two."

"I can imagine."

"But enough about me." He lowers himself into his chair. "You have been meeting with Dyvik

Sandströmm and Magnus Flagge."

With his accent, I can't tell if he's asking me or telling me.

"Yes, I have. But there's been a complication in the matter."

He leans back in his seat, his face broadcasting that he is not glad to hear that. "Do explain."

"I need something from you. Something important," I say. "No questions asked, I just need you to help me."

"This already sounds like a tall order."

"Then it's a good thing I'm talking to the most powerful man in Brusandhåv."

"Power is tricky, Henraek. I thought I made that clear when you were last here." He looks out the window for a moment. "If applied properly, it's as if it never existed. But if one takes it for granted, it can undo the fabric of the very society it seeks to protect and—"

"Ødven, look," I say, not having time for this. "Not to be rude, but I don't need your lofty pontifications right now. Are you going to help me or not?"

He runs his tongue over his teeth and the resemblance to a wolf before prey is uncanny. "That all depends."

"On?"

"What I have to do and what I get in return."

I lean forward in my chair, knitting my fingers together so he can't see me squeeze them repeatedly, working myself up to speak. *You're doing it, Henraek. This is the moment when everything changes. This is the moment you become everything you railed against. You are now your own enemy.*

And somewhere in my head I hear Belousz's voice echoing. I shove it all down into the recesses, take a deep breath, and look Ødven square in the eyes.

"I need you to get me and my boys to Eitan, as soon as possible. We need protection while we're there. And I need you to end your support for Brighid."

Ødven stares at me in silence for what feels like an eternity, or maybe it only feels like silence because my blood is crashing so hard against the inside of my skull that I can't hear anything else.

"That is in fact a tall order," he finally says. "It would take some arranging, finding a suitable replacement for you in Rën, someone who knows the groups, someone who can integrate themselves with–"

"Cut the shit, Ødven." I don't mean to yell but I can't help it. I swear I can hear the woman outside his office gasp. This is probably the only time in memory someone has yelled at him. The expression that plays over his face says I better have something fantastic to follow that up with if I don't want to become a sacrifice to his wolf god. "We both know all you have to do is send a message and a boat will be waiting for us. It's that simple but you're drawing it out because you want to display your power in front of me. I get it. I've dealt with it for the last seven years, I'm sure I'll see it for many more. But you need to talk straight to me."

He barely parts his lips when he speaks. "And why would that be?"

"Because you want Nyväg, and I want my people safe."

He doesn't respond, just gives a slight nod of assent.

"They have members spread around the country, and they are planning to attack."

"They have attacked before and they can attack all they please. None will ever make a difference."

"This one will."

He scoffs at me, the prick. He actually scoffs. "You're asking me to give up a significant overseas territory just to defend myself against a handful of dissidents. Why should I care if they launch another attack?"

"Because I planned it for them. I showed them how to bring Ragjarøn to its knees."

I feel sick as soon as I say it, but his expression tells me I have him. I know I have him. He needs to know about Nyväg and I need to get home. What will happen to the people here, I have no idea, and my soul hurts for them, but I have lost too many that I love and cannot bear the thought of any more. I cannot wait for Andrei and his boat, and I cannot leave the boys behind.

His laugh dies halfway up his throat. "Continue," he says.

"You do all that for us," I say, my voice surprisingly steady, "and I'll tell you everything you need to know about Nyväg."

22.
EMERÍANN

The next few mornings, I jump out of bed, I'm so excited to get to work on the power system. I wish Henraek could see what we're doing, what we're going to accomplish and provide for Eitan. I hope that he can come back soon. Maybe I can bring it up with Brighid. I'm sure she could sell it as part of getting the power system done faster.

I take a few winding roads out to the site, enjoying the feeling of the truck cresting the small curves through the city on my way to the foothills. Driving on my own is a strange sort of freedom I never would have expected to either take for granted or now relish. But nothing ever ends up like you expect it to, I guess.

When I pull up, there are already sixty-plus people working, most of them Ødven's men from Brusandhåv. According to Brighid, they were shipped down here because they'd already installed these at home and it would make the process quicker. Some operate threshers, clearing out the remaining brush and grasses, while others work at configuring the wiring in the central dome unit. With so many people working, this whole thing is already going way faster than I expected. I figure it's like a house too, where the outside seems to go up in two days, but it's all the inside work that takes the most time. I flipped through the schematics a couple times yesterday and the wiring diagrams made my eyes cross quick enough for me to stop after a minute. The overall area is larger than I expected, given how advanced Tathadann technology was, but it probably takes a lot of space to cool the machines after they produce all the power. Or something. What the hell do I know about any of this? I'm a bartender and an instigator of unrest, not a foreman. Still, it's nice to be outside, unwatched, for a change.

One of the younger workers comes up to me, waving his hand to get my attention.

"There's man who makes delivery and needs it put." His accent is thick, his gesturing doing most of the talking for him.

"What is it?" I squint and try to make out the truck but it's too far away.

"Says it's curing pods?"

"What the hell is a curing pod?" I say.

He makes some odd gestures with his hands, like he's trying to form a person out of clay or something, but eventually gives up. "I don't know how to say. Where to put?"

I fire up the hologram device, asking him to repeat the name in his language.

It doesn't sound familiar. I flip through the schematics, looking for a curing pod, partially to see what the hell it is and partially to see where the hell it goes. The kid looks at me impatiently, but I can't figure out what he's talking about. I'll have to find someone who can communicate better.

I point to a space across the field. "Tell him to put it there and we'll figure it out. OK?"

He nods a couple times.

"Great, thank you."

He jogs back to his post on the far side of the field.

Now that the kid isn't here waiting for an answer, I can take my time in looking through these holograms and try to understand what the hell is going on.

The initial ones are mostly land surveys, diagrams of how the plant will be laid out, the large central generator with smaller pods spread out around it. But as I get deeper into the files, I start finding schematics for the machines, detailed wiring diagrams, and power flow illustrations. It looks like the central dome generator isn't actually connected to the auxiliary ones. That seems counterintuitive, even for someone whose understanding of creating energy comes mostly from listening to guys who worked at a nearby power station and drank at Johnstone's. Why wouldn't you connect them all?

A loud bang echoes across the field. I flinch and reflexively look over my shoulder, irrationally worried that the insurgents overtook the high-rises and have mounted an attack. Then there's another bang as the crane attached to the back of the delivery truck sets a smaller pod on the ground.

I go back to the diagrams. The translation software on these devices can be wonky at times, but from what I can gather the smaller ones are the curing pods the kid was talking about. But how the hell do you cure energy?

I thumb deep into the files until I find the central dome diagram. The interior wall along the top of the dome has a bunch of sockets that attach to something that looks almost like a range of showerheads, except these have small notches on them. No, not notches, I can see when I zoom in, but hooks. Claws. Like they're holding something. That can't be right. Because having hooks on the things on the ceiling for grabbing things would mean that the dozens of fasteners I see on the side walls, which at first glance looked like braces for thick ropes of conducting wires, would be restraints for whatever is being grabbed, not fastening wires.

But why would you need restraints in a power plant? My palms start to sweat.

The holograms waver as I scan through them, my thumb flicking in time with my pulse. I try to relax my eyes, absorb what I'm seeing and learn through osmosis, but I still don't understand exactly what I'm looking at.

Until I find a demonstration video.

I hit the small triangle and the image begins to move. The narrator speaks in a tongue I don't understand – apparently the translation feature only goes so far – but I can follow along well enough. The central dome is completely constructed, with all the wires and tubing in place. The camera moves through the small cutout window and inside the dome, where all the devices hang from the ceiling like clawing hands. And around the edge of the dome, held still by the restraints, are people. More than a dozen, all of them fairly young.

What the shit is this?

I glance around, looking for one of the workers so they can explain it to me, but everyone is busy.

The camera in the video pans around the dome, showing all of their faces. They wear terrified, unmoving expressions, but their fingers twitch and curl so they're obviously not sedated.

"Hey," I yell to a group of workers a hundred yards away. They're in the middle of positioning a dome and don't hear me until I yell a couple more times. One finally looks up and I wave him over. He starts to trot toward me.

I glance back to the screen as he arrives and the devices in the video are shuddering and moving downward. Everyone's eyes widen. I want to scream at them to jump, to fight, to resist. The fact that they never move is incredibly unsettling. It's like they're frozen by horror, but also accepting of it. The devices come to rest a few inches in front of everyone's chest before sliding forward and pressing against the skin, leaving shallow puncture wounds. The casing around them vibrates, the small hooks clicking around the edges. The tubes that circle the dome start glowing – first a dull, barely noticeable color, then emitting stronger and stronger light until it almost hurts to watch. Then it all stops.

And all at once, everyone's head snaps back, their

fingers stuck in rigor mortis claws. The space in front of their chest vibrates, but it's impossible to see air vibrating. I'd normally say that's just Henraek's melodramatic way of describing something, but I can physically see the air moving. I pull the device closer and squint, and that's when I realize that it's not the air that's vibrating – there's something coming out of the people, streaming through the puncture wounds. Something invisible, but not.

I drop the schematic device to the ground and step away from it, just as the worker gets to me. He picks it up and offers it, but I can't hold it.

"What the hell is this?"

"A power station, ma'am."

"No," I snatch the schematics and slam my finger on the screen. "This. What the hell is this?"

He watches a second, then looks up at me, confused. "Committing ändes?"

"It looks like this thing is, I don't know, sucking something out of their body. Like, their, I don't know, their soul or something."

"Soul?"

"Yeah, like…" I gesture vaguely, so many thoughts and hideous images crashing together inside my head that I'm having trouble coming up with a coherent movement.

"Ah, yes," he says. "In Brusandhåv, we don't have 'soul.' That is southern religion term. This," he says, "this we call ände. Almost same thing, but without religion. It's better that way."

I can't do anything but stare dumbfounded at him. "Better?"

"In Brusandhåv, we commit our ände in our thirty-fifth year. It provides energy for the country and is personal honor to contribute to that."

"Y-You," I stammer a couple times, feeling my knees turning to water, "you give your soul to the party?"

"Not soul. Ände."

"Holy shit." I crouch down on my knees. My whole body has started sweating and it feels like someone is squeezing my head. They give their soul – I don't give a shit what they call it, it's the soul – to the party. Not metaphorically – literally. And just for energy.

"It is a small personal sacrifice for the greater good of the people," he says, like it's a totally normal thing to be discussing. Then he unbuttons his work shirt and shows me his chest, his skin pale except for a dozen scarred marks that circle his breast bone. He's displaying a mark of pride.

Everything begins to telescope before my eyes. Maybe my brain is short-circuiting trying to comprehend what he's saying. And then it snaps into sharp focus.

This is what Brighid wants to do to Eitan. In order to bring us back online, she wants to get the citizens to give up their souls.

"Do you need anything else, ma'am?" the worker says.

My head snaps upright. I'd forgotten for a second that he was here.

"No, no. Go back to work."

He heads back to the group of men, leaving me alone.

My hands feel absent, or like they belong to someone else. The crane lowers another dome and the ground beneath my feet shakes.

Brighid lied, and I was wrong. She is not the one we've been looking for. She is an abomination to the Tobeigh name. She is a Morrigan, through and through. She sees us as commodities, not people. We should serve our purpose then be disposed of.

She needs to be stopped.

I will stop her.

No one else is around to save Eitan, so I'll have to do it myself.

23.
HENRAEK

After leaving my meeting with Ødven, I could feel everyone's eyes on me. No one was looking at me, but everyone was watching. Judging. Following. Tracking. Waiting. Plotting.

Through the streets of Vårgmannskjør.

On the train, during the two-hour ride and three hours of delays, which, from what I'd seen, was incredibly uncommon and therefore absolutely appropriate for the day.

At the central station, through the handful of weary travelers.

Along the cold, windy streets of Rën.

Intellectually, I know it's crazy, but I can't help but feel it: the ghost of betrayal floated behind me, tugging at my skin, wrapping around my arms, weighing me down.

But at the same time, I feel lighter now, my step a little higher. Because I am sorry – truly sorry – for Dyvik and Magnus. Hell, for the people of Brusandhåv.

But this coup is threatening to steal my son – my sons
– away from me. I know Cobb will follow Donael to
the ends of the land and walk on water if Donael tells
him he can.

I remind myself that Dyvik and his people might
be misreading the will of the people. The people of
Eitan suffered for years and continue to suffer on a
daily basis. Most of what I saw in Vårgmannskjør was
people smiling blithely, albeit vacantly, and staying
warm inside the public assistance centers. Yes, they
may be sedated, but sometimes not feeling isn't such
a bad thing. There are many people in Eitan who
wish they could no longer feel.

After hemming and hawing, and me threatening
to walk out and give him nothing, Ødven promised
that we would have transport by tomorrow. Still, I
stop by the market on my way to our lodging to pick
up some extra food. Since they've adjusted to the
cuisine up here, the boys are eating like they're never
had real food before, which, I suppose, they haven't.
Not like this.

The man behind the counter glances up when I
enter. He's maybe ten years older than me. I nod to
avoid him suspecting I'm dodging his attention then
try to keep my head down on my way to the cooler.
The store reminds me in some way of Toman's place
in Macha, though it's not nearly as ostentatious or
gratuitously nice as his. This one, like the town and
country, is dignified but austere, minimalist and
considered. Though I'm tired of being cold as balls all
the time, I have to admit that I like the lack of crap
around here. Everywhere you go in Eitan, there are

piles of stuff. Rubble, discarded furniture, abandoned cars, bodies. There's shit everywhere, yet no one has enough to live. It's one of the great paradoxes on my homeland, exacerbated by years of tyranny.

Stacks of smoked fish filets sit on the refrigerated shelf on the side. I grab a piece of wrapping paper and a pair of tongs then pick out a few. In the reflection of the cooler, I can see the man staring at me, a sober expression set on his face. I hunch up my shoulders and grab a jar of the jam Cobb now loves and two packages of crispbread for Donael. When I pull a carton of juice out of the refrigerator, I can see the man is still looking at me. Part of me wants to continue to shop for things I don't need, wasting time until he gives up. But part of me wants to rush over to him, grab him by the hair, and smash his face against the counter until he learns it's impolite to stare.

What I do, is take a deep breath, then carry my groceries over.

He rings up my items while keeping an eye on me. I stare at the counter, feeling my jaw tighten.

"I know," he says.

The spring trap in my fist sets. I swallow. *What are you going to do if this man heard about your trip to Vårgmannskjør? You knock him out: then what? You kill him to protect yourself: what do you do with the body?*

"You know what?" I push the words through my teeth.

"About you." He leans forward and I'm ready to swing. Then he says, "I've known Dyvik since he was føga." He holds his palm at his waist, suggesting a child.

"Dyvik's good." I purse my lips and nod. "A good man."

The man sets the fish on top of the bag, folding his hands over my food. "He is a good man. But he doesn't understand the way things work."

I reach for my groceries but his hands haven't moved. He still has more to say, apparently.

"How's that?"

"He needs something to rail against, and Ødven Äsyr is an easy target. Years ago, all the lands, they were divided into small communities. It was nice that you had your own people, but communities are meant to grow. That meant the territory lines between people were always being blurred, which led to fighting among each other. Been like that as long as I can remember, everyone killing each other over some little parcel of land." He gestures outside. "Once Härskare Äsyr was touched by Evivårgen and had his vision, he stopped all that fighting and united the people, made everyone the same. Same country, same rights, same land. Everyone was equal. Everyone stopped killing."

The man loses himself inside his head for a minute, revisiting those scenes that I never want to have to witness, before navigating his way back to the market. He pushes my bag of food toward me and gives a sad smile.

"But you don't have any say in your life," I say. "Doesn't that bother you to have someone hundreds of miles away dictate your actions?"

"I have no say?" He waves his hand around the store. "I choose to come to my store or not. I choose to love my wife or not. I choose to be kind or not. Ødven? He decides policies and taxes. He does not decide how I live my life. Only I do that."

"That's one way to look at it."

"That is my choice. Dyvik, Magnus, the others? They don't understand that. But I hope they live long enough to."

I nod, I take my bag, and I head back to my family.

My stomach sinks when I open the door and find the house empty. I call out for the boys but hear nothing in return. I focus on each step as I walk to the kitchen, telling myself to breathe and calm down, don't let the panic creep in too quickly. When I set the bag on the counter, I close my eyes to sharpen my hearing and listen.

Murmuring outside.

I go into the living room and check out the window. They're in the side yard, on the opposite side of where I'd come from. Donael is holding the football in his extended arm, the rest of his body turned away. Cobb comes running up, cocks back his leg, then swings it. His foot doesn't come anywhere near the ball, instead throwing his whole body out of balance so that he tumbles down on the grass. Donael helps him up and gives him pointers before they try again.

Seeing them like this, so safe and so caring, releases some of the tension in my chest. I appreciate what the man in the market said, and I know I made the right choice.

I'm heading back to the kitchen to put away the groceries when someone pounds on my door. I snap open my hunting knife and hold it at my side as I approach.

When I swing it open, I find Dyvik standing on my front step, red-faced and breathing hard.

"Where the hell have you been?" he says as he walks past me into the house. He glances down and sees the knife at my side. "You going to kill me?"

I swallow. "Pounding on my door like that, sure, the thought crossed my mind."

"I was looking for you all day."

"I had to take care of some things."

He reaches into his jacket and my hand instinctively tightens around the handle of the knife. Then he pulls out a small envelope.

"They tried to deliver this to you a couple times but you weren't here. I held it for you at the store to keep it safe," he says. "It came on the boat from Eitan."

I take the envelope from him, feel the energy emanate off it.

"I have to meet Magnus," Dyvik says, though there's a hitch in his voice. "Unless you need me to stay here."

"No." I slide the envelope in my back pocket. "I'm fine. Go ahead."

He hesitates, then nods, turns, and leaves. As soon as the door closes I tear open the envelope.

Another piece of the same fabric, the liner. I unfold it and realize I'm actually holding my breath. Then I see the words, the letters written in her blood, and I feel the floor rushing up toward me. My knees slam into hard wood the same color as Emeríann's dried blood.

A barrage of images clatter against each other inside my skull. A thousand faces shifting and sliding over one another. The shit-eating grin on Ødven's face. The peace radiating off the man in the market. The awe washing over Donael's when listening to Magnus talk about Nyväg. The admiration and undying love on Cobb's any time he's around Donael. The surprise and shock on Walleus's when I plunged the needle into his temple. The terror on Emeríann's as they pulled us apart on the stage during what was supposed to be our most triumphant moment.

I have no idea what expression must rest on my face. How could I possibly accurately summarize the expression of all things finally coming together in one startling moment?

I think she might be what we've been looking for, Emeríann said. Her first letter was wrong. They're going to rebuild Eitan.

I have a sinking feeling inside my chest, knowing that I have given up Dyvik and Magnus for nothing. Emeríann and Brighid are guiding Eitan toward renewal. They don't need my help.

My head is pounding, like the skin is contracting against my skull until it will finally shatter the bones. What do I do now? Can I call it off with Ødven, say I talked them out of it and at least spare their lives? Or do I take the boys back to Eitan anyway, Nyväg be damned? How the hell am I supposed to work myself, my boys, and Dyvik and Magnus out of this without anyone getting hurt?

From some great distance, I hear Donael call my name.

I reread the letter again to make sure I have it right. It's almost too good to be true, that after years of fighting and scraping to survive, something is finally going our way. I'm seeing it more clearly now. There is no clean way out of this. I need to get us out of the country before anyone learns of my deal with Ødven. This will prove to be the longest day ever.

Donael says my name again, but this time it's not calling out: it's screaming.

I jump to my feet, the letter falling to the floor. Through the window, I see the boys standing stock-still in the yard, Donael shielding with his body. They're staring out at the street with horror. I run to the door and only now I realize that all the noise I thought was inside my head is actually outside.

I throw the door open and see Ragjarøn troops storming the neighborhood, streaming from three large transport vehicles idling in the middle of the street. Two of the soldiers smash the windows of Dyvik's store. Two others kick in the door of Magnus's bar. Another group rings around the front of a house two blocks down, getting into formation crouched down behind their riot shields. I pause for a second, wondering what they're doing, then realize that Magnus lives there. The troops advance toward the house, but before they reach the door, a large chair crashes through the front window, catching two of the troops and knocking them to the ground. The other troops rush the door and even from two blocks away I can hear Magnus shouting and grunting inside, glass breaking and wood beams shattering. One of the troops flies out of the front door and tumbles into the street, but three more auxiliary troops rush inside.

"Dad," Donael screams behind me.

I spin, fists ready to smash anyone who comes near my sons, but see they are blessedly alone.

"What the hell is going on?" Donael yells, and I don't have the energy to scold him.

"Get inside," I tell them.

Donael flings his arms at the scene. "What is this? What's happening?"

"I don't know, Donael." I hurry over to them, then herd them toward the door. "But you need to get inside."

"Are they going to come here?" His voice sounds like it's about to crack. Cobb clicks maniacally and wraps himself around my leg.

"I'm not going anywhere," I tell them as authoritatively as I can.

"How do you know? They taking everyone from Nyväg."

His words are a cold blade in my chest, knowing what's on his jacket. "I'm not going anywhere," I repeat. "Now get your asses inside and hide under your beds. Stay away from the windows."

I move them toward the door as a great roar erupts behind us. I shove them inside and yank the door closed, then spin around. Magnus breaches his front door with three Ragjarøn troops trying to restrain him, a fourth one close by. Magnus tries to pull his arm away but his energy is quickly draining. The extra troop yanks something from his weapons belt and sprays Magnus in the face. The big man takes two halting steps, then collapses face first on the street.

I hear another man yell and his voice cuts through me like a garrote. Two troops have yoked up Dyvik's arms, holding them high over his back in a restraining position. He tries to fight, but every time he struggles it puts more pressure on his shoulders. His face is bright red, as much from the screaming as from the blood after the troops beat him. As the troops maneuver him toward the transport vehicles, his eyes catch mine for an instant. I freeze in place, caught vulnerable, exposed for what I really am. I expect him to spit, to scream out *traitor!* as I've been called a thousand times before but know how much worse it would cut now because now it's true. I truly am a traitor.

But instead, his eyes hold mine tight and he mouths three words.

Run.

Hide.

Fight.

He doesn't know. No one knows. Which is somehow, in some way, so much worse.

The troops walk him to the transport vehicle and load him into the back while five others gather around Magnus and lift him.

And then the front door of the vehicle opens, and out steps Slåtann. He surveys the scene, appraising his men's work with a stoic expression, until his gaze falls on me. A smile tugs at the corner of his lips, though he doesn't acknowledge me.

He knows. My enemy knows me better than my compatriots do.

I take three steps back, reach behind me and open the door, then retreat into our house.

I close the door and the noise from outside dies. The house is deathly quiet. Too quiet. Unnervingly quiet. A hundred feet from where I stand, people are being ripped from their houses, families torn asunder, businesses destroyed. Yet here I stand, in this foreign land, safe. Protected even. I feel a ripple spread through my throat, a scream that has been building for years barreling up from the darkest, dankest, most roiling part of my gut, and I spin around and open my mouth to scream, to finally exorcise myself of everything I've done.

And there stands Donael. Not under his bed, like I told him. In the middle of the living room, where he has a sightline right out the window, in full view of Slåtann's transport vehicle.

"He looked at you but didn't shoot," Donael says. His voice is strange, alien in its lack of affect. It's like he's not even my same boy.

"He saw us on the boat." My mouth moves though I don't tell it to. I wonder if he also thinks I sound like an alien. "He knows who we are."

Donael starts to speak then cuts himself off when something passes over his face. His features settle, jaw clenched as if the last piece has finally clicked into place. In the space of two seconds, he has aged five years.

It's the look of realization.

"Donael," I say, but he turns around without a word and walks into Cobb's room. I cringe preemptively, expecting the door to slam in anger, but there's no noise at all, leaving me alone in the living room. A raid rages outside our quiet house, but somehow the silence is much, much worse.

24.
EMERÍANN

I say goodbye to Brighid as I leave our compound and head in the direction of the work site. I take my normal route, the traffic lights synching in that uncanny way where, if you squinted, you could easily imagine that you're reliving the same day over and over on an infinite feedback loop. Then, when I'm far enough away from the compound and anyone who might see me, I bust a hard left, my tires jumping the curb on the median, and head east, the opposite direction of the site. I push down the gas pedal and head to a bar called Render's. It's too early for a drink, but I have no idea where Lachlan's living now, after everyone scattered. The one thing I do know, you want to run into Lachlan, you go to Render's and wait.

This would definitely not qualify as my type of bar, deep inside the winding shantytowns of Amergin. The floor is caked with scabs of dirt, the liquor is completely unorganized, and someone has actually set up a memory stand in the corner, complete with a lagonael booth. That it's the complete opposite of any place I'd go makes it a great place for me *to go* right now, because I don't want to be found.

I know better than to take up space at a bar without giving them some money so I ask for a cup of coffee. The bartender looks familiar, but he's a Brigu, and they share similar features. Know him or not, he still gives me a look that could flay skin when he hears my order.

"OK then, how about you put some bourbon in it?" I say. This seems to do the trick.

I wrap my hands around the cup and set my face over it, feel the steam waft up over my skin, the fumes of what is probably bathtub bourbon screech up my nostrils. Surprisingly, when I take a sip I barely notice the taste of the liquor, which immediately pisses me off because I think he gave me a soft pour. Then the alcohol kicks in.

"You make this yourself?" I say to the bartender.

He looks surprised that I asked. "Doesn't everybody?" He has the faint Brigu accent common to the neighborhood, one that is as guttural as it is musical. He turns to tend to his other customer, a man who apparently replaced his missing arm with spare parts he found in an alleyway.

For all that is holy, Lachlan, get your ass in here.

Two hours and two coffees later, the front door opens. My head feels slushy when I turn to look, but – praise be, Nahoeg – I finally recognize that silhouette. The bartender starts preparing his drink before he even saddles up to the bar.

"That one's trouble," I say, though it comes out a little more slurred than it was in my head. I push the coffee aside. "Dunno if you want to serve him."

"Holy shit," he says, coming over to me.

"Lachlan Parnell, how the hell are you?"

"When did you get here? What happened after the ceremony? Where are Henraek and the others?" His questions come rapid fire and I flinch a couple times, like I can physically dodge them. He cocks his head. "Are you drunk already?"

"Only because your ass took so long to get here. Couldn't be a punctual lush for once?"

"I just got in from the border."

"Back to running jewels?" I shake my head. It's dangerous work, and probably not worth the money.

"Can't stay in here to work, and me wee one still needs to eat." He takes his drink from the bartender and asks him for a regular coffee for me – emphasis on regular – then sits down on the next stool. "What are you doing out here?"

"It's a long story but I have to tell it quick. I need to be somewhere."

I give him the short version: the raids, the first ambush, the squatters, the soul farm.

When I finish, Lachlan lets out a low whistle and waves to the bartender for another drink. I slide him my coffee cup too. I need to sober up a bit more before I go to the work site. Showing up late is one thing. Showing up late and wasted is something else.

"What are you going to do, then?" Lachlan says.

"I'm going to take her down," I say. "But I need help from you and your crew."

"My crew?" He barks out a laugh. "Shit. Your gal pal took care of most of me crew. Most of everyone's crew."

I feel my stomach sink. I'm responsible for that too.

"Some of them skipped town, went back to the hills to find work," he says. "Some left just trying to stay alive. Most are dead or detained."

"How many people are left?"

He shrugs. "Dozen. Maybe fifteen. Only half of them are in the city, though." He looks at me over the top of his drink. "And none of them are going to be happy to see you, since you were with her so much."

"She forced me to go with her. I didn't have a choice."

"I know that. And I understand being in a hard situation. Hell, running around with Forgall for years? All we got was hard situations. But not everyone else is so understanding."

"I thought..." I don't even know how to explain what I thought. What I'd hoped for was to not be wrong, to think that Eitan finally, finally had better days ahead of it. Maybe I got caught up in that, in thinking that I could be the one to help bring those better days in. Maybe it was my ego that led to it. "I don't know. It was a mistake to trust her in the first place. I take responsibility for that."

"Awful magnanimous of you, sweetheart, but some mistakes you never stop paying for. I'm not saying no one's going to ride beside you, but don't be surprised if no one's keeping the streets empty for you."

"What do we do, then?"

He takes a long drink. "What we always do," he

says. "We fight."

"Are you fighting with me?"

"Much as I can."

"How much is that?"

"I'll ask around, see what I can do to help. But I can't promise anything. I'm sorry, but I told you before that things are different now."

"Then I'd better plan on doing it on my own."

"I can help you, do whatever I can in the planning aspect." He nods toward outside, what I'm assuming is his home. "But I've got me kid now. Not like during the Struggle when I could disappear for days on a whim. I can't go getting myself killed any more."

"No, I know." I pat his hand. He helped more during the uprising than he really should've, but once he starts, it's hard to get him to stop. "I appreciate it."

"What I think the real question is," he says, wagging his finger, his thinking motion, "what's the nerve point? What's the thing you hit that knocks down everything else?"

I nod, running through options in my head.

"And," he says, "what can you do with one person?"

"I'm so stupid," I say. "That's it."

"That's what?"

"I know how to stop her." I clink my coffee cup against his drink. "But I'm going to need your help afterward."

"I just said I don't know if I'll be able to do much."

"I don't need you to do anything," I say. "I just need to use your name."

• • •

The work site is a flurry of activity when I arrive. As it should be, because it's midday and I should've been here three hours ago.

I park my truck and hop out, already barking out orders as I fire up the hologram device, checking what's been accomplished against what's scheduled so this will be finished within a few days. Electricians work frantically inside the central dome, while other workers hustle to assemble the curing pods. A cold chill settles over me as I'm walking to the central dome, like I can feel the residual pain people have endured in these machines. Ragjarøn and Brighid aren't any better than the Tathadann. All of them have a total disregard for common suffering, thinking only about profits or statues or their inalienable right to seize whatever they deem appropriate. When I'm named Queen of the Struggle, I'll change that all. Give the land and the power back to the people.

The thought makes me laugh as soon as it passes through my head. Me being named to lead. I'm a goddamned pariah now, and the remaining rebels curse my name according to Lachlan. I suddenly have sympathy for Henraek, thinking about how much it hurt him, all those people calling him a traitor all the time. Not having the respect of those who I've fought alongside sucks pretty goddamned bad. The next time we meet, I'll have to ask Lachlan exactly how bad it is.

"Where have you been?"

I startle as soon as I hear the voice and look up to find Brighid standing outside the central dome. It's a good three times as tall as her, easily sixty feet in diameter. You could park two transport vehicles inside with room to spare.

"Why, are you following me?" I say, because I can't immediately think of a better response.

"Following you? No, I came to check in and see if you needed help. But I'm more than happy to let you deal with all of this by yourself if you're going to be a cunt about it."

Maybe the accusatory thing wasn't helpful.

"I'm sorry. I wasn't feeling well. It took me a bit to get here."

She approaches me warily, sizing me up with every step. "You were fine this morning when you left the compound."

I give a fake smile. "Do you want details on what it was like each time I had to stop on the side of the road, or will you take that it I had to stop a lot?"

Still, she stares at me, her eyes probing inside my skull, trying to see what I'm thinking. Then she says, "You can be real disgusting sometimes, know that?"

I shrug. "I asked which one you wanted. You could've chosen."

She shakes her head. "Why isn't this finished yet?"

"Because it's a gigantic project." I gesture to the field of people. "Everyone's working their asses off. It'll be done soon. What's the rush?"

"Because Eitan needs to see results. If we want them to trust us, to follow us, we need to give them something to believe in. We need to give them electricity and water. Now." She considers me for a long moment. "Is there anything stopping us from doing that?"

I swallow, then shake my head.

"OK," she says, then starts off toward one of the smaller domes, but not before looking at me long enough to make me question whether I was found out.

There's no way she would know I met with Lachlan. Despite fighting with us for those six months, I doubt she even knows where that neighborhood is. It's rare that I even go there.

After all, to them I'm a traitor.

I walk up to my room that evening with the hologram device in one hand and a cup of coffee in the other, preparing to stay up all night studying these schematics and refining my plan. But when I open the door, I find something on my pillow again. From over here it looks like a snake. A dead snake.

That goddamned woman. The mole. She knows where I am. She either followed me over here, or there are other moles in Brighid's inner circle that have told that cunt where I lay my head. But that bitch is not going to scare me.

I cross the room, ready to snatch up the snake so I can shove it in her mouth when I find her.

I stop short as I get to the bed, my skin suddenly cold and clammy.

It's not a snake lying on my pillow. It's a clutch of long brown hair, braided in three strands, from that poor little girl from the warehouse.

A yellow flower tie holds one end together. A piece of scalp clings to the other.

25.
HENRAEK

Donael forks idly at his dinner, more taking apart his fish flake by flake than trying to eat. He hasn't said much for most of the evening, despite me trying to provoke conversation. Even Cobb has been subdued, and while I normally would savor any kind of peace and quiet in the house, this is just uncomfortable.

It doesn't help that a Ragjarøn soldier passes by our window every five minutes. They've been patrolling the streets after the raid. Three troops have been stationed by the labor farm to protect it.

"When did you know you were going to join the Struggle?" Donael says.

Cobb and I both stop eating at the same time. The air tightens around me.

"What?"

Donael sets down his fork, any pretense of eating now gone. "You heard me."

"First off, I don't appreciate that tone. Second, I don't know what that has to do with anything."

"I'm just curious. Don't I have a right to know about important things in your life? You are my dad."

I flinch slightly, try to gauge any sharp edges in that last phrase.

"Is this about you thinking you'd be allowed to join Nyväg's youth brigade?" I watch him carefully, but he doesn't give any reaction. "What's it called, the ungdømstrüpper?"

"What are you talking about?" he says.

"Donael." I set my fork down. "I'm not stupid. I saw the pin on your jacket."

"Why were you snooping around my room?"

"I wasn't snooping around your room. I managed to stay alive all these years because I'm pretty damn good at observing things." I clear my throat. "It doesn't hurt that the both of you are physically incapable of putting away your belongings."

He mutters something I can't hear.

"So," I say, "is that what this is about?"

"What do you mean 'think I'm allowed'? I can't make my own decisions?"

"About that? No. No, you can't. You're too young to understand what revolution entails."

"How? I lived through it, didn't I? With you and Mom during the beginning, then with Walleus during all that crap afterward. I saw what happened. I saw what it did to people."

"Then you should understand why I'm saying no." Cobb leans away from me, back into his seat. I close my eyes and take a breath to calm myself. "I'm sorry. I didn't mean to yell. But this is not something I'm negotiating on."

Donael picks up his fork and resumes fussing with his food. Cobb waits a minute then follows suit. A soldier walks past our window again. I've seen them more often this evening than earlier in the day, almost as if they're keeping an eye on our house. It makes me wonder if Ødven told them to protect us, or if he said to watch us and report anything suspicious. It's hard enough to determine the line between caution and distrust, even more so when you're an outsider and prone to question people's motives as a matter of course.

"Are you afraid?" Donael says, quiet enough that he can pretend he didn't say anything but loud enough to know I'll hear him. I start to answer *Yes, of course I'm afraid, I'm afraid for you every minute of every day because people get killed just walking down the street when an iron beam is knocked loose from a building, and that's without purposely putting yourself into harm's way by signing up for a well-intentioned revolution that is more like a mission to become martyrs.* But before I can say anything, I hear the rest of the sentence: "That I'll become a traitor like Walleus?"

And in an instant, my whole body changes, intense, conflicting feelings thrumming through me. Cold fury coils inside my arms while righteous indignation stalks inside my chest. As if he knew anything, as if he'd experienced any of what war is truly about, anything to think that he feels he has the right to lecture me about it.

Throughout all that though, slipping between the cracks, there is the vicious, vibrating feeling of shame. Because my son has marked Walleus a traitor, as I had many times before, and I know that I am no better than Walleus. So my son will eventually think I am a traitor.

But does he know?

I keep my jaw tight as I respond, mostly as a way to focus my anger but also to keep myself from screaming and scaring them.

"You have no right to judge anyone for their choices until you understand what they were going through when they made that choice." I'm not sure if I'm saying this for his benefit or my own.

"But you said he was the reason the Struggle failed. If he–"

I slam my palm on the table, the impact knocking off my fork, which tinks on the wooden floor.

Tense silence sifts down over the room, punctuated only by the trill of the phone. Our breath courses in and out. The phone trills again.

"You have no right, Donael."

I stand and grab the phone before the third ring, don't ask who it is, just pick it up.

At the table, I can see Donael's chin trembling, the muscles of his jaw writhing. When he was younger, this was the prelude to one of his famous tantrums, where he'd throw himself on the ground and scream and cry and flail his limbs around like an octopus, trying to hit any- and everything within his range. But now it just houses bright, burning anger.

"Tomorrow morning." I recognize Slåtann's voice on the phone. "Take the early train to Vårgmannskjør. I'll be waiting for you at the harbor. Pier twelve."

He hangs up without waiting for a response.

When I sit down at the table, the expression on Donael's face is gone, as if he just flipped a mental switch and said *No, I'm not angry any longer, I'm fine now.* His face is blank, impassive.

"I'm sorry. That was over the line." His voice is as atonal as his expression. "It's probably better not to talk about some things."

"Donael…" I start, then trail off.

"I'm tired. I'm going to bed." He retreats to his room, Cobb falling in line as always. The door closes, lock clicks.

Just make it to tomorrow morning. Less than twelve hours to get through.

The soldier passes our window, looking in this time. His eyes meet mine and it appears he's trying to impart some sort of message, some understanding, but I don't get it and then he's gone and I'm sitting in the empty room and the air has a different quality to it. It's not silence; it's the echo of nothing. I go to the cabinet and grab the bottle of liquor that's been left here, the local drink I had in Ødven's office. Not my favorite but right now anything will do. I take a swig from the bottle and it makes my hair stand up. I take another drink then drop the bottle on the table, bend down, and pick up the fork even though I'm not hungry. The sunlight glints off the prongs, and, for a second, I imagine what it would be like to grip the handle tight, raise it high, then plunge the sharp tongs deep into my thigh.

I wonder if it would hurt. I wonder if it would be a relief.

26.
EMERÍANN

The first thing I see when I wake is the crack in the ceiling above my bed. I trace it with my eyes from the spot near my head down into the corner, where it disappears into the wall. It's not a small crack in the plaster, like something that would happen over the years of the house shifting and settling, but more of a fracture, which makes me wonder what caused it. A concussive blast from a bomb. A tree limb ripped loose during a storm.

My next thought is: I opened my eyes.

Shit. Shit shit shit shit shit.

I spring up in bed, the hologram device clattering to the floor. Goddammit, I fell asleep. I'd been up most of the night studying schematics of the power system and I must have drifted off at some point.

I'm late. I'm so late. And I'm in such deep shit.

I yank on pants and a shirt, snatch the hologram device from the floor, and grab two takeaway cups of coffee for the road, then sprint out to my truck, hoping I can still pull this off.

I arrive at the labor farm, sucking down the last of the coffee and wishing I'd grabbed a third cup. My body should still be buzzing with caffeine after drinking several cups last night to stay awake while going over the plans, analyzing and re-analyzing and trying to learn in a few hours what should take months and months... but hours are all I have. Hell, hours are all *we* have. I hurry toward the central dome.

The sky is a muddy brown out here, even with full morning coming almost four hours ago. Only a handful of the workers are around right now, since most of the main work has been done. I've had to kick some asses to get it finished and made a couple enemies, but they made it happen. One worker inspects the exterior of the central dome, which is set up and wired, ready for its first testing later today. The curing pods have been assembled, half of them wired up and ready to test, electricians getting the others prepared. The rest of the people are working on the conveyance mechanisms, which will transport the power from this plant into the city. I think they're retrofitting a facility in Findchoem to handle, store, and disperse all of this, but that's not part of my instructions.

Brighid is supposed to be out here after lunchtime, which is when we're scheduled to do the test. I was supposed to arrive here at least three hours before that, to give myself extra time, but apparently I shot that plan to shit. Right now, I've got about an hour to work and get everything ready. You would think that reversing and rerouting the flow of energy shouldn't be that hard – basically turning a lever the opposite way – but I'm not an engineer. So I hope like hell this works.

I don't know why it took me so long to think of this. It seems so obvious in retrospect. What better way to save Eitan from Brighid's plans than to destroy the very thing that she threatens us with? Because the energy that comes with harvesting the soul is stored in one central unit before shuttling it out to the pods, reversing the energy flow will essentially overheat that central unit. As it overheats, the seals that connect the tubes will begin to degrade, which makes them prone to rupturing. And when they rupture, you want to make sure your ass is far away and behind something that will act as a heat shield because it's going to be a big goddamned boom.

Now I only have to hope my half-cocked plan works and will reverse that power.

I'm booting up the hologram device to get moving on these wires when I glance up and see the worker is no longer inspecting the dome. They're looking at me. And they're not just any worker.

It's that bitch with the long brown ponytail.

"You bastard," I say as I approach her.

"Shut your mouth, traitor," she spits. "You gave us all hope that we could be our own country again. All you two wanted was the power for yourselves, and now you sleep under the same roof as the enemy."

"I *am* trying to help. That's all I've been doing for the last two years."

"And look at you now," she says. "You're lucky

Henraek and his boys were taken by Ødven. He'd sooner cut all of their throats than be seen with you."

You cunt.

I drop the hologram device and charge her, bending down and driving my shoulder into her gut. We slam back against the outside of the dome. I swing at her head, trying to smack it against the metal, but she shifts to the side, throwing me off-balance, then puts her feet on my chest and mule kicks. I fall to the ground, crushing the hologram device as I roll away. The device crackles and fizzles, throwing hot electric sparks on the dry wheat field. That is not going to be good.

I'm about to stomp out the device when something crashes against my face, spinning me around. My left cheek is on fire, and when I run my hand across it, it comes back dark red. I glance down at the ground and see a spanner wrench flecked with my blood. I hear her feet pawing at the ground as she bounds toward me, and in one motion I bend to grab the spanner and swing up and out, catching her right in the jaw. I can hear the crack of bone splitting. She crouches down, her hand cupping her fractured jaw, exposing the back of her head.

I grip the spanner tight. She's down. She's defenseless. She's practically begging for it. But echoing in my skull is the sound that poor girl in the water distribution plant made just before I shot her. That pitiful, completely vulnerable sound at knowing she was about to die, either by my gun or by the plant collapsing on her. That girl was part of the Tathadann and we were at war.

This woman, this is murder. They tried to murder

us. I am not them.

I don't even see her lash out. I only see the explosion of white dots as her foot connects with the side of my knee, buckling my leg. The pain is so bright I can taste it. I fall to the ground, bringing my injury beside me to protect it, then feel it light up again as I roll away when she tries to stomp my wounded knee. She raises her leg again, ready to fully tear the ligaments inside my knee and render me lame, but I scream and straighten my leg as hard as I can, my heel plowing straight into her kneecap. Even through my boots, I can feel it slip aside and I shudder as the bones crumple on impact. She falls backward, roaring like a wounded animal.

As she lands on the ground, I see the halo behind her head. Flames lick at the sky, nearly three feet tall.

Oh shit.

I push myself to my feet, favoring my good leg. The fire covers a good forty square yards, but it's spreading like water. This whole field is dry grass, ready to burn, and within twenty minutes, it will be one giant lake of fire.

And that bitch is now immobile in the middle of it.

Goddammit.

I hobble over to her, doing my best to crouch down so I can get my hands under her armpits.

A finger of smoke brushes against my nose, the heat already warming my face. She swings at me but it's half-hearted at best. She's in too much pain and contorted at too-awkward an angle.

"Cut the shit or I'm leaving your ass here," I tell her.

"I'm going to kill you when we get out of this," she says, her voice hoarse.

"The same thought crossed my mind."

I'm able to drag her five feet closer to the car when I hear someone yell my name.

I drop the woman and pivot on my good leg, only to see Brighid racing across the field, her truck parked at an odd angle, hanging half-off the street. What the hell is she doing here so early?

"They got here too?" she shouts.

"Who?"

"The rebels. Cantonae's people." She pulls up to me, breathing hard. "They bombed three sites in Eitan."

"What? How do you know who it was?"

"They were coordinated. A pipe-bomb at a bar, three pulse charges to free the captured ones in the high rises, and they just set fire to a home." She looks past me at the field, the fire spreading faster and faster. "The city's burning again."

Oh shit. It's not the insurgents. It's Lachlan.

Brighid looks down at the woman at my feet. Her face shifts, recognition setting in.

"The ponytail," she says.

And before I can tell her no, we need to leave, before I can open my mouth and push out a single word, she reaches behind her, aims her pistol at the woman, and fires once. The woman's head snaps back, a single red hole in the middle of her forehead as she flops backward. Blood leaks from her skull into the dirt beneath her, the flames making it bubble and sizzle within seconds.

The bottom of my stomach drops away. Another person killed because of me. She could have been saved. This is not how we'll rebuild. This is not what Eitan deserves. This ends now.

Brighid yanks at my arm and I suddenly feel the heat of the flames anew.

"Let's go," she says. "Now."

"Why did you come here?"

"What?" she says, half-turned and completely confused. "Seriously, let's go now."

"Why did you come here? To Eitan? To this field?"

"What the hell are you talking about?"

A small container left in the field explodes, throwing a shower of sparks into the air. I duck on instinct and feel the pain, electric blue and shimmering, spread through my knee.

"I came here to save you," she says, and there's something in her voice that I can't isolate, almost like she's wounded by me even asking.

"No, you didn't." I try to keep my voice level but it's a wild animal, out of my control and rising quickly. "Don't you dare say that. You have done nothing but lie to me since you got here."

"Do you have smoke inhalation or something?"

I push her hard, and she stumbles back a few feet before steadying, her hands reflexively protecting herself.

"What the hell is your problem?" She points at the fire raging all around us. My eyes begin to water. "You want to die here? Fine. Stay and die. I came to make sure you were safe."

"No, you didn't," I scream at her, swinging a hand

wildly and catching her on the cheek. "All you've done is manipulate me to do what you want! This machine is going to use our souls like firewood."

"Acceptable sacrifice, you stupid bitch." She swings back but I'm expecting it. I duck beneath it, lash out with a rabbit punch to her ribs and connect once, twice, then she grabs my arm and wrenches it backward. "Daghda always thought he was so goddamned smart, but he never led Ardu Oéann to be anything more than an afterthought to other countries."

She pulls up on my arm, sending a storm of electricity through my shoulders. It's enough to almost make me puke.

"Under me, we will step outside of Ødven's shadow and we will be bigger and more prosperous than ever before. We won't be a country." She puts her lips beside my ear, which lets me get my foot positioned between her legs. "We'll be an example to every other country. And everyone will know the name Tobeigh."

"You're willing to sacrifice everyone just so people know your name," I spit. "You are insane."

"No, I'm not," she said. "I'm ready."

You bitch.

I swing my foot up as hard as I can, catching her right between the legs. I can actually hear the sound of breath leaving her, and I swing around as soon as she lets go of my hand and charge at her, my hands going for her throat. But even then, she somehow grabs my wrist and spins me around, pushing me toward the central dome. I scramble to break loose, but she's cinched me into a hold. My heels leave ditches in the dirt beneath us. I try to flail my arms, do anything to get free of her hold. She just guides me forward, swearing in some language I don't speak.

We're five feet from the central dome, the metal heated enough from the surrounding fire that I can feel it radiate at this distance. She's going to push me in and leave me. I'm going to die in the middle of this potter's field.

And then it hits me.

I dig my heels in as hard as I can, pushing back on her with every ounce of strength in my body. She pushes forward just as hard, and because she's stronger than me, she moves me. One foot. Two feet. Three.

We're an arm's length from the dome. If I reached out and touched it, my fingertips would probably sizzle.

But I don't reach out. I drop to my knees.

The sudden change of balance throws her off, and she tumbles forward, skittering across the metal of the central dome. I scramble to my feet and grab the door, feeling my fingerprints melting smooth, then slam it closed and yank down the lever and lock it from the outside.

In the small porthole window in the door, I can see her spin around, her eyes wide with surprise before shifting to anger, then fear. She slams her hands on the door impotently, her mouth screaming terrible things, but I can't hear anything other than the fire spreading, the land being razed.

She won't burn alive in there – she'll cook.

"You made me believe you," I scream at her. "You made me believe you were my friend, but you don't care about any of us. We're just kindling to you." I doubt she can hear anything I'm saying, but I can't stop screaming that over and over at her, until I start coughing and choking on smoke.

Her palm slams against the window, fingers extended, like she's trying to touch me. Tears roll down her cheeks, and I start to feel bad for her. I'm the monster for doing this.

Then I remember what the dome that will be her tomb is meant for, and I don't feel so bad. I turn around and hobble toward my truck. The air is cooler as I move away from the fire, my skin prickling with sweat.

Still, under the crackling flames and rushing sound of wheat catching on, I swear I can hear her calling my name.

27.
HENRAEK

I wake to the sound of my alarm, already prepared to take the boys to the freighter in the harbor, though I still don't know what to tell them. Then I hear a second noise and realize it wasn't my alarm: it was the sound of shattering glass.

I scramble out of bed and into the living room. Outside the windows, shouts echo through the streets, followed by gunshots and screaming. A Ragjarøn soldier doubles over, pushing his hands against his stomach to staunch the bleeding, but it's all for nothing as one of the villagers jumps toward him, bringing down a long lance through his back. The soldier coughs a splatter of blood then hits the street, face first. The man jams his foot against the soldier's back and yanks on the lance. A spurt of blood shoots out, and he unleashes a war whoop and sprints after another soldier.

It's Nyväg. Members from other towns, ones who live here quietly. They've come to take out the

Ragjarøn troops, to show Ødven that they won't be cowed and they won't bow before him, that they'll die on their feet, not live on their knees.

Watching that gets my blood flowing, my adrenaline spiking with that feeling of do-or-die, knowing that history will look kindly on those who would rather be forgotten than remembered for giving up and giving in.

It also makes me think that I need to get the boys and get the hell out of here.

A noise behind startles me. I spin around, hand cocked and ready to break someone's nose, but there's no one there. Another noise, and I realize it's the clap of boards against skulls in the field beside our lodging, not a rebel who has discovered my duplicity. It surprises me that the noise hasn't woken the boys.

"Donael?" I call out. "Cobb?"

No response.

I call out to them again, heading toward their room. Each gunshot outside makes my heart beat faster.

"Donael," I yell as I slam into his door. "Boys."

The room is empty, his bed made, as if he'd never slept in it. I look in the closet, in Cobb's room, in the bathroom, in the living room, in my room, knowing somehow that each place will be empty but needing to prove it to myself. And each time, I'm proven correct.

I run outside, into the fray. It's not a large battle, but more than I want to be in unarmed. A Ragjarøn soldier rushes toward me and I take two steps back. He continues on, readying himself to tackle a Nyväg fighter. By instinct, I yell, "Watch out!" just in time for the fighter to spin around, barbed-wire-wrapped board in hand, and unleash an uppercut swing against the soldier's jaw. The soldier crumples on the street. The fighter looks at me, but I can't get a read on his expression and hurry away before he has the chance to out me as a traitor or conscript me into fighting with him.

I need to find my boys.

I sprint up the street to the park where they played football and find only a few bodies lying speared or shot.

I run to the docks and find only sand slowly giving way to the sea.

I check three more places they play, then Magnus's and Dyvik's houses, but there's nothing. Not my boys, not their boys, not even Lyxzä wielding a shotgun.

Someone screams behind me, and I turn just in time to see the top of a Nyväg fighter's head explode in a burst of red. I sprint back to the house, slamming the door behind me and locking it. I head back to Donael's room and stand in the middle of all the order, everything in its right place. I know I yelled at them for not cleaning up, but they've never listened to me before so why would they start now?

But Donael's room, it doesn't look cleaned up like it does when I threaten them during normal chores. It looks arranged, as if for a specific reason. Like someone would do when they don't plan on returning.

Slowly, as if I can will it into not being true if I take long enough to do it, I turn to look at the back of the door. Donael's jacket is no longer there, nor is Cobb's. The shelf beside it is empty as well. Their gloves, their hats, their boots, the goggles and balaclavas I got them from the general store to protect from the wind and snow and cold – everything's gone.

My knees give way and slam against the floor, weighed down by my heart and by knowing that this is all my fault.

No.

I slap myself in the face once, twice, three times.

You stand up. You did not make it this far to give up. You did not find your boy by taking the easy way or stopping when things became hard. You fought for what you love, because that is what you are. A fighter.

I grab my jacket and cold-weather gear, then shove my hunting knife in my waist band.

I know where they are.

I throw open the door and make a beeline down the street, walking through gunshots and bayonets and brandished knives. They won't touch me. Anyone who comes near will meet a quick and violent end. The door to our house yawns open, but I don't give a shit. I'm never coming back here again.

I'm going to Skaö to get my boys back from Nyväg. With or without Ødven's help, we're going home. Where we belong.

28.
EMERÍANN

Speeding back into the city, the scene is eerily familiar. It looks like the three bombings from Lachlan and his people have energized the citizens again. People fighting in the streets. Platoons of fatigued soldiers – Ragjarøn grey this time instead of Tathadann brown – swarming in to subdue crowds, dragging away those who resist. Part of me wonders if this is all Eitan's future holds, if people here are only happy when they're rioting and at war. If peace would actually be the worst thing for the city.

But I think just as quickly that the citizens deserve to have that choice. To not be pawns in Brighid's game.

I ditch the truck on the side of the street. I'm never going to use it again, and it's easier to navigate Amergin on foot. I keep my head low as I pass along the sidewalks, littered with trash and debris beneath a dull, grey sky. It's a stark contrast to the open fields and muddy skies of the power system site, where you could pretend that the air was fresh and clean instead of heavy with the cloying scent of rotting garbage.

At the openly advertised lagonael den on the corner, I turn right, a few blocks down from the bar where Lachlan practically lives. Though I hadn't expected him to be able to help with the bombings, I'm all but dead if he doesn't come through now. Once Ragjarøn hears about Brighid, they will search every alleyway and avenue of the city until they find me. And what's left of the rebels are already salivating at the thought of my head on a pike. The only people who don't want to kill me are ordinary citizens, but they also wouldn't kill someone to protect me.

Which leaves me one choice: run.

When I get to the bar, I glance around the street, checking for soldiers or insurgents. All I see is degenerates, Brigus, Amergi, and lagons. So, pretty much the usual. I open the door and duck inside.

The bar looks the same as last time. I nod to the bartender, who pours a small drink and slides it to me.

"For good luck," he says.

I snatch it and drink it down.

He nods at the man sitting at the bar.

"You're Emeríann?" the man says.

"I am. You're with Lachlan?" He says he is. "I thought he was supposed to be here."

"It's busy out there. He got caught up." The man throws back the rest of his drink then nods toward a back door. "Ready?"

I hook my thumb behind me, toward the street. "Aren't we going that way?"

"Only if you want someone to see you. Which

means they track my car. Which leads them right to my colleagues. Which gets half the smugglers in Eitan marked for death." He holds out his hands. "I'd suggest the alley where no eyes are prying."

My skin tingles. Something feels off about this. It could be that gasoline bourbon the bartender brews. It could be the whole vibe this neighborhood gives off. It could be that I'm about to smuggle myself into a foreign country thousands of miles away in a vain attempt to find my love who has no idea I'm coming and who might not still be alive. Or it could be that this man wants to kill me.

But given how many people out on the street are actively hunting me, I don't know that I have a choice.

I nod to the man, follow him out the back.

And as the door closes, I hear the bartender say *Hořte v pekel*. My skin prickles.

The insurgent who planned the ambush. The one who blew off the back of his head in front of me. That's who the bartender looks like. Now that I hear him say it, I realize they could be brothers.

I'm about to say something when a man steps from the side of the alley with a metal pipe in his hand.

Oh shit.

I scan the alley quickly, looking for anything I can use against them. Then the man shoves me from behind just as the other rears back his pipe, ready to split my head open. I drop to the alley floor when he swings, the pipe whishing so hard and close to my head I can hear it pass through the air. But it misses me, and instead plants inside the face of the man who shoved me.

He falls down like someone pulled the plug, his forehead clipping the back of my leg.

The other man, shocked at missing, stands idle for a second. I come up on my knees, feeling the searing pain from the woman's kick, the electric burn of Brighid wrenching my arms back, and punch as hard as I can. It's not my best, but it connects square in the man's crotch. He doubles over, sucking in wind, and the pipe clatters to the ground.

I snatch the pipe and use it to push myself to my feet. The man is still writhing on the concrete, his face smeared with offal.

I swing the pipe three times and his writhing stops. My pipe gets wedged against the underside of his skull, inside the collapsed pieces of bone, and when I yank it out there's a sucking sound that almost makes me puke. The blood that pours from his head mixes with the runoff that makes the concrete slick and slimy. I wipe his rotten blood from my face but only feel it smear.

There's no place to go. If I go inside, the bartender will kill me. If the insurgents catch me, they will kill me. If Ragjarøn catches me, they will kill me. I have to run. And run and run and run.

I take off out of the alleyway, knee exploding with every step, pipe still in hand because I have no idea who will cross my path, whose head I will have to cave in to save my own skin.

And as I turn the next corner, someone grabs me. I scream *No!* and ready myself to spin and swing when I hear Lachlan's voice.

"What happened?"

He's here. Only him. Only Lachlan.

"The bartender. He tried to have me killed."

"What." His voice drops a full octave.

"That insurgent I told you about, that was his brother. They said they were with you, that they were supposed to take me out." I swallow hard, blink away the image of the man's head. "Lachlan, I just caved in a man's skull with a piece of pipe."

"I guess it's Thursday, then. Which means I'm about to go kill the shit out of that other cocksucker." He starts to turn back toward the bar but I grab his arm and yank him.

"I need to go. You need to get me the hell out of this city. Please," I say. "You can take care of him later. But I need to leave. Now."

He shakes away whatever he was thinking, squeezes my hands. "Right, right, of course." He hurries over to the car idling in the middle of the street and opens the trunk. "Climb in, sweetheart. Your chariot's arrived."

"In the middle of the street?" I gesture all around us. "What if someone sees?"

"You think anyone here gives two shits what anyone else does?" He nods inside the trunk. "I've got two bottles of water and some jerky in there. Made it special, just for you."

Before I climb in, I wrap my arms around him, squeezing hard, then lock myself in the trunk.

An hour later, with the rapid turns long behind us, the road seemingly straight and smooth, I open the trunk a little. Fresh air rushes in through the crack and it's like being born again. I nudge it a little wider, enough that I can see the outside and try to get a bead on where we are. It's all fields, with the mountains still looming in the background. We could be anywhere or we could be nowhere. But as I bite off a hunk of jerky, I see something far in the distance. Twisting black threads rising from the mountains. It's not the other side of the mountains, though: it's Eitan, burning again. Burning as it always has. And maybe, burning as it always will.

Then a dark shape rushes past me, startling me enough to swallow the chunk of jerky. I pound my chest as I try to work it down. As the tears dry, I can see that the shape was a foerge, one of the birds of prey out here, carrying some small rodent in its claws. The name makes me think of Forgall, my fallen friend.

The foerge glides to the top of a skeletal tree, flapping its wings to hover above a bunch of sticks. Small black blobs jut out of the sticks, babies pecking at the rodent in their mother's claws. The mother finally drops the food down, then flaps away to find more.

I lower the trunk, settling back into the darkness, but a small stream of light still bleeds through.

29.
HENRAEK

It is cold out here in the Jötun Mountains, cold enough to make a man consider becoming religious, because this is clearly some sort of punishment for a life ill-led.

The hours spent traveling here were the longest of my life, constantly replaying every conceivable thing that could have happened to the boys in my absence. I know Dyvik said the reason their center was built out here was because it was the safest location in the country, but none of that means shit when my boys might be in jeopardy.

I push open the doors to the train before it's even fully stopped, my feet slipping on the slick platform. There are piles of snow here, waist high. I can't imagine what it's like once winter proper comes. I hurry out of the station, headed toward the small outcropping of buildings in the distance.

Then I hear an echo that chills more than any icy blast cascading down from the mountaintops.

It's the echo of gunfire.

I start running, doing my best to avoid the icy patches in the road, only falling twice.

When I come to the edge of the buildings, I feel a swirl of disorientation, as if I'd traveled in a gigantic circle and ended up back in Rën. The buildings are the same style, though taller, and the arrangement is slightly different. But what terrifies me is that the *sounds* are the same.

The streets ring out with rifle shots and shotgun blasts, with pained screams and shouted directions of attack, with the injured groaning and the scared crying.

Groaning, because some of the bodies lying in the streets wear the grey fatigues of Ragjarøn.

But crying, because some of them wear regular clothes. Because they are not soldiers, or even civilians.

They are children. They are Donael's age, and younger.

Ragjarøn is hunting and fighting and killing children.

The side of a building shatters not two feet from my head, ripping me out of my horrified stupor. I throw myself down behind a pile of snow, which will do nothing to protect me from a bullet but keeps me out of the line of fire.

What am I supposed to do? How will I save my boys?

I hear someone yell, then heavy footsteps coming in my direction. I huddle down farther, trying to make myself as small and inconspicuous as possible because I have absolutely no play in this.

Then a shadow passes over me, and a body hits the ground beside me, his back rounding and absorbing the blow as he rolls to his feet.

It's one of Magnus's boys. Axel. He has a rifle tucked against his shoulder, then pops up to standing, takes aim, and fires off a round of shots before ducking back below the snow drift.

"Henraek," he says, almost as if he'd expected to see me here. "Where's your weapon?"

"I- I-" I sputter. "I don't have one."

Axel reaches inside his jacket and pulls out a handgun, checks the magazine, then hands it to me. "Won't help much against their rifles, but it's something."

"I'm not here to fight." As soon as I say it, bullets rake the building above us. I jump up by instinct and pop off a few shots to push them back, only realizing what I've done once I crouch back down and see Axel smiling at me. "I came here to get my boys."

He nods gravely and I feel my hands disappear.

"What happened to them? Where are they?"

Before he can speak, more bullets pepper the wall.

Those cocksuckers. Axel goes to stand but I yank the rifle from him, jump to my feet and spray the area to the right, then left, then center, concentrating on a car where the shots were coming from. Five seconds of firing and one tags the gas tank, making the whole car jump three feet in the air when it explodes in a great ball of fire.

I duck back down and shove the rifle at Axel.

"Where are they." I'm not asking anymore.

"They fled into the mountains yesterday with our leader, Hemdälr."

My body sinks, my vision narrowing to pinpoints. So close, yet so far. Everything I love remains perpetually just out of reach.

"I thought this was where the camp was." I wave around, indicating the city.

"It is. But when Ragjarøn stormed the city yesterday, most of the camp fled." He motions across the street, where I now see two boys hidden in a third-floor window, their rifle barrels barely poking out from behind curtains. Snipers. God damn, if these boys haven't been well trained. "A handful of us stayed behind to hold off the troops, let our people get to safety."

"Then they can't be that far if it's only been a day." I can still catch them. I can find them and I can bring them home. There is still hope.

Axel shrugs. "Hemdälr is local. He knows these mountains. He was born here." He pauses to let off a few shots, then comes back to me. "All I know is that they're headed north to some village called Umåyø. We're supposed to reconvene there once we've eliminated the troops, then make our way to someplace Hemdälr told us about."

"And then what?"

He gives me a look scarily reminiscent to his father. "Keep moving or train to fight back."

Ragjarøn will continue to send troops. The boys won't be able to outlast them forever. And every day that passes, my boys trek farther and farther away from me. I can't let them go. I can't wait.

"Which way is north?"

He points it out for me, just beyond the buildings to our left.

"I have to go," I tell him. "I have to find them."

I try to return the handgun but he shoves it back, then fishes out another magazine for me. "You're going to need it."

I nod, then borrow the rifle from him and take out two more cars with a few well-placed shots. Consider it my parting gift.

"Good luck," I tell him.

"You too."

I crouch down and wait. Then, when a lull in firing comes, I sprint across the street, zigging and zagging to remain a hard target. When I pass the buildings on the other side, I stand more upright, letting my legs move faster.

Within two minutes I'm away from the buildings and all the fighting. The terrain has changed quickly. Where before there were flat, paved surfaces, there are now skull-sized rocks tossed around as some sort of path. I slow down and catch my breath, looking up at what's before me.

I can't even see the top of the mountains, shrouded in fog, thousands of feet above me. A valley runs in between two of the taller peaks, a harsh V carved in the middle of the severe terrain. Simply looking at them chills my blood, imagining the cold and the wind and the ice.

But my boys are out there. I don't know where they are, but I will find them.

I pull down my goggles. I pull up my balaclava.

And I start walking.

"I'm coming, boys," I say to the mountains towering above me. "I'm coming."

ACKNOWLEDGMENTS

I owe huge thanks to more people than I could fit on this page, but I'll try anyway.

Thank you to my wonderful publishers – Phil, Penny, Nick, Mike and Marc – for believing in this book.

Thank you to my wonderful agent, Stacia Decker, for helping make this book readable.

Thank you to my so-so friend, Rob Hart, for having an idea so great I had to steal it (but seriously, go buy his books, they're awesome).

And infinite thanks to my lovely wife, Amanda, and my beautiful children, Donovan and Ruby. You're the reason for everything I do.

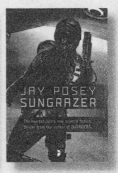